The Fallen Princess

The Gareth and Gwen Medieval Mysteries

The Bard's Daughter
The Good Knight
The Uninvited Guest
The Fourth Horseman
The Fallen Princess
The Unlikely Spy
The Lost Brother

The After Cilmeri Series:

Daughter of Time
Footsteps in Time
Winds of Time
Prince of Time
Crossroads in Time
Children of Time
Exiles in Time
Castaways in Time
Ashes of Time
Warden of Time

The Last Pendragon Saga

The Last Pendragon
The Pendragon's Quest

Other Books by Sarah Woodbury

Cold My Heart: A Novel of King Arthur

A Gareth and Gwen Medieval Mystery

THE FALLEN PRINCESS

by

SARAH WOODBURY

The Fallen Princess
Copyright © 2014 by Sarah Woodbury

www.sarahwoodbury.com

Cover image by Christine DeMaio-Rice at Flip City Books
http://flipcitybooks.com

To my Taran

A Brief Guide to Welsh Pronunciation

a 'ah' as in 'rah' (Caradog)

ae 'eye' as in 'my' (Cadfael)

ai 'eye' as in 'my' (Owain)

aw 'ow' as in 'cow' (Alaw)

c a hard 'c' sound (Cadfael)

ch a non-English sound as in Scottish 'ch' in 'loch' (Fychan)

dd a buzzy 'th' sound, as in 'there' (Ddu; Gwynedd)

e 'eh' as in 'met' (Ceri)

eu 'ay' as in 'day' (Ddeufaen—this would be pronounced 'theyvine')

f 'v' as in 'of' (Cadfael)

ff as in 'off' (Gruffydd)

g a hard 'g' sound, as in 'gas' (Goronwy)

i 'ee' as in 'see' (Ceri)

ia 'yah' as in 'yawn' (Iago)

ieu sounds like the cheer, 'yay' (Ieuan)

l as in 'lamp' (Llywelyn)

ll 'shl' sound that does not occur in English (Llywelyn)

o 'aw' as in 'dog' (Cadog)

oe 'oy' as in 'boy' (Coel)

rh a breathy mix between 'r' and 'rh' that does not occur in English (Rhys)

th a softer sound than for 'dd,' as in 'thick' (Arthur)

u a short 'ih' sound (Gruffydd), or a long 'ee' sound (Cymru—pronounced 'kumree')

w as a consonant, it's an English 'w' (Llywelyn); as a vowel, an 'oo' sound (Bwlch).

y the only letter in which Welsh is not phonetic. It can be an 'ih' sound, as in 'Gwyn,' is often an 'uh' sound (Cymru), and at the end of the word is an 'ee' sound (thus, both Cymru—the modern word for Wales—and Cymry—the word for Wales in the Dark Ages—are pronounced 'kumree').

Cast of Characters

The Living

Owain Gwynedd – King of Gwynedd (North Wales)

Rhun – Prince of Gwynedd (illegitimate)

Hywel – Prince of Gwynedd (illegitimate)

Cadwaladr – Owain's younger brother

Gwen – spy for Hywel, Gareth's wife

Gareth – Gwen's husband, Captain of Hywel's guard

Taran – Owain's steward

Cristina – Owain's second wife

Mari – Gwen's friend, Hywel's wife

Evan – Gareth's friend

Llelo – Gareth and Gwen's foster son

Dai – Llelo's younger brother

Meilyr – Gwen's father

Gwalchmai – Gwen's brother

Iorwerth – Prince of Gwynedd (legitimate)

Ifon – Lord of Rhos

Gruffydd – Castellan of Dolwyddelan

Sioned – Gruffydd's wife

The Dead

Tegwen –Hywel's cousin, Cadwallon's daughter

Ilar – Tegwen's mother

Bran – Tegwen's husband, Ifon's older brother

Marchudd – Ifon's eldest brother

Cynan – King of Rhos, Ifon's father

Gwladys – Owain's first wife (mother of Iorwerth)

Prince Cadwallon – Owain's elder brother

King Gruffydd – King of Gwynedd, Owain's father

1

October 1144

Gwen

"This won't be a pleasant sight, my lady." Rhodri helped Gwen dismount. He'd come to Aber Castle to find Gareth, but Gwen's husband had risen from his bed long before dawn, leaving to ride with Prince Hywel and his men on patrol.

"It never is," Gwen said.

Rhodri set her gently on the soft sand, its usual yellowish-brown color turned to gray in the pre-dawn light. The cart intended for carrying away the body rumbled to a halt behind them, and another soldier, Dewi, jumped off the seat, leaving the stable boy who'd been driving the cart to wait with it and hold the horse's head.

The tense expression in Rhodri's face didn't ease, so Gwen added, "I'm well, Rhodri. Truly." Many women struggled with their health during pregnancy, but other than an annoyingly strong sense of smell, Gwen hadn't had any difficulties so far beyond a few unpleasant mornings, particularly in the beginning, and an increased need for sleep. Even at this late stage, with the baby due at the end of January, some people still didn't notice right off that she was carrying a child.

While the men shooed away the crowd of onlookers, Gwen circled the body, trying to disturb the scene as little as possible. She considered the corpse from all angles—though as it was well wrapped in a cloak, there wasn't much to see. From the closeness of the weave, the cloak had once been very fine. It was dirty now, of a color that she thought should have been blue. The hood half-covered the face, implying that one of the onlookers had drawn it back and then, when death had been definitively determined, hastily thrown it over the face again.

Gwen braced herself for the need to see who this was and bent to lift away the cloth.

At the grotesque appearance of the face, Gwen's breath caught in her throat. Then a hand touched her shoulder, and she jumped a foot. "By all that is holy—"

"I'm sorry! I'm sorry!" Llelo said. "I didn't mean to startle you."

Gwen let out a burst of air. "What are you doing here? Is Dai here too?"

"He's a laze-about," Llelo said, answering her second question first. "I came for the clams. Are you all right?"

"Why does everyone think I'm not well? I've seen dead people before."

Llelo frowned, staring past her to the body. "Not like this one, I don't think."

Gwen deliberately hadn't looked again at the dead woman's face. Instead, she gestured towards a group of children looking anxiously in their direction. "They shouldn't be here."

"They're the ones who found her," Llelo said.

Gwen inspected her young charge. He'd grown four inches since he'd come to live with them and loomed over her. If she were to stand, he'd be taller than she was. *Thirteen years old going on twenty*, as Gareth had said privately to her more than once. Upon the death of his father, Llelo had needed to grow up quickly in order to care for his younger brother, Dai. Gareth had discovered both boys in an English monastery last May and taken them under his wing.

The boys had spent most of the summer with Gwen on Anglesey while Gareth was in Ceredigion serving Prince Hywel, but they had all gathered at Aber this week to celebrate *Calan Gaeaf*, what the Church called All Saints' Day. It was the end of the harvest season and the beginning of winter. In the traditions of her people, at this time of year the veil between the next world and this one thinned. Tomorrow night, *Nos Galan Gaeaf*, or Hallowmas, the spirits of those who'd died would walk the earth. Gwen shivered to think that this poor soul could be among them.

"Since you're here, you might as well help," Gwen said. "The children will talk to you. Find out what they know while I see who this is."

"You can tell it was once a woman," Llelo said, with all the morbid fascination of the young.

Gwen waved her hand at him. "Off you go." Asking Llelo to help her might turn out to be the worst idea she'd had this month, but since he was here, it was better to keep him busy.

Gwen turned back to the body, no longer able to avoid looking at it. As Llelo had said, it was that of a woman, but beyond this simple observance, Gwen didn't know that she'd ever seen a stranger circumstance. For starters, the woman's body wasn't bloated with water like it should have been had she drowned. Instead, her skin was dried out, leathery and brown like an old apple, more bones than flesh, though flesh still adhered to the bone. The woman could have been dead for months, if not years. The cloak that wrapped her wasn't wet either, which Gwen would have noticed earlier if she hadn't been so distracted.

On the ride to the beach, Gwen had conceived two scenarios that would have put the body here this morning. One would have been a drowning, though the sea had been calm last night, despite three weeks of solid rain. The second and more complicated possibility had been that the body had been buried in the sand somewhere—a dune or a cliff face near the water's edge—and over time, wind and tide had worn away the sand that covered her grave until it was fully exposed and the body fell into the sea.

In that case, the body could have washed up here because of the way the water moved in and out of the Menai Strait. Both possibilities would have involved a recent death, because that was the only way the body would have remained intact enough to wash up on the beach in the first place.

And if the body had washed up on the beach, even many hours ago, it would have been wet from head to toe. That wasn't the case, which meant that someone had placed it here.

With these thoughts spinning in her head, Gwen put her hand flat on what remained of the woman's belly. The fabric of her dress was damp, like laundry left out on the line all night, but it wasn't sopping. Gwen looked up, meeting the eyes of several villagers, who gazed at her with expressions ranging from curious to revolted to worried. She, herself, was among the worried. She didn't know who this was, but she knew nobody was going to be happy when she discovered the woman's name. Somewhere, sometime, someone had lost a daughter. It would be Gwen's task—and Gareth's and Hywel's—to find out who that was.

"Who found her?" she said.

Llelo lifted a hand to gain Gwen's attention and brought the group of children closer. "They did, all together."

"Did you touch her?" Gwen studied the children's faces as they shook their heads vehemently in turn. She ended up looking intently at a medium-sized boy of about nine with a mop of dark hair and dark eyes.

"No, my lady." He shook his head too.

Gwen looked sideways at him. "Not even a little?"

"It was I who pulled back her hood, Lady Gwen." A burly villager stepped forward. "Once I saw that she was dead—long dead from the looks—I went to find Rhodri, there." He gestured to where Rhodri guarded the pathway between the body and the cart.

If he'd come to the same conclusion Gwen had—that the woman hadn't drowned—he'd realized that it was along that trajectory that evidence, if there was any evidence, would be found. All of the men-at-arms at Aber, whether they served Prince Hywel, his brother Rhun, or King Owain, knew from experience that Gareth would want to inspect the entire area personally and would be displeased if it had been marred by the curious and the careless. Beyond Rhodri, Dewi had gone back to the cart and was talking to someone, though since the man had his back to her, Gwen couldn't tell who it was.

She glanced up at the sky. The sun was coming up over the hills to the southeast, revealing a cloudless sky, unusual for so late in October. A warm breeze was blowing into her face from the south. She'd woken to dozens of mornings like this on Anglesey over the summer, and for a moment she wished that she was back at her little cottage, wiggling her bare toes in the warm sand instead of on this windswept beach crouching over a dead body. "When is low tide, Llelo?"

"Just now, Ma," Llelo said. "That's why we all came down here this morning. After the rain we've had, we were looking forward to a good haul of clams."

Gwen focused on the damp sand around the body. The high tide mark was another ten feet further up the beach, beyond where the woman lay, which meant that she'd been laid down on this beach sometime after midnight. Otherwise, she would have been washed away with the tide. That led Gwen to conclude—though Hywel would say it was far too soon to conclude anything—that whoever had laid her here had wanted her to be found. Otherwise, he should have left her where he found her, wherever that was, or put her closer to the water's edge so the tide could have taken her out to sea.

"Can we move her now?"

Gwen looked up and struggled not to let dismay show on her face. Adda, the commander of one of King Owain's companies, had arrived at Gwen's side with Dewi in tow. Adda bent over the body, his hands on his knees. Dewi wore a look of revulsion on his face.

"I'm sorry, sir, but we really can't," Gwen said.

"Why not?" Adda said.

"Because she didn't drown."

"What do you mean?" Adda said. "Sailors and fisherman often wash up on our shore when they don't end up on the Great Orme."

Adda was right. The villagers knew to come to the beach after a storm to look for valuable items they could salvage from boats lost at sea, even if they had come for the clams today.

"The body is barely damp, Adda," Gwen said as gently as she could.

Adda pressed his lips together.

Gwen didn't know either man well. But while Dewi seemed something of a simpleton, Adda was far from stupid, even if he annoyed her by being pompous and overbearing.

It should have been clear to an experienced man such as he that the woman had been dead long before today, but he was also a stubborn man with fixed opinions. Gwen encountered men like him all the time. They were older, set in their ways, and did not welcome the notion that a young woman might have anything to contribute to a murder investigation.

"Perhaps while we wait for Gareth to arrive, Dewi and Rhodri could survey the beach?" Gwen gestured to the area around the body. "I know that we've disturbed the sand with our footprints, but they could look for tracks from a cart or from a man walking as if he was carrying something—her—on his shoulder? Given how dried out the body is, she wouldn't have been very heavy for a grown man, but his boots should have sunk deeper into the sand than if he carried nothing."

Adda raised his eyebrows. "Sir Gareth would want the body removed from the beach first."

Gwen just managed not to grind her teeth. She'd given him a long speech and was trying to be as polite as she could. "My husband, and Prince Hywel, of course, will be very grateful to you when they return for moving the investigation forward in their absence. I'm sure they will personally want to hear from you whatever you discover." She gave him her sweetest smile and tried to keep her expression as sincere as possible.

Adda's chin still stuck out stubbornly, but as Gwen had hoped, he grunted his consent. It was unlikely that Adda would tell her anything of what he found now that she'd wounded his pride, but Gareth would tell her what Adda had to say as soon as he heard it. There was only so much she could do here all by herself, and she did need Adda's help.

Adda motioned for Rhodri to join him and Dewi, and Gwen went back to studying the body, finding it hard to reconcile its condition to its presence on the beach. She fingered the cloth of the woman's dress. Blue like the cloak, with a close weave that was still fine to Gwen's touch, it was embroidered at the bodice and had a full skirt, the hem of which would have trailed behind the woman as she walked. Her linen shift and underdress were also embroidered. Even without the garnet ring strung on a gold chain around the woman's neck, Gwen would have known by her clothing alone that this was no serving girl. She'd been noble or at the very least had dressed like it.

Whoever had left her on the beach hadn't just dumped her here, either. He'd arranged the woman's long braid of reddish-brown hair so that it trailed down her right shoulder past her hip. In Wales, girls trimmed their hair until they reached womanhood, keeping it shoulder length and easier to care for, after which they never cut it again. Comparing this woman's braid to Gwen's own, and taking into account that not every woman's hair grew at the same rate, the dead woman had been at least five years past womanhood when she died.

A dirty band of fabric that might once have been white was tied around her head. A dark patch on it—dried, of course—had Gwen carefully unwinding the cloth, tugging on it to unstick it from the right side of the woman's head and knowing before she saw the mat of blood in the woman's hair that someone had to have hit her very hard to cause the wound. The same dark stains that Gwen guessed were blood instead of mud or the decay of time marred her dress at the right shoulder too.

Gwen gently worked her fingers underneath the matted hair and found the wound. As Gwen traced the edges of shattered bone, she came upon an abrupt indentation in the center of the wound as if a sharp point had been driven into the bone.

Gwen sat back. Trying to gain control of her thoughts, she blocked out the image of the woman as she was now in order to take stock of what the girl had once been: she was more than eighteen years old, possibly noble, and had been dead for years. Gwen ran her thumb along the woman's slender wrist. The flesh still adhered to the bones and, like the rest of her arm, wasn't a uniform medium brown. The skin was mottled all along the arm—darker in some places than others—but a thin band of darker skin went around each wrist. Given the unusual state of decomposition, Gwen didn't want to speculate if these were bruises or a natural result of the desiccation of the body. Gwen had never seen a body like this one, so she honestly didn't know what was normal in such a case.

Other than the head wound, of course, which clearly wasn't.

For the first time in months, Gwen felt her stomach rebelling. She swallowed down the bile at the back of her throat, grateful now that Rhodri had woken her from a deep sleep, and she hadn't had the opportunity to eat anything before she rode to the beach.

"Gwen!"

She looked up at the sound of her husband's voice. Gareth had appeared in the gap between two dunes, accompanied by Prince Hywel and ten other men. Gwen had drowsily kissed Gareth goodbye before he'd ridden out of Aber Castle with Hywel. At the sight of him now, her spirits lifted, alleviating some of the sickness in her stomach. Gareth and the other men reined in and dismounted near where Gwen had left her horse and the cart had been parked.

Gwen's pleasure faded, however, as Adda stepped in front of Hywel, talking quickly. They were too far away for Gwen to make out Adda's words, and apparently Gareth wasn't interested in hearing what Adda had to say because he strode past him, crossing the last few yards of sand to where Gwen waited. He was careful—as Gwen had been—to take a circuitous route so as not to disturb the already churned up sand more than he had to.

Gwen rose awkwardly to her feet and gestured to the body in the sand. "As you can see, we have had some trouble here."

Gareth slipped an arm around her waist, holding Gwen close for a moment while she pressed her cheek to his chest. To Gwen's dismay, tears pricked at the back of her eyes, and she shook her head to stop them from falling, determined not to lose her composure just because Gareth had arrived and she no longer needed to keep it.

"Are you all right?" He kissed her temple.

"I have lost count of the number of people who have asked me that this morning," Gwen said. That wasn't entirely true; in fact, she'd kept a careful count. Gareth was the third.

"You didn't answer my question," Gareth said, but he must have decided that if she could talk back to him, she really was fine, because he released her and crouched in Gwen's place beside the dead woman.

While Gwen related what she'd discovered so far, Gareth went over the body as she had. Hywel, on the other hand, once he dismissed Adda, stood chewing on his lower lip, his arms folded across his chest and every line of his body revealing his tension and unhappiness. Gwen had assumed that the strange state of the body and the length of time since her death would make it difficult to identify the woman quickly, but the prince's expression said otherwise.

"Do you know her?" Gwen said.

Hywel breathed deeply. "I don't want to; I shouldn't be able to."

Gareth looked up from his examination. "My lord?"

Hywel didn't answer. He seemed to be struggling with himself somehow.

Gwen stepped closer, looking at him with some concern. "Whoever she is, we're here to help, like we always are."

"After all these years, I can't believe she's dead." Hywel scrubbed at his hair with one hand, his gaze never leaving the body.

"Who's dead, my lord?" Gareth said.

"My cousin, Tegwen," Hywel said.

2

Gareth

Gareth looked from Hywel to the body and back again. "This is your cousin? How can that be?"

Gwen was staring open-mouthed at Hywel. "But—but—Tegwen ran away. We all know that she ran away!"

Hywel shook his head, sadness and regret in his face. "It seems we might have been wrong about that, Gwen." Then he looked at Gareth and said, "My uncle, Cadwallon, was her father. He never had any sons, and Tegwen was his only child."

Gareth straightened from his crouch and stepped close to his lord to ensure that none of the onlookers could overhear him. "I know who Tegwen was, my lord, but she's been missing these five years. Are you suggesting that she didn't run away with a Dane as we all thought but has been dead this whole time?"

"I can only tell you what I see." Hywel gestured helplessly to the body. "That's Tegwen. I'd swear to it."

"How could she have ended up here?" Gwen stood with her hand to her mouth. She seemed unable to look away from the dead woman, so Gareth stepped past Hywel to stand beside her, his hand resting gently at the small of her back.

Gareth couldn't blame the two of them for being shocked. This was the last thing he wanted to see today too. From the head wound, this was murder, and even if it happened a long time ago, it couldn't be ignored. Neither King Owain nor Hywel would allow it. For Gareth's part, he was loath to spend the short time he had with Gwen working on a murder investigation, particularly one involving a beloved member of the royal house of Gwynedd.

Tegwen's disappearance five years ago had been dramatic enough to have become legend. Gareth had heard the stories and couldn't blame the people for reveling in its retelling. Who wouldn't enjoy a tale of a young princess who defied her family and ran away with a handsome Dane? The fact that Tegwen had left her husband and daughters behind was usually (and conveniently) forgotten.

Gareth had heard a version of the story in the great hall at Aber just last night, set to music and much embellished, with the names changed and an added mythological element that included a dragon. The singer hadn't been Meilyr or Gwalchmai, Gwen's father and brother, and as Gareth had heard this version before, he hadn't paid much attention. He'd been with Gwen at the time, and they'd had eyes and ears only for each other.

Neither King Owain nor his guests were going to enjoy what appeared to be the real story: Tegwen hadn't run away with a Dane. She'd been murdered instead.

Gwen slipped her hand into Gareth's. "We have more to observe, but it might be better not to do it in front of all these people. Can you get them to leave? Rhodri and Dewi tried, but nobody seems to have listened."

Gareth surveyed the beach. Although most of the dozen onlookers had the decency to move at least ten feet from the body, and no one else was hovering over it like they were, Gwen was right. "I'll see what I can do. Ignore them and do what you have to do to help Prince Hywel."

With a worried look at Hywel, who seemed to be frozen where he stood, Gareth headed up the beach towards his men in what wasn't his usual stride. His boots dug into the soft sand, and he knew he'd be dumping the fine grains out of them for weeks to come. As he crossed onto drier sand, Gareth called for the men to gather around him.

"This has turned into a more delicate situation than Prince Hywel first thought it would be, and we need to contain this scene," he said. "Many of you have had the misfortune to participate in incidents like this before. I must stay beside the prince for now, but I need to know everything that happened on this beach between yesterday evening and this moment." Gareth pointed with his chin at his friend. "Evan, if you could see to interviewing the people here? You know what to do. At a minimum, I need them to stay further away from the body. A crowd of onlookers watching his every move is the last thing Prince Hywel needs right now."

"Of course, my lord."

Gareth turned away, taking a breath and letting it out to settle himself as he looked down the beach to where Hywel and

Gwen were talking quietly over Tegwen's body. Hywel seemed to be recovering from his initial shock, which had been uncharacteristic of him to begin with. None of them had encountered a murder since last spring when a Norman spy had dropped a body at their feet in the bailey of Earl Robert's castle at Newcastle-under-Lyme. While Gareth had been a key player in that investigation, his task had been hampered by his unfamiliarity with the area and a general prejudice against the Welsh displayed by most every Norman he encountered. At least here at Aber that wouldn't be a problem.

Always considering himself to be one of Gareth's men, even though he was only thirteen, Llelo had gathered a handful of children to him and was bending forward to speak to them, his hands on his knees. Gareth patted him on the shoulder as he passed him on the way back to where Hywel and Gwen waited. "All right there?"

"Yes, sir," Llelo said.

"Let me know what you discover," Gareth said.

"I already promised Gwen I would," Llelo said, looking slightly affronted that Gareth would tell him his job. Gareth held back a smile.

Gwen had mentioned designating tasks to the other two attendants on the scene, Rhodri and Dewi, but they seemed to have disappeared. As Hywel had dismounted from his horse, Adda had tried to explain to him how inadequate to the task of investigating the death Gwen had been. Gareth had brushed past him with a disdainful look, but he probably should have found out if Adda had discovered anything important. Contrary to Adda's opinion, Gareth was pleased with how Gwen had taken charge in his absence and how quickly the investigation had moved into full swing.

"I gather that you don't recognize Tegwen yourself, Gareth?" Gwen said as he reached them.

He shook his head. "I never met her."

"She disappeared a few months before you began your service with me, Gareth," Hywel said.

"And you, Gwen?" Gareth said. "You must have grown up with her."

Gwen bit her lip. "Not really."

"Tegwen was the same age as I am." Hywel had returned to his usual matter-of-fact manner, pacing around the body with his eyes on the ground as he talked. "She was the result of a liaison between my uncle, Prince Cadwallon, and a girl named Ilar, the daughter of a man-at-arms turned knight of my father's generation. His name is Gruffydd."

Gareth's brows drew together. "Do I know him?"

"You should," Hywel said. "Tegwen's grandfather still lives. He's the castellan at Dolwyddelan."

Gareth's expression cleared. "He's a good man. He was very helpful last year when Anarawd—" Gareth broke off as Hywel glanced at him, his mouth twisting in wry amusement.

"Yes. Exactly," Hywel said. "Ilar died birthing Tegwen, so Gruffydd and his wife raised her themselves. My grandfather appointed Gruffydd to be the castellan at Dolwyddelan at Uncle

Cadwallon's request, in remembrance of Ilar and so Gruffydd could raise Tegwen as befitted her station as a princess of Gwynedd."

Gareth would have wondered why Cadwallon hadn't brought the child to Aber and raised her himself if he hadn't been a prince. Any peasant would have, but Cadwallon was a warrior and was often absent from home. It was common practice to foster out royal children, either at birth if the mother was dead and the parents hadn't married, or at the age of seven when a child began to prepare for his adult life.

"That was why I barely knew her," Gwen said. "I was only eleven when Cadwallon died, twelve years ago now. Tegwen lived mostly with her mother's family, and I saw her in court only a few times."

"When she was fifteen years old, Tegwen married Bran ap Cynan, whose father was the Lord of Rhos." Hywel looked at Gwen. "You attended the wedding, didn't you?"

Gwen shook her head. Rhos, a sub-kingdom to Gwynedd with the lord's seat at Bryn Euryn, was a little more than ten miles from Aber Castle. "My father provided the entertainment, but Gwalchmai was a small child, and Meilyr left me at Aberffraw to mind him. Don't you remember? You came home with your head full of new songs, though you'd sung none of them because your voice was still changing and my father didn't trust it."

"I was fifteen myself." Hywel had gone back to a crouch beside the body, his head bent.

Gareth wasn't sure if he should speak since it appeared that Hywel was struggling to control his emotions again. He cleared his throat. "My lord, why are you so sure this woman is Tegwen?"

"By her dress, her belongings." Hywel threw out one hand, the gesture halfway to despair, pointing at the necklace at the woman's throat. "She never took that necklace off. It was a gift from her husband."

The body lay as Gwen had left it, the cloak spread out in the sand, and now Hywel flipped back the edge of the cloak to reveal a hem embroidered with tiny red lions, half obscured by sand and dirt. "This is her cloak. The lions were a tribute to her father's personal coat of arms. My father gave it to her the day she became betrothed to Bran. I don't know what has been done to her or how she came to look like this, but ..." Hywel's voice trailed away.

It was obvious to Gareth that Tegwen could have discarded the cloak and necklace at any time between her wedding and her disappearance, making this a completely different girl, but he kept his lips together. It would be one thing if what she was wearing was the only piece of evidence, but if Hywel thought he recognized her shape as well, Gareth wasn't going to argue with him.

He'd never seen Hywel so shaken by a death. It worried him that if this was Hywel's reaction—a man who wore stoicism and cynicism like a cloak—the effect of the news of Tegwen's death on the rest of the inhabitants of Aber would be far more tumultuous.

Gareth put his hand on Gwen's arm. "Gwen, you should ride ahead and tell the king that we will be bringing Tegwen's body into Aber as soon as we've finished examining the scene."

"What? Why me? Gareth, please—"

Gareth moved his arm up to her shoulders and bent his head so he could speak gently in her ear. "It has to be you. Right now, the three of us are the only ones who know this woman may be Tegwen. The news of her death would be better coming from you, since you've seen and touched her, than from any of the people here. The last thing we want is to arrive at Aber with the body and surprise King Owain with the news. We're lucky it's still early in the morning. You know how fast gossip spreads. In another hour, the news that the body of a richly dressed woman was left on the beach this morning will have reached half of Gwynedd. We have to reach the king before he hears of it from someone else and wonders why he's been kept in ignorance."

Gwen groaned audibly. "I'll have to wake him."

"I know," Gareth said. "But maybe that's for the best too. He won't be in the hall yet. He shouldn't have to learn of Tegwen's death with his people watching."

Gwen wrinkled her nose at Gareth. He hoped she wasn't angry at him, even if he was right, but she didn't complain further and then shot him a bright-eyed look over her shoulder as she turned to head up the beach to where the horses were picketed. At a gesture from Gareth, two members of the guard intercepted her, and she accepted the help of one of them to mount her horse. She lifted her hand to Gareth one last time and rode away, a guard on either side of her.

Turning back to Tegwen, Gareth stood on the other side of the body from Hywel, waiting for him to finish his examination. Hywel had crouched to feel at the head wound, and after a moment, he looked up at Gareth. "Help me turn her."

Gareth crouched beside his lord and pushed up on Tegwen's right hip to roll the body up onto its side. As Gwen had said, the sand was damp beneath her, and though the moisture had seeped into her clothing, the cloth covering her front was relatively dry. Neither Gareth nor Hywel acknowledged this observation to the other, just laid her gently back down to the sand.

Hywel picked up one of Tegwen's narrow wrists, stroking gently. "It's broken."

"Do you think it happened before or after her death?" Gareth said.

Hywel turned the hand over and back. "I can't say. The skin is discolored, but so is her entire body. It has been too long since she died for me to read events clearly." He gestured down the length of her. "She didn't die here, that's for certain."

Bodies that had been moved always made for more difficult investigations. "She was struck on the head, but I don't see how that relates to a broken wrist," Gareth said.

"Maybe it doesn't. Someone could have dragged the body roughly once she was dead," Hywel said.

"Could the damage have happened as recently as last night?" Gareth picked up her other wrist. The bones were so dry and brittle that he feared he would break more of them and destroy whatever evidence they had. "You could see how easy it would be to do."

"The head wound occurred prior to death," Hywel said, "and I would say with some certainty that it caused her death, but I have never been faced with a body in this condition before."

Hywel pointed to Tegwen's feet, and Gareth moved around the body in order to inspect the heels of her boots. He knelt in the sand to lift up one heel and then the other. "I see scuff marks. I could match them to the scene if she'd died yesterday, but after all this time, it will be impossible to trace."

"She was murdered; that's what matters most." Hywel straightened and stepped back from the body, his hands on his hips. "This will enrage my father."

"Will he ask us to discover who killed her?" Gareth said.

"Who else?"

"Even after all this time?" Gareth said.

"Hallowmas is tomorrow night," Hywel said. "The discovery of this death will make everyone uneasy. How much worse will it be if my father does nothing to find her killer?" Then Hywel shrugged. "Even if he doesn't ask, I will insist we try."

That was as Gareth had assumed, though he'd felt the need to ask. He rose to his feet too, brushing the sand from his knees. "It's hard to know where to start."

Hywel scowled. "We should treat it no differently from any other murder. If we ask enough questions, eventually we will ask the right ones of the right people, and we will learn things we didn't know before. All cases can be solved given time and a little luck."

"Make that *a lot of luck*," Gareth said.

Hywel looked over at him, his gaze sharpening. "I need to know that you will put your full efforts into this, Gareth. I can't have you doubting what we do."

Gareth tamed his skepticism and reluctance in an instant. "Of course." At Hywel's continued hard look, Gareth added, "I apologize, my lord." He blew out his cheeks. "But I must point out that we will have to reexamine everything we knew about her. She was a princess and your cousin. You might not like what we find."

"Knowing the truth is always better than believing a lie," Hywel said.

Gareth nodded. It wasn't the first time Hywel had said those words, and Gareth believed he meant them. "Then I have my first question, and it needs to be put to you: Gwen said that Tegwen married Bran, a prince of Rhos. Why don't I know of him? Is he a younger son who hasn't participated in your father's endeavors?"

"Was that before your time too?" Hywel said, surprise in his face. And then he shook his head. "No, it couldn't have been."

"Was what before my time?"

"Bran was the heir to the throne of Rhos," Hywel said. "His older brother, Marchudd, died after Bran married Tegwen, and then his father died—of old age, mind you—between Marchudd's death and Tegwen's disappearance. I can't remember the specifics at the moment, since Bran had taken charge of the cantref long before that. Then Bran himself was murdered three years ago by an arrow through his heart as he journeyed along the road from Caerhun to Dolwyddelan."

Gareth's brow furrowed as he thought back to three years ago and what he'd been doing at the time. He'd been a member of Hywel's company for almost two years by that point. "Tegwen was married to *that* Bran?"

"Indeed," Hywel said.

Gareth looked away, his mind churning. "I remember that he died. In fact, wasn't he ambushed not far from where Anarawd's company was ambushed?" At this second mention of Anarawd's murder, Gareth didn't look at Hywel and hurriedly continued, "Why wasn't I among those investigating his death? Where was I? Where were you?"

"You were with me," Hywel said. "We spent most of that year in Ireland, remember? I didn't learn of his death until my father told me of it six months after it happened. By then, with no trail to follow and nothing to investigate, he didn't see the point in wasting my time with an inquiry."

"Who benefited from Bran's death?" Gareth said.

Hywel gave him a dark look. "That is the one question that we never ask, and you know it. Bran was the Lord of Rhos and had no sons. Who do you think benefited?"

"His younger brother. I see, but surely—" Gareth broke off what he'd been about to say: *but surely his brother wouldn't have murdered him?* But surely he would have, if it meant gaining the lordship.

"Bran was the second son of his father, and Tegwen had given him only daughters." Hywel had gone back to studying the body of his cousin. "The elder brother died, as did many of our men, during the wars in Ceredigion, and upon Bran's death, the third son, Ifon, inherited."

Given that King Owain himself had inherited Gwynedd under identical circumstances—the untimely death in battle of an older brother—it was no wonder that he didn't want to delve too deeply into Bran's murder and the subsequent inheritance of the cantref by a third son. How King Owain had for so long tolerated having his younger brother, Prince Cadwaladr, anywhere near him was a mystery to Gareth. All that stood between Cadwaladr and the throne of Gwynedd was Owain himself. Then again, King Owain might think it was better to keep an eye on the treacherous prince than to have him far away doing God knew what.

Until Prince Hywel had elevated Gareth to the captain of his guard and given him lands of his own, the politics of Gwynedd had concerned him only as far as they concerned Hywel. More recently, Gareth had started paying more attention.

"I wouldn't worry too much about the younger brother," Hywel said. "Ifon hasn't a violent bone in his body. I can't see him having anything to do with his brother's death. Or Tegwen's, for that matter."

Hywel's comment violated their oft-spoken motto, *never assume*, but Gareth let it go for now. He'd met Ifon, and Hywel's assessment was accurate up to a point. Still, while Ifon might not have an impressive intellect or the same skill with a sword as his older brother, Gareth had worked for Hywel long enough to know that the face a person showed to the world often belied his true character. You could never know what was in another's heart, especially when he rarely talked about himself or put himself forward.

"My lord, I have news." Adda finally reappeared with Rhodri and Dewi in tow.

A look of disdain crossed Hywel's face at the sound of Adda's voice, but since Hywel still faced Gareth, Adda didn't see it. Hywel rolled his eyes at Gareth and then cleared his expression before turning around. "Good. Let's hear it."

"I was unable to find any witnesses to this incident." Adda held his back straight and gazed at a point to the right of Hywel's left shoulder. "I did discover tracks that I believe are from a cart. They start twenty yards up the beach from the body and continue past where we left the horses. If I am not mistaken, there are two sets: coming and going."

Gareth took a step closer. "Rhodri and Dewi brought a cart when they arrived with Gwen. How can you tell the difference between the tracks?"

"The other set goes off towards the west," Adda said. "They are deeper, too, as if the cart carried a load."

Gareth nodded. "Excellent work." Adda's observations were far more insightful than Gareth would have given him credit for.

Prince Hywel looked Adda up and down as if seeing him with new eyes too. "What happens after the tracks reach the road?"

"It is impossible to trace them, my lord," Adda said, still stiff.

"Did you stand watch last night?" Prince Hywel said.

"No, my lord," Adda said. "Mine was the morning shift."

"Find the man you replaced and bring him to me once I return to the castle," Prince Hywel said. "You are dismissed."

"Yes, sir." Adda saluted and departed with Dewi.

Rhodri had been hovering on the margins of their conversation and didn't leave with Adda even though the older soldier shot him a look that indicated he should. While Hywel bent to Tegwen's body and began wrapping her back up in her cloak, Rhodri stepped towards Gareth. "My lord, if I may have a word?"

Gareth nodded and moved with Rhodri to one side, out of earshot of Hywel. "What is it?" It wasn't that he wouldn't share the information Rhodri was bringing him with Hywel but that there was a solemnity to Hywel's movements that Gareth didn't want to disturb.

"I wanted you to know that I wasn't on duty either; I was here. I brought my boy to the beach this morning. My family are fishermen, and it's his heritage, you see."

Having seen to Tegwen, Hywel signaled to several of the men to come help him carry Tegwen's body to the cart. Gareth turned back to Rhodri, who hurriedly continued, "I didn't notice her until the children pointed her out, seeing how it was still dark when we arrived, and it was at least an hour that she lay on the beach before there was enough light to see by. The lanterns don't shed much light beyond a small circle, you see."

"You don't have to apologize, Rhodri," Gareth said. "She'd been dead a long while before today."

Rhodri ducked his head. "It's not that. It's this." From his pocket, Rhodri brought out a coin pendant with a hole shot through it and strung on a length of leather thong. "Within a few moments of our arrival, my boy found this lying on the path. He picked it up, thinking to keep it, but I reckon that it isn't his to keep."

Gareth took the pendant and held it out flat in the palm of his hand, a cold wave of dismay flooding his chest. It was clearly old and so worn that Gareth couldn't read the writing on the coin or make out the image on its face. It would have been worn as a necklace and passed through many hands to reach his. "Thank you, Rhodri, for your honesty. I will show this to Prince Hywel."

"I thought it might be the dead woman's, you see," he said. "I couldn't by rights keep it."

"See to your boy. This can't have been an easy day for him." Gareth dismissed Rhodri and returned to Hywel's side. The prince had by now seen his cousin safely ensconced in the cart. Gareth waited patiently for Hywel to finish adjusting the cloak so it covered Tegwen completely and then caught his lord's attention, touching his sleeve and stepping away from the group of men who had gathered themselves for the somber journey to Aber Castle.

Hywel's expression turned wary at seeing the concern on Gareth's face, and when Gareth handed him the necklace and explained where it had been found, the muscles in Hywel's jaw tightened. He turned the coin over in his fingers, licking his lips and as reluctant as Gareth to speak.

Finally, Hywel said, "You know as well as I do to whom this belongs."

"I will name him if you won't," Gareth said.

Hywel shook his head. "Uncle Cadwaladr, what have you done now?"

3

Hywel

*U*ncle Cadwaladr.

Although Hywel had never liked him, his very existence had been haunting Hywel for over a year now. At first, it had been because he hired a company of Danes from Dublin to ambush and murder King Anarawd of Deheubarth and Hywel had been instrumental in proving his culpability. Since then, Hywel had taken over Cadwaladr's castle and lands in Ceredigion, and the legacy of his uncle's every decision had been dogging Hywel's steps. Cadwaladr had been a bad ruler, alienating the populace and fomenting discontent such that they didn't trust *those foreigners from Gwynedd*, of which they viewed Hywel most definitely as one.

And the worst thing was that Hywel could see Cadwaladr in himself. A few different pieces to his life—and a few different people in his life—and he and Cadwaladr could have been very much alike.

Long ago, when Gwen and Hywel were no more than eight and nine, Gwen had openly chastised Hywel for his behavior for the first time. Hywel had taken a kitten from the daughter of one of the kitchen staff and hidden it from her in his room. He hadn't hurt it, but when Gwen learned that the kitten was missing, she'd come to him, all fire and outrage.

At first he'd tried to brazen it out, but then he'd succumbed to her glare and shown her where he was keeping it and that it wasn't hurt. Gwen had then asked him, *why would you take pleasure in hurting others?*

Such a simple question, and one that he'd at first refused to answer, though his heart had sunk into his boots. He hadn't known why he'd stolen the kitten. It had been a game to him with no real consequences from his end, since he'd intended to return it eventually. But he'd hated the disappointment he'd seen in Gwen's eyes. She could see right through him.

Everyone else he could charm—and he'd charmed Gwen plenty too, he knew—but not when right and wrong were at stake. If not for Gwen—not just that time, but all the times she pointed him in a better direction from the one he was taking, though usually more subtly than in that first instance—Hywel wondered if he wouldn't have turned out like his uncle.

Hywel knew himself to be perfectly capable of killing. He'd done it in battle. He'd killed Anarawd, who was to have been his brother-in-law, and not lost more than a night or two of sleep over it. He'd justified his actions, as all men did, by telling himself that what he'd done was *right*, because to believe anything else would be to undermine his very existence.

But Cadwaladr was a different animal entirely, and Hywel didn't think he was just telling himself that in order to feel better about hating his uncle. Cadwaladr really did care only about himself: how he felt, what his position was, how other people viewed him. He'd been spoiled by his mother, or so Hywel understood. Hywel had no idea what that was like, since his own mother had died at his birth, and he'd been raised by a series of nannies and foster mothers.

Just like Tegwen.

Until he was seven years old, Hywel hadn't even lived with his father, who had fostered him and Rhun out to a man named Cadifor, with estates on the Lleyn Peninsula. Hywel's father had brought the boys to him when Cadifor's wife died, and he deemed them old enough to take their place at court. Hywel had hoped that Cadifor would bring his sons to Aber to celebrate the harvest, but three years running he'd stayed home, and given the lateness of the hour, Hywel supposed he would do the same this year too.

Hywel didn't think it was an estrangement keeping them apart, or at least he hoped it wasn't. Hywel would have to go to him if many more months passed without them seeing each other. He'd get Rhun to come. If Hywel had offended his foster family in some way, Rhun would help smooth it over.

Hywel's men-at-arms clustered together near the cart, and Hywel tried to focus on each one as they spoke to him of what they'd found—or rather, not found—on the beach. He hadn't put Cadwaladr's pendant coin away. He wouldn't keep it himself; when Gareth returned from collecting Llelo, Hywel would give it to Gareth to hold. It wasn't that Hywel's scrip was too full but rather that the thought of having something near him that belonged to his uncle turned his stomach, even if that something was evidence against him.

Hywel clenched his fist around the coin. He could admit that he hated Cadwaladr, and part of him rejoiced at the idea that he'd caught his devious uncle out in more wrongdoing, but Hywel feared it too. The next break between King Owain and Cadwaladr might well be the last, and then there was no telling what Cadwaladr might do. If he were cast out, Hywel's father would have no more control over him.

Though, judging from today, the control that King Owain did have was no more than an illusion.

Unable to contain his body when his thoughts were in turmoil, Hywel spun away from the cart and climbed to the top of the adjacent dune. He could see Aber's towers from here and, facing the other way, the Lavan Sands, Anglesey, and the Irish Sea stretching into the distance. This was home. He and Gwen had ranged all over the cantref as youngsters. He'd missed the quality of the air and the sea while he'd been away. He'd missed the mountains.

He'd come back from Ceredigion to breathe this air and see this view. He'd needed to see his wife, Mari, too, and had been looking for a respite from the pressures and the petty conflicts that marked his life. He desperately wanted to bring Mari south with him when he returned. She was smart and capable, and he surely needed every capable hand he could find.

His father had taken the lordship from Cadwaladr and given it to Hywel as his own and as a test of Hywel's character. He needed Hywel to hold it, for Hywel's own sake and as a buffer for Gwynedd against the Normans in Pembroke and the ambitions of King Cadell in Deheubarth. It burned Hywel to admit that within a year of receiving ownership, he was perilously close to losing it. Enemies confronted him on all sides, and while he was gaining experience every day, it wasn't happening quickly enough.

Gareth was a good man—a good leader—but he knew even less about governing a people than Hywel did. Ruling a kingdom wasn't the same as winning it. It was as if his father had sailed with him in a boat halfway to Ireland and then shoved him out of it, saying, "Swim." By God, Hywel was swimming as hard as he could, but Ceregidion wasn't Gwynedd. The people there had spent far too much time among Normans to understand how true Welshmen lived and acted. The lesser lords plotted and connived, always looking for a weakness.

Hywel hadn't known what real leadership was until this year, and it terrified him to think he didn't have it in him. So far, Hywel's father hadn't said anything to him about the men he'd lost or the money he was spending. He had to think that, for now, his father believed that having Hywel in charge of Ceredigion was better than having Cadwaladr, whom he was punishing. But if Hywel didn't get control of the cantref soon, he might find himself yanked by the neck hairs back to Gwynedd.

"My lord?" Evan approached the base of the dune and looked up at Hywel with a concerned expression.

"What is it?" Hywel glanced down at him, hastily rearranging his thoughts and smoothing his expression in case what was going on inside his head showed.

"We await your orders, my lord."

"I'm coming now." Hywel took a last look at the view and then slid down the dune, holding his arms out for balance so he wouldn't land ignominiously on his rear. As he reached level ground again, one of the guards who had departed with Gwen returned.

The man dismounted by the cart and went down on one knee before Hywel, far more formally than was usual for his men, but the occasion seemed to have touched everyone and demanded it. "I am so sorry for your loss, my lord."

Hywel looked down at the man's bowed head and then snapped his fingers, indicating that he should rise. The man was in his middle thirties and had served Hywel's father before transferring to Hywel's company. "Thank you, Cynan. How do you know I have experienced a loss?"

Cynan straightened his back and looked at Hywel, his expression confused. "Isn't this the body of Princess Tegwen?"

"Did Gwen tell you that?"

"No, my lord." Cynan licked his lips. "I apologize if I shouldn't have looked at her while you were examining her, but I did look." He made a helpless gesture with one hand. "She's wearing Tegwen's garnet and her cloak."

"It's been five years since anyone has seen her," Hywel said. "How is it that you remember what she wore?"

Color rose in Cynan's face. "She was beautiful, my lord, and full of life."

Evan had been listening to their exchange, and now he stepped closer, bowing his head as Cynan had. When he looked up, his face wore a stunned expression. "My lord, please. I couldn't help but overhear that you believe this is Tegwen. But it can't be. She ran away with a Dane."

"Apparently, she didn't." Hywel studied the faces of his men, acknowledging that the body's identity was no longer a secret and he shouldn't pretend his men didn't know. "Does anyone remember who it was that saw her sail away?"

Dewi, the driver of the cart, raised his hand. "I believe it was her maid."

Cynan's brow furrowed. "I thought it was a guard on duty at Bryn Euryn."

That was as Hywel remembered too. "Did you speak of this to anyone at Aber just now, Cynan?"

"No, my lord." Cynan shook his head. "It was my understanding that it was Gwen's task to inform the king. I delivered her to the castle and said nothing to anyone before returning. It was what I thought you expected of me."

"Good man." Hywel rested a hand briefly on Cynan's shoulder. "I would appreciate it if you would keep her identity to yourselves until my father announces it in the hall."

There were nods all around, and then Hywel turned to see Gareth hiking up the beach with his foster son. Gareth glanced up and saw Hywel looking at him. He raised one shoulder in a half-shrug, his expression showing the same resignation and acceptance of his fate that Hywel himself felt.

"We came home looking for a respite from our troubles, my lord," Evan said, "only to have trouble find us instead."

Hywel allowed himself a slight laugh. "You would think we'd have learned by now to expect it."

4

Gwen

The early morning activity in the castle came to a sudden halt the moment Gwen rode underneath the portcullis and reined in before the gate. Her brother, Gwalchmai, appeared at her side to help her down from her horse. Because he often entertained the hall late into the night, it was rare that he was awake at this hour, so he had to have been watching for her. A moment later, her father, Meilyr, hurried from a side doorway, puffing with every step. His belly had expanded into a paunch in the last year since they'd returned to Aber, and of late his shortness of breath had her worrying about his health.

"Well? Can you tell me what's happened?" Gwalchmai had grown over the summer too, undoubtedly trying to keep up with Llelo, and was now tall enough to look into Gwen's eyes. "We heard that a woman's body has washed up on the beach."

"It didn't wash up, but that's all I can tell you right now. Prince Hywel sent me back to Aber to speak to the king. Father—" Gwen broke off as she greeted Meilyr with a kiss on the cheek. They had come a long way since the cold silences, sometimes lasting a week, that had haunted their relationship before her marriage to Gareth. She'd grown up, and if her father's heart had expanded along with his belly, she couldn't begrudge him the long, mellow evenings that had caused the change. "I can't say anything about it until I see him."

"You should speak to Taran first," Meilyr said. Lord Taran was the king's steward and closest confidant. "I will accompany you." He pinned his gaze on his son. "Gwalchmai, you stay here."

Gwalchmai opened his mouth to protest, but Gwen put a hand on his arm. "This is serious. I will tell you all about what has happened afterwards, though you may hear rumors before I get to you. It's not going to be a secret for long."

Gwalchmai settled back on his heels with a suppressed sigh but didn't protest again. Gwen left her horse with him and entered the keep with her father, who held the door for her. The keep housed the great hall and had two wings leading off of it, guarded by stone towers at each corner. Taran's room was the door closest to the great hall in the east wing, while the king's rooms were further along the corridor.

Unlike in past years, Gwen wasn't resentful of her father's presence. In fact, she was grateful for it. He might be accompanying her because he wanted to know what was going on as much as because he was worried for her, but telling the king that his long-lost niece was dead was not a task she relished taking on all by herself.

"Someone is dead?" Meilyr stopped outside Taran's door.

"I'm afraid so. It's someone he cared about," Gwen said.

"He was in a mellow mood last night when he retired," Meilyr said.

"I'm sure it was in part because you and Gwalchmai sang so well."

Meilyr bowed his head in silent thanks. "I suspect tonight's entertainment will be more in the way of forgetting our troubles than to celebrate the harvest."

Gwen's father was right that the king's good humor at seeing all of his people gathered in his hall wasn't going to last beyond the next few moments. "Better that than not to have any music at all. This is not a message I would ever choose to bring to the king."

Meilyr straightened his tunic. "Are you ready?"

At Gwen's *yes*, he reached up to knock on Taran's door, but it opened before his knuckles hit the wood so that Meilyr almost rapped on the steward's nose.

"Meilyr! Gwen! What are you doing here? I heard voices outside my door and wondered who it might be."

"I'm sorry to disturb you," Gwen said.

"How may I help you?" When he'd opened the door, Taran had still been adjusting his sleeves inside his coat, and now he pulled them straight with quick jerks.

Gwen licked her lips and glanced quickly at her father, who gave her a slight nod. "One of the guards woke me earlier to tell me that a body had been found on the beach," she said. "He was looking for Gareth, but since Gareth and Prince Hywel were on patrol, I went to see it in their place. Once they returned, the prince recognized who it was and sent me to inform the king before he could hear about it from someone else."

Taran smoothed his mustache, his eyes on Gwen's. "Just say what you have to say, child. I can tell that you are bringing bad news."

Gwen glanced right and left to make sure they were still alone in the corridor. "Hywel believes the body to be that of Tegwen, the king's niece."

Taran took a step back, his heel bumping the bottom of the door behind him. "That's not possible. She's been gone these five years. She ran away."

"She may have done so," Gwen said, "but it seems she didn't get far."

Meilyr, too, was staring at Gwen. "She ran away with a Dane. She was seen getting into a boat with him."

"I know that was what we were all told," Gwen said. "As I said, it may have been true. But somehow she has ended up on Aber's beach five years later."

Taran was standing with a hand pressed to the top of his head. "You are sure it's Tegwen?"

"Hywel is certain or he wouldn't have sent me." Gwen took Taran's free hand and squeezed it. "It's more complicated than that, too, because it's obvious that she's been dead a long while. Her body is all dried out like—" Gwen cleared her throat, "—pardon me for saying it, but like an old apple."

"Then how do you know it is she?" Taran said.

"Hywel is sure, my lord," Gwen said. "I am only doing as I was bidden."

"How did she die?" Meilyr said.

"Someone bashed her skull in," Gwen said, and at Taran's horrified look, added, "I know. It's awful. Here we've spent the last five years believing that even if she ran away with a Dane, it was her choice, when all the while she's been dead in Gwynedd with her murderer walking free among us."

Taran closed his eyes and breathed deeply through his nose, letting the air out through his mouth. Then he opened his eyes, his usual manner of quiet competence returning. Releasing Gwen's hand, he said, "Come. We should go to the king. He won't like being disturbed, but he would prefer it to not being woken."

That had been Gareth's reasoning too, and Gwen was glad now that she had come, even if it was one of the worst tasks she'd ever been set. She tugged her cloak closer around her, chilled even though the corridor wasn't cold. In her mind's eye, she kept seeing the dent in Tegwen's skull and the blood. Death came to everyone, of course. Each person lived with it every day, but it was hard to know that it had come by murder to Tegwen. As Taran had said, they'd all imagined her happy with her Dane. The truth was going to be like a bucket of cold water thrown over Aber.

As they walked down the corridor to King Owain's quarters, Gwen was glad she had the two older men to buttress her on either side. During the short ride from the beach, she'd been dreading knocking on King Owain's door, especially if Cristina was beside him. Unlike Gwen and Gareth, the queen and king didn't always share a bed. Cristina had her own room on the floor above, and she slept there roughly half the time. Gwen had overheard Cristina telling one of her ladies-in-waiting that the king snored. Cristina could endure it less well now that she was heavily pregnant with their first child and not sleeping well herself.

It was Cristina, more than King Owain, who would resent an unexpected visitor outside her door. Gwen suspected the reason was less that she didn't like being woken than that she didn't like anyone to see her before her maid had dressed her and fixed her hair. Coupled with her difficulty sleeping and her pregnancy, Cristina was all the more to be avoided in the morning.

Taran rapped his knuckles on the door. "My lord? May I have a word?"

Gwen heard the thud of King Owain's feet hitting the floor and his lumbering tread to the door, which opened to reveal his burly form, wild golden hair going gray, and heavy-lidded eyes. With so many visitors at Aber for the celebration of Hallowmas and Calan Gaeaf, the king had experienced a succession of late evenings and had consumed more mead than was his usual custom. He enjoyed his comforts, but Cristina and he retired early most nights, especially since she'd fallen pregnant.

Gwen knew what that was like. Some days, she could barely keep her eyes open during the evening meal, and she would have slept until noon if her duties hadn't called to her.

"What is it?" King Owain hung on to the doorframe, one arm above his head.

Gwen tried not to wilt under the king's glare. He didn't have the look of a man with a full measure of patience. Swallowing hard, she braced herself to tell him straight out. "A body was found on the beach this morning. I have seen it, and Gareth and Prince Hywel are examining it now. The prince believes it to be the body of Tegwen, your niece, whom we believed ran away with a Dane five years ago."

There. That had been as succinct a statement as she could make.

King Owain, for his part, stared at Gwen through several breaths without responding. Then he looked to Taran, who nodded, his jaw tight, and then back to Gwen. "You found a body on the beach that Hywel believes to be Tegwen's? How is that possible?"

"My lord, Hywel recognized her."

"Did she drown?" King Owain said.

"No, my lord. From the condition of the body, Hywel judges that she has been dead many years." Gwen knew she was a coward for not owning that estimate herself, but King Owain would accept Hywel's authority more than hers in this instance.

"Then how could he possibly recognize her? She would be nothing but bones."

There it was again, the point that they would be addressing over and over again. In Wales, it rained all the time. The ground was moist year round, and anything and everything that spent any time outside rotted away, even items still in use. Clothing, rope, wooden posts that held up a roof. Gwen herself was still having trouble accepting the strange condition of the body. Not to mention the disturbing fact that someone had found it and then left it on the beach.

Gwen bowed, loath to explain further but knowing that she must. "Her form is dried and desiccated. But even I, who didn't know Tegwen well, can recognize her now that Hywel has named her. She was wrapped in the cloak you gave her upon her betrothal to Lord Bran."

King Owain wasn't buying it. "If she has been dead for years, how is it that she lies on the beach?"

"That is something we cannot yet explain," Gwen said.

The king ran a hand through his hair and looked behind him to Cristina. She'd been listening to their exchange, sitting up in bed with the blankets pulled up to her chin.

"It could be another girl dressed in Tegwen's cloak," Cristina said.

King Owain's eyes flicked back to Gwen's, and then he returned them to his wife's face. "Yes, of course, my dear. Don't upset yourself. Whatever happened to this girl, Tegwen or not, it happened a long time ago." He'd taken a step towards Cristina as he'd spoken to her but now turned back, moving into the doorway, closer to Gwen. He pulled the door nearly closed behind him, with only a sliver of empty space between the door and the frame. He didn't want Cristina to hear him. "Do you have any indication as to how she died?"

Gwen found her gaze dropping to her shoes so she wouldn't have to see King Owain's expression when she told him. "My lord, her hair is matted with blood and her skull crushed."

"So on top of everything else, this is murder," King Owain said.

"The location of the wound makes a fall from a horse unlikely but not impossible," Gwen said. "Hywel may already have discovered more about it, but he sent me to find you so you wouldn't learn of this from someone else."

King Owain pursed his lips. "Wait for me in the hall. I would speak to you further."

Gwen curtseyed. "Yes, my lord."

The king looked at Taran. "We'll have to inform Gruffydd."

"He and Sioned should be arriving at Aber this afternoon." Taran's mouth turned down. "They'll be bringing Tegwen's daughters with them." After Bran's murder, Tegwen's grandparents had taken her two daughters in to raise, as they'd raised Tegwen upon Ilar's death.

"That is a conversation I am not looking forward to." King Owain went back into his room and shut the door.

The three companions in the corridor heaved a mutual sigh of relief. "That went better than I had any right to expect," Taran said.

But as they turned away to head to the great hall to wait for the king as he'd requested, a crash resounded from within King Owain's bedroom. "A chair has met its demise, I would say," Meilyr said.

Taran walked steadily down the hall. "Cristina will see to him."

"Coward," Meilyr said.

Turning his head to look back at them, Taran shot Gwen and her father a grin. "Definitely." Then he sobered and stopped a few feet from the end of the corridor. "Putting entirely aside the matter of Tegwen's death and that we've been deceived all these years as to the manner in which she left us, why would someone remove her from her grave and leave her on the beach?"

"I do not know, my lord. I don't even know if that's what has happened," Gwen said. "I think we won't know until Gareth and I—and Prince Hywel, of course—start asking questions. It may be difficult to discover the sequence of events, however, given how long ago she disappeared."

"I will give you any assistance I can—" Taran turned to look towards the doorway to the great hall.

Gwen waited a beat. "What is it?"

Taran cleared his throat, and it was only when he wiped at the corner of his eye that she saw the tears on his cheeks. "She was a dear girl. I liked the thought of her in the arms of some mighty Dane. She deserved to be loved and protected."

"What about Bran—?" But Gwen had asked the question to Taran's back. Two strides had taken him into the hall where he was immediately besieged by men wanting to know what had happened.

Meilyr rested a hand on Gwen's shoulder. "Let him go. He'll speak to you again when he's ready."

Gwen swung around. "Do you know what he's talking about? Obviously if everyone accepted that she ran away with a Dane, something was wrong with Tegwen's marriage to Bran."

Meilyr's mouth thinned. "I do not know the details."

"I don't need the details as much as I need to know what you're thinking," Gwen said. "I can fill those in later from someone who knew her better."

"You may recall that I played at the wedding?" Meilyr said. At Gwen's nod, he continued, "She was not a happy bride."

When her father didn't elaborate further, Gwen said, "Is that all?"

"To tell you the truth, I didn't inquire at the time. It was none of my business. Gwalchmai wasn't even four. I had my own troubles."

"We all did." She fixed her father with a look. "So you can't tell me any more than that?"

Her father was silent for a moment and then said, "Let's just say there were rumors that Tegwen didn't come to the marriage bed a maiden."

Gwen raised her eyebrows. Her father did think she had grown up if he was willing to speak so openly to her. "Such is the case with many girls, or so I understand, but it isn't usually something the rest of Gwynedd knows about."

Meilyr's lips pressed together. "Taran believed that Tegwen was a sweet girl, but I never got that impression. Maybe she was quiet, but still waters can run deep. Of course, I didn't know her as well as Taran did, and we left Gwynedd not long after her wedding."

For all that she and Tegwen had been close in age, Tegwen had never befriended Gwen, having friends of her own of a nobler class, and it hadn't been Gwen's place to join them. In fact, until today, Gwen hadn't thought anything much about Tegwen at all and struggled to recall a substantial memory with Tegwen in it. Hywel had known her better, but then, Hywel had always made it his business to acquaint himself with every girl, eligible or not, cousin or not, within a hundred mile radius of wherever he was living at the time.

Hywel appeared to have put that life behind him with his marriage. Upon entering the hall with her father, Gwen spotted Hywel's wife, Mari, sitting at the high table among some of the lords of Gwynedd who'd come for Calan Gaeaf. Since Gwen was supposed to wait for King Owain there, she excused herself from her father and made her way to where Mari sat. Gwen wouldn't normally have merited a chair at the high table, but since it was early in the morning and plenty of seats were empty, she sat when Mari patted the chair beside her.

"Tell me," Mari said, "where is my husband?"

"He's standing over a body," Gwen said. "I suppose I can tell you because everyone is going to know shortly, but Hywel believes it to be the remains of his cousin, Tegwen."

Mari put her hand to her mouth. "How can that be? She ran away with a Dane five years ago."

Gwen wondered how many times she would hear that exact phrase today. The story was legend. After Gwen had returned to Gwynedd last year, she'd even heard girls giggling about their marriage prospects with the caveat *you can always run away with a Dane* if the man didn't turn out to be all that a girl wished. Gwen hadn't realized where the phrase came from until today.

"Or maybe she didn't," Gwen said. "I know that's the story, but Hywel is very sure that the body is the remains of Tegwen or he wouldn't have sent me home to Aber to tell King Owain of it."

"Do you mean to say that Tegwen has been alive this whole time? Do you have any idea where she's been living? How could we have not known of her?"

Gwen shook her head. "No, no. That's just it. She hasn't. It looks as if she died years ago—maybe even the very day she disappeared." The more Gwen thought about it, the more likely that scenario seemed to her. Running away with a Dane would have put Tegwen out of reach, but surely someone would have heard a rumor of her at least once in all these years. Gwen herself had gone to Dublin last year (which was a polite way of putting it, given that Prince Cadwaladr had abducted her) but she hadn't seen Tegwen among the court. Admittedly, she hadn't thought to look either. "For some reason, someone left her body on the beach early this morning."

Mari's face had gone very white, and Gwen pressed her hand. "Did you know her?"

"Yes, I did." Mari took a sip of warm mead, and some color returned to her face. "My uncle Goronwy and her grandfather were well acquainted. She and I were the same age, and she visited my uncle's estates often." Her brow furrowed. "You are of an age with us, more or less. Why didn't you know her?"

Gwen explained again why she hadn't, though she was beginning to wonder if the issue wasn't so much that Tegwen hadn't been at court as that Gwen hadn't sought her out when she'd visited. At the time, Gwen's life had revolved around Hywel. Gwen's only other excuse was that Tegwen had married Bran at fifteen, and Gwen had left Gwynedd with her father shortly thereafter, on the heels of King Owain assuming the throne after the war in Ceredigion.

"Mari, when did you last see her?"

Mari rubbed at her forehead with her fingers as if she had a headache. Gwen felt one coming on too. "Perhaps ... a few weeks before she disappeared? She confided in me that she thought she might be pregnant again."

"Did she seem happy?" Gwen said.

Mari looked at Gwen through narrowed eyes. "Yes, of course. Why are you asking me this?"

"Mari, Tegwen's skull was fractured. We suspect—Hywel, Gareth, and I—that someone hit her very hard and killed her. Do you have any idea who could have done such a thing? Or why?"

Mari rubbed at the back of her neck and looked down at the table.

"What is it? What don't you want to tell me?" Gwen said.

Mari let out a sigh. "When I last saw Tegwen, she told me that she'd learned a terrible secret about her husband. It was tearing her apart."

"What was the secret?" Gwen said.

Mari shook her head. "I tried to get it out of her, but she wouldn't tell me. She didn't want to cast aspersions on Bran's character."

Gwen frowned. "If I thought about her at all, I assumed her marriage was unhappy since she'd run away. You're saying it wasn't?"

"The truth is, when we were girls, Tegwen fell in and out of love every week depending upon which man had talked to her most recently." Mari shrugged. "I suppose I was like that at fifteen too, but Tegwen never learned constancy. When she told me she no longer loved her husband, I didn't think anything of it because she'd said as much to me at least once a year and then changed her mind if he bought her a new dress. Still, she seemed different, more somber this time."

"Is that why you believed, as we all did, that she ran off with a Dane?" Gwen said.

"Not exactly," Mari said. "I thought she'd run away with the man she'd loved before she married Bran."

That coincided with her father's comment, but Gwen still felt a little overwhelmed by what Mari was telling her. She really hadn't known Tegwen. "Tegwen loved someone before Bran? I mean, more than just a passing fancy?"

"Oh yes," Mari said. "So much so that she pleaded to King Owain—though he wasn't king at that time—for him or his father to intervene and prevent the marriage, but neither saw a reason to go against the wishes of her family. I don't know if anyone else other than a few of her close friends knew about this other man. I never met him or even knew his name, but if he was a Dane and not well-born, it would have been an impossible match for a princess."

"It may come out now that he never existed," Gwen said.

"Oh, he was real," Mari said. "I know that for certain."

"How?" Gwen said.

"She was all mysterious smiles and knowing looks whenever anyone talked about a man whom they were interested in. She referred to him only as 'B', and the letter didn't stand for Bran."

"I don't see why they didn't elope in the first place," Gwen said. "In seven years, their marriage could have been as legal as any other."

"She was a princess," Mari said.

Gwen looked at her friend out of the corner of her eye. "Was she unfaithful to Bran after the wedding?"

Mari bit her lip. "I think so, but not right away. You met him, didn't you?"

"I suppose." Gwen shrugged, casting her mind back to that long-ago time. "I must have seen him when he came to Aber or Aberffraw."

Mari raised her eyebrows. "You must not have been paying attention. Bran was incredibly handsome. All the girls favored him. Tegwen ended up admiring him too. And he treated her very well initially."

"So Bran did love her back?"

"Bran wanted her because she was beautiful and Prince Cadwallon's daughter," Mari said.

"So 'no'," Gwen said. "What about Tegwen's lover?"

"Whoever he was, he broke it off with her when she married Bran. It was only at the end that she took up with him again."

Even as a married woman, Gwen found this story shocking. She knew that women weren't always faithful to their husbands. Husbands certainly weren't faithful to their wives, though a wife had the right to compensation and to divorce her husband if he lay with another woman three times. In turn, if Bran discovered Tegwen with another man, he was justified in beating her. "Did Bran find out?" Gwen said.

"I don't know," Mari said.

"Wait—I didn't really hear you when you mentioned it the first time, but did you say that she was pregnant when she disappeared?" Gwen said.

"She told me she was," Mari said.

"Was the child Bran's?" Gwen held her breath.

"I don't know." Mari said the words so quietly Gwen almost didn't catch them. "The two daughters she gave him definitely were his, but I don't know about the child she was carrying when she disappeared."

"No part of any story I have heard about Tegwen up until now mentions that she was pregnant." Gwen sat back, her mind churning at the information Mari had given her. For all that Gwen had traveled the length of Wales, lost her mother to childbirth, spent the last years as a spy for Prince Hywel, and was now a married woman, she could still be surprised by the behavior of those she lived amongst. "And you never knew the name of her lover?"

Mari shook her head. "I'm sorry. Tegwen would never tell me more than the scantiest details about him, not even after she'd found solace in too much wine and her tongue loosened."

Gwen looked carefully at her friend. "Was that a habit of hers, to drink too much?"

Mari's eyes were sad. "Married to a man who didn't love her, pregnant with a child she didn't want ... it isn't only men who choose that route."

Gwen swept a hand down her own belly. She couldn't help but smile as her child chose that moment to kick.

Mari was watching her closely. "You can't understand it, Gwen. Nor can I. But Tegwen deserves our pity, not our judgment."

"You misunderstand, Mari. I don't judge her, and I do pity her. I also know that with a few different twists of fate, her situation could have been mine. Wasn't Gareth in the same position as this lover of Tegwen's—worse, even, as he was banished from Cadwaladr's retinue and sent to wander Wales until he could find a lord to take him in?"

"I suppose," Mari said. "Come to think on it, I could have shared her fate as well, except that it was I who was impoverished, not the man I loved."

"And now you're married to a prince!"

The two friends clasped hands.

"I will do my best by Tegwen," Gwen said. "I promise."

5

Gareth

As he trudged up the beach beside his young charge, Gareth eyed the small sack Llelo had slung over his shoulder. "Are we having clams for breakfast?"

Llelo shot him a woeful look. "I didn't have time to dig up very many. It's not enough to share with more than a few people. I should give them to the king, shouldn't I?"

"Lucky for you, King Owain doesn't eat clams for breakfast," Gareth said. "Bring them to the kitchen for boiling and you can eat them at the cook's table. I know you spend half your life at it already."

"That's because I'm always hungry!"

Gareth shook Llelo's shoulder. "I saw you huddled with the children. I would think that there might be a few nightmares among them over the next day or two."

"Is it true that the body is that of the king's niece?" Llelo said.

"You heard that, did you?" Gareth said. "I can't say for sure. Prince Hywel thinks so."

"How could she come to look like that?" Llelo said. "If she drowned, her body would have been bloated, but if she died a long time ago, wouldn't her body have rotted away?"

"How would you know about that?" Gareth said.

Llelo shrugged. "I've seen plenty of dead animals. I found the remains of sheep we lost during a previous winter. Usually they're just bones by the time I get to them."

"Right. Of course." Gareth nodded, acknowledging that his thirteen-year-old self would have known as much, which was why it always stumped him when he came across adults who had no experience with dead bodies. Common folk who lived off the land or worked it had a very different perspective on life and death than the nobility. "Regardless of how recently she died, whether last month or years ago, her body was kept in a dry place and all the moisture leached from her before she could rot."

"Like if you leave a dead frog in the sun?" Llelo said.

"Even so," Gareth said.

Llelo's brow furrowed. "I came upon a cave once with a dead sheep inside. The body was all brown and dried out like this body. The wool was still soft!"

Gareth nodded. "That sounds like the right kind of place. You probably don't remember since you were so young, but we had a dry spring and summer the year Tegwen may have died. Crops failed, even on Anglesey, because of it." Herders had found the high pastures in the mountains parched along with the lowlands. Creeks and pools that had never failed in living memory had lacked water. Gareth had suffered himself in his trek to Dolwyddelan, finding places to fill his water skins in short supply.

The boy driving the cart that would carry Tegwen's body to Aber Castle had turned the horse around so it faced away from the beach, and Prince Hywel stood by the cart bed. Evan nodded at Gareth as he approached and stepped closer. "I have given a report to Prince Hywel."

"I will hear it from him and then from you," Gareth said. "Good work."

While Gareth moved to stand beside Prince Hywel, the men formed up behind them. Everyone would walk back to the castle behind the cart to honor the burden it was carrying. "Tegwen will receive the ceremony due her, even if five years too late," Hywel said.

"I'm sorry, my lord," Gareth said. "I wish there was something I could say to make this easier."

"We can find out who murdered her," Hywel said. "It's the least I can do. I failed her in life; I refuse to fail her in death."

"How did you fail her?" Gareth said. "It's hardly your fault that she's dead."

Hywel sighed. "She told me she didn't want to marry Bran, and I didn't help her talk to my father. I knew Bran had little regard for her and was marrying her because she was Cadwallon's daughter, but—" The muscles around his eyes tightened.

"Marrying for love is rare among noblemen," Gareth said.

"Not in my family," Hywel said. "We all marry for love. Why do you think my father sacrificed the Church's regard to marry Cristina?"

"He wanted to unite the last remnants of his family—"

"He loves her," Hywel said simply. "I love Mari. Rhun will find a wife soon too, and if he chooses a woman he doesn't love, my father will not accede to his request."

Gareth loved Gwen more than life itself, so he could understand what Hywel was saying. And it was certainly true that a Welsh woman of whatever status generally had more say in whom she married than a Norman noble woman. A couple's ability to elope was codified into Welsh law. King Owain's own sister had eloped with the much older King of Deheubarth, which was how Gwynedd had become involved in Ceredigion in the first place. While her husband was absent, negotiating a treaty in Gwynedd, a Norman force attacked her castle and killed her by hanging her from the battlement.

"So why didn't your father discourage Tegwen's union with Bran?" Gareth said.

"I don't know. Maybe her marriage is what made him think about his own unions differently," Hywel said. "I didn't know my father as well then as I do now. It's hard to think of him as ever being wrong about anything."

Gareth didn't know what to say to that. King Owain had thrown Gareth into a cell a year ago, having accused him of a murder he didn't commit. Hywel must have guessed what he was thinking, because he shot him a sardonic glance. "Except when he's angry, my father is usually a good judge of character."

"Was Bran a good man?" Gareth said. "I'm getting the sense that he wasn't."

"I didn't know him well." Hywel shrugged. "Many would say that my character leaves much to be desired, and yet my father trusts me, and I have ever sought to serve him. Perhaps the same could be said of Bran."

Gareth bowed his head, granting Hywel his point. "Given that Bran is dead, he cannot be our immediate concern. He was not the one who left Tegwen's body on the beach."

"We know who left her body on the beach," Hywel said.

"Cadwaladr," Gareth said.

Hywel scowled. "The question now is what drove my uncle to do so five years after Tegwen's disappearance."

"Five years after he killed her," Gareth said.

Hywel held up one finger. "We don't know that. We don't know anything about the circumstances of her death, and until we do, we will not speculate."

"Yes, my lord." Gareth acknowledged Hywel's authority in this matter, but just because they weren't going to talk about it didn't mean Gareth couldn't think it.

The cart started rolling forward, and after a pause for it to get a few yards ahead, Hywel lifted his horse's reins to get him moving. Gareth did the same.

"My lord, if I may, you were only fifteen when Tegwen married Bran," Gareth said, changing the subject in order to abide by his prince's wish. Maybe they didn't have to talk about Cadwaladr now, but they would have to face his involvement eventually. Gareth knew it was petty of him, but he couldn't be happier to learn of Cadwaladr's culpability. The man was a menace—to himself and to his country. King Owain was going to have to face his treachery eventually, and to Gareth's mind it was better to do so sooner rather than later, before he betrayed them more completely than he already had.

"I was a man," Hywel said. "That should have been enough."

Gareth shook his head. Even if Hywel was chastising himself for his failure now, the man he was then would never have interfered in the marriage of his cousin, no matter how much he loved her. Hywel's concern for Tegwen did shed new light on his intervention in his sister's marriage to Anarawd, who by all accounts hadn't been a good man either. In fact, it might explain everything.

Llelo tugged on Gareth's sleeve. "Da." Llelo had started calling him that in the last week since Gareth had returned from Ceredigion. It was a familiarity that warmed Gareth's heart, and he hoped their coming baby wouldn't put Llelo off or make him jealous. Every child needed an older brother—two in this case—though Dai, for all his youthful enthusiasm, was taking longer to warm up. "I found out one more thing. One of the boys I talked to lives to the west of the beach. He—Ceri—heard a cart pass by as he was returning from the latrine in the middle of the night. Carts never pass by at that hour, so he ran after it to see who it was."

Hywel came out of his reverie and looked past Gareth to Llelo. "Did Ceri recognize the driver?"

"It was too dark to make out the features of either the driver or a second man who walked ahead of the cart. Both were well-wrapped in cloak and hood. But he knew the horse."

That was the kind of news Gareth lived for. "Go on."

Llelo's eyes were bright. "The horse pastures on a steading west of the Aber River and just south of the road to Penrhyn."

Gareth looked at Prince Hywel. "Do we know who lives there?"

Hywel's brow furrowed. "I'm trying to think. I should know." He looked at Llelo. "Once we get Tegwen settled at Aber, we'll want to speak to the boy and his parents. Do you know where they live?"

Llelo nodded. "Yes, my lord."

Which was only as Gareth would have expected. He and Gwen had taken on Llelo and Dai out of charity, as two boys lost in the expanse of England, but it was the boys who'd added joy to their lives. Llelo had turned out to be thoughtful, responsible, and mature beyond his years. He was also curious and energetic, and combining all those qualities together had produced a boy who dug clams in the early hours of the morning and knew every farm and homestead—and their inhabitants—from here to Bangor.

Although Gareth had been absent all summer in Ceredigion and hadn't witnessed it himself, Gwen reported that Llelo and Dai had ranged all over the region since they'd come home. At Aber, they'd joined the pack of boys that included

Gwalchmai, Gwen's brother, and Iorwerth, the king's eldest son by his first wife, Gwladys. Under Cristina's rule, the boys had found Aber Castle less hospitable than before her tenure. Particularly now that she was pregnant, she had shown resentment towards King Owain's sons by other women, and the boys had learned very quickly that life went more smoothly when they stayed out of her way.

"Stay close so I don't have to hunt you down later. And don't speak of this to anyone else. I believe this investigation will be one of the more—" Gareth glanced at Hywel, who'd gone back to ruminating on his failings, "—delicate ones we've undertaken."

"Yes, Da," Llelo said and fell back to walk behind Gareth with the other soldiers.

It was only a half-mile from the beach to Aber Castle: a short walk, if somber. The driver brought the cart to a halt before entering the castle, and King Owain came out from underneath the gatehouse to greet them. He paced towards Prince Hywel, who bowed along with everyone else at his approach. Gareth and the other men held that position until Hywel raised his head.

"Sire," Hywel said.

"I'd like to see her for myself before you take her inside," King Owain said.

Hywel stepped to the cart bed and gently peeled back the hood that covered Tegwen's face.

King Owain reached out a hand, hovering it over her hair and hesitating. "Do you really think this is she, son? Her features are unrecognizable, and her hair has more red in it than I remember."

"Perhaps. But you haven't yet seen the whole of her." With two fingers, Hywel carefully opened the cloak at her throat and lifted up the garnet ring that rested on its chain. "This was hers, as was the cloak." He pointed to the embroidery on the hem.

King Owain recoiled slightly but recovered after a moment and moved closer again. This time, he rested a hand on the top of her head. "What became of you that your life ended here?"

As a kinswoman, Tegwen's welfare had been King Owain's responsibility more than Hywel's. King Owain's father, also named Gruffydd like Tegwen's grandfather, had been king at the time, but Owain had already shouldered much of the responsibility for the kingdom by the time Tegwen married Bran. Her death was made all the worse by the fact that he'd pictured her happy, far away in another land. They'd mourned her at the time as they would have mourned any similar loss, but this was a different kind of grief.

Pain was etched into the king's face as he turned to his son. "Gwen says Tegwen was murdered."

"It seems so, Father."

King Owain touched the side of Tegwen's head, feeling at her scalp as they all had. Hywel didn't stop him. A crowd of people had followed the king out of the castle, gathering around the cart and the soldiers who'd accompanied it from the beach. Gareth didn't know that he'd ever seen a people as silent as they, not even at chapel, as they watched their king stand over the fallen princess.

Finally, King Owain sighed and covered Tegwen's face again. "You will find out who did this."

"Yes, Father."

And with those simple words, King Owain once again delegated a sensitive and difficult task to this younger son. With a wave from King Owain, the driver of the cart urged his horse through the gate and into the courtyard of the castle. Hywel hung back to confer with Gareth, allowing his father the opportunity to walk behind the cart alone. "We need to move quickly. Hallowmas is only a day away. My father will want to see real progress between now and then."

Gareth didn't know how that was going to be possible, but he would certainly try. He didn't say as much to Hywel, however, merely nodded. Once inside the castle, he signaled that his men should see to their duties. They dispersed, and Gareth tossed the reins of his horse to one of the stable boys who came forward to take them.

"While I speak to whoever had guard duty from midnight to dawn," Hywel said, "you find Gwen. Meet me in my office."

"Yes, my lord." It was on the tip of Gareth's tongue to suggest that he join Hywel and speak to the guard with him, but then he thought better of it. There was a glint in Hywel's eye this morning that told Gareth it would be best for everyone if he did as he was told and didn't question his orders without a very good reason to do so.

Thus, he left Hywel to his task and went in search of Gwen. He found Meilyr first. There was a time when any interaction with

Meilyr had been awkward and uncomfortable for both of them, but either Meilyr had mellowed since Gareth's marriage to Gwen or Gareth had. Or both. Gareth found himself actually glad to see his father-in-law.

"A bad business," Meilyr said by way of a greeting.

"Indeed," Gareth said.

"I accompanied Gwen to see the king," Meilyr said.

"Thank you for that," Gareth said and meant it. "It was a difficult task. If I couldn't be with her myself, I'm glad you could."

Meilyr didn't seem to know what to say to that, but his lips pressed together as if he was pleased.

"We don't know much more than we did before," Gareth said. "I'll be off in a moment with Prince Hywel in pursuit of the few leads we currently have."

"I assume you will limit my daughter's involvement in what will surely be a lengthy investigation," Meilyr said.

"Of course." Gareth bowed slightly. "I appreciate your concerns." He said this even though he knew as well as Meilyr that a man limited Gwen at his peril. Then Gareth smiled to see the woman herself appear in the doorway of the great hall.

"There you are." Gwen came down the steps and hurried across the courtyard towards him.

Gareth broke away from Meilyr to meet her halfway. He caught her in a tight hug and then released her. "Your father was just telling me of your ordeal."

"I survived." She nodded towards the cart. Only now were men lifting the body from it. "You brought Tegwen home, I see."

"She'll lie in a room in the barracks until we can bury her," Gareth said.

Meilyr cleared his throat, causing Gwen to turn to him. "Hello, Father."

"I don't like to see you involved in this, Gwen. Not with my first grandchild on the way."

Gareth smirked but then looked away, hoping Meilyr hadn't noticed. Meilyr hadn't changed so much that pomposity was beyond him.

"I will do nothing to endanger the child, Father." Gwen put a hand on his arm and went up on her toes to kiss his cheek. "Gareth will make sure that anything dangerous takes place as far away from me as possible. I won't even leave Aber. I promise."

"That's what you always say," Meilyr said, grumbling.

"And I always mean it," Gwen said.

Gareth looked down at Gwen. "Prince Hywel asked that we meet him in his chambers."

She took Gareth's hand while smiling at her father. "We can talk later."

Meilyr waved his hand at his daughter, a growl still on his lips. "Take care of her."

"Yes, sir," Gareth said. As they walked back inside, he touched Gwen's rounded belly and kissed her cheek. "Are you really all right?"

"I'm fine. A little sad that this has happened."

"Hywel has already impressed upon me the urgency of sorting out at least something of what happened to her by tomorrow evening," Gareth said and related the details of what they'd discovered since she'd left the beach, including the information about the cart and Cadwaladr's pendant. He concluded, "King Owain will certainly bury her before the sun sets tomorrow evening."

"It is making everyone uncomfortable that her body turned up right before Hallowmas. They fear her ghost," Gwen said.

Gareth eyed his wife. "Do you?"

"Of course not, but maybe Cadwaladr does," Gwen said.

Gareth's brows came together. "Why do you say that?"

"Because he left the body on the beach!" Gwen said. "Why do that unless he was afraid of her somehow?"

"He kept the body hidden for five years," Gareth said. "Why would it bother him now when it didn't before?"

"That I don't know," Gwen said, "but people are already saying in the hall that she walks among us. Someone saw a white light along the road last night, and in another hour, half the castle will have seen it too."

Gareth nodded slowly. "I would be more afraid of the man who murdered her than of Tegwen herself."

"You would," Gwen said, "but you don't believe in ghosts."

"Why leave her on the beach now, though?" Gareth said. "Cadwaladr has to know that five years on, the only possible outcome of bringing her death to light is to stir up trouble."

"Maybe he preferred trouble to retribution," Gwen said, "though I think there has to be more to it than that."

Gareth raised his eyebrows. "What more?"

"I think we're looking at this wrong. Cadwaladr may not have felt he had a choice but to move the body," Gwen said, "since it may be that he only recently found it."

Gareth stopped outside Hywel's door, looking down at his wife. "*Cariad*, how could that possibly be right? Cadwaladr would know where he left the body." And then his eyes narrowed as he understood what she was saying. "You think the man who killed her and the man who left the body on the beach aren't the same person."

Gwen nodded. "As much as we all would like to see Cadwaladr hang for Tegwen's murder, I am wondering if there aren't two opposing minds at work here: one belongs to the man who hid the body, the killer. Knowing we all thought Tegwen happy somewhere else, he never wanted her found; the second man feels the exactly the opposite: he wants the body as far away from him as possible and doesn't want to be reminded of it ever again."

Gareth rubbed his chin. That Cadwaladr was to blame for Tegwen's death would wrap this investigation up in a neat bow. He didn't want Gwen to be right, but the more he considered what she'd said, the more he had to grant the possibility that she was.

Gwen's brow remained furrowed in concentration. "I confess that the latter sounds more like Cadwaladr than the former."

Gareth urged Gwen across the threshold of Hywel's office and closed the door behind them. Hywel was alone in the room. "Have you caught the killer yet?"

"Not quite," Gwen said.

"Gwen has decided that the killer and the man who left the body on the beach are two different people," Gareth said.

"Is that where we are now?" Hywel said.

"It's an idea," Gareth said. "Under the circumstances, it is one you may prefer."

Hywel's mouth twisted into an apologetic smile. "I had considered it." Then he looked at Gwen. "Thank you for speaking to my father. It went well? He didn't eat you, I see."

"He was angry at first but then was more sad than anything else." She looked around the room. "How did you convince Mari not to join us?"

Hywel grimaced. "Breakfast did not sit well with her."

Gwen focused on Hywel's face. "I noticed that she was picking at her meal." She took a step towards the prince. "Mari is with child?"

Gareth's mouth fell open. That wouldn't have been his first thought, but then, he apparently wasn't thinking clearly this morning in many ways.

Hywel's face split into a grin. "We think so."

"That's wonderful." Gwen threw her arms around Hywel and hugged him. Then she backed off, holding both of his hands. "But I just spoke with her. She said nothing to me."

"We swore to each other that we wouldn't mention it, not to anyone, until we were sure," Hywel said.

Gwen hadn't told Gareth she was pregnant until she was sure either, and they'd both held the news in for half the summer during Gareth's absence. It did no one any good to raise hopes only to dash them later.

"You can tell her I guessed," Gwen said. "And I didn't get a chance to tell Gareth yet, but she's already helped this investigation. She knew Tegwen better than any of us, I think." Gwen gave an account of her conversation with Mari to the men.

Hywel began to pace in front of the window. He left the shutters open except in the bitterest of weather. Today it was warmer outside than in. "I spoke to the men on guard. Those on duty after midnight saw nothing and heard nothing."

"Except for the light that passed by on the road," Gwen said.

Hywel stopped his pacing. "What was that?"

"The talk in the great hall is that one of the guards saw ... well ... an ethereal light passing along the road in the early hours of the morning. He has the entire hall convinced that it was Tegwen's ghost."

Hywel snorted in disgust. "That's just what we need: a haunting. Next thing we know, the shade of Tegwen will be meeting Bran at midnight in the woods, since he had the poor judgment to get himself killed too."

Gareth nodded. "Ill-fated lovers."

"My lord, I am loath to bring this up, but when do you plan to tell your father about Cadwaladr?" Gwen said.

Gareth sent a look of thanks in Gwen's direction, but she was focused on the prince and didn't see it.

Hywel resumed his pacing. "I say we wait to speak of Uncle Cadwaladr until we track down this horse and cart and determine where the body came from." He glanced at Gwen. "Gareth and I will see to that while you find out about Tegwen's last days."

Gwen put her hands on her hips. "You give me all the thankless tasks. Do you have any suggestions as to how I might accomplish that?"

Hywel ignored Gwen's irritation. "Everyone has gathered at Aber for the holy day. The sudden appearance of her body will bring memories to the surface. Gather them."

"More specifically," Gareth said, "Mari spoke of Tegwen's unhappy marriage and of a lover. Who was he? Where is he now? What might he know of the events leading up to her disappearance? Someone here has to be able to tell us more about her life."

Gwen looked thoughtful now instead of defiant. "Yes, my lord."

"Meanwhile, Gareth and I—" Hywel halted his pacing, his expression clearing with the promise of activity, "—are off again."

Privately, Gareth was still wondering if the body really was that of Tegwen and not someone else wearing her clothing and necklace, but one look at Hywel's face had him swallowing down any argument. He would go where his lord pointed, as he always did.

6

Gwen

Gwen grumbled to herself as she said goodbye to the men and walked out of Hywel's office. She'd promised her father that she wouldn't leave Aber; she had known before she met with Hywel and Gareth what the end result would be. More and more of late, her condition was preventing her from doing what she wanted to do. It wasn't because she couldn't be as active as in the past, necessarily, and certainly Gwen cared little about what people thought, but the worst thing would be to do something strenuous and damage the baby. She would never forgive herself if she miscarried the child.

The frustrating confinement of Gwen's pregnancy would be easier to accept if Mari was pregnant. Although Mari had never been as adventurous as Gwen herself, they'd kept each other company during the long summer without their men. Gareth had journeyed with Hywel to Ceredigion in the south, and from the little Gareth said, Gwen knew that Hywel was consumed with solidifying his hold on his lands in the wake of Cadwaladr's treachery last summer. He and Gareth had fought more than one battle already in pursuit of that goal, and she was terribly afraid that they would be fighting many more.

Because the Norman influence was greater in the south, most of the pressure on Hywel's rule came from them, not Cadell, the King of Deheubarth. Hywel's forces had raided the Norman castle of Aberteifi (which the Normans called Cardigan) and come away victorious, having burned the castle to the ground. The repercussions of that raid were still to be felt, which was why Hywel (and Gareth) would be staying in Gwynedd for only a few months before heading south again after the Christmas feast. Gwen already felt the pang of longing at the thought of Gareth leaving again. They hadn't had enough time together. They never had enough time together.

And if he left, Gareth wouldn't be with her when their baby was born. She had already been on her knees praying for inclement weather that would prevent Hywel from leaving Aber and for the baby to come early.

Gwen stopped in the corridor with one hand on the wall and the other on her belly, feeling the baby shift under her hand. Gwen could hear the hubbub in the great hall and needed to compose herself before joining it. Too many times since Gwen had discovered her pregnancy, she'd found the fear of the future engulfing her. She feared dying in childbirth. She feared Gareth's death in battle. As always, she told herself to put aside her fear, because it would prevent her from living in whatever time she had left. That, however, was easier said than done.

The great hall remained nearly as full as it had been earlier that morning. Gwen didn't see Mari at the high table and stopped, unsure where she should look for her friend. Mari hadn't been sleeping in the room adjacent to Hywel's office either. Then Gwen felt a hand on her arm.

"Lady Gwen?" It was Mari's maid, Hafwen. "Princess Mari asked me to tell you that she has gone to lie down in the manor house. She requests that you attend to her later but that she needs to sleep now."

Gwen nodded. With the enormous crowd of people coming into Aber, Mari and Hywel had already been planning to move from where they normally slept in the room adjacent to Hywel's office to the manor house where they would be sharing a room with Gareth and Gwen. An entire family of King Owain's relations who lived near Dolbadarn would be occupying Hywel's usual chambers.

Stymied for the moment, Gwen hovered on the edges of the crowded room. King Owain was holding court on the dais for all the well-wishers who'd come for a feast but found themselves attending a funeral instead. He hadn't summoned her to him as he'd said he would, but they'd both been so busy, he hadn't had the chance. Gwen spared a thought for Tegwen's body, lying now in the barracks, and decided she'd better stay in the hall rather than hide away there examining what was left of the princess. The conversation among the inhabitants of Aber consisted of nothing but talk of Tegwen. Gwen would start upon the task Hywel had given her: to listen to what people had to say.

The hated Cadwaladr sat at one end of the dais, basking in the attention of his followers. If anything, he was growing more handsome as he aged, and no hint of baldness had yet touched his head, unlike his elder brother, who was losing his blonde hair faster than it could gray. Even Cristina, for all her fiery will, couldn't stop what nature had decreed. For once, Cadwaladr's wife and children had accompanied him to Aber. Alice de Clare, daughter of a Norman, could have felt out of place in this very Welsh castle, but she sat beside her husband and ate her food, never a hair out of place, keeping one eagle eye on the active six-year-old Cadfan and the other on her one-year-old daughter, currently in the arms of her nanny.

Since Hywel had burned Aberystwyth and taken the lands for himself (at his father's bidding), Cadwaladr and Alice had been living on Cadwaladr's estate in Merionydd. Like Rhos, it was a cantref of Gwynedd. Its proximity to Aber gave them a much shorter distance to travel for the festival. With Alice sitting beside him, a maligned wife if there ever was one, Gwen felt a little bad about hating Cadwaladr as much as she did. She didn't feel so badly, however, that she wasn't looking forward to the moment Hywel held out the pendant coin to him and asked Cadwaladr where he'd been last night. That pleasure, however, had to be deferred until they knew more about the circumstances surrounding the disappearance, death, and reappearance of Tegwen.

A pity.

"I've been watching for you." The voice came low in her ear. "What do you see? What are you looking for?"

Gwen turned her head, startled to find her queen, Cristina, at her side. Gwen glanced again towards King Owain, chastising herself for being so unaware that she hadn't noticed her queen's absence from the high table. "My lady, to what do I owe this honor?"

Cristina dismissed Gwen's obeisance with a gesture. "I may sit where I like, with whom I like. Owain doesn't like to trouble me with difficult issues these days, but I would like nothing more than to be distracted by this new intrigue. I assume you do not fear my involvement in this matter? You don't think I had anything to do with Tegwen's death or the discarding of her body on the beach?"

"Of course not, my lady." Gwen meant what she said, for once. Cristina certainly wasn't gallivanting about Gwynedd last night, hauling Tegwen's body from wherever it had been hidden and leaving it on the beach in the small hours of the morning. "How are you feeling?"

"As well as could be expected for a woman about to deliver her first child," Cristina said. "Your time will come."

Gwen bowed her head in acknowledgement of their shared experience, interested that Cristina had even brought it up.

Cristina, however, was not to be distracted by the coming baby. "Do you think you can divert me from what I want to know like a hapless miscreant? I am not fooled by your innocent gaze, my dear."

Gwen looked down at the trencher she didn't remember putting in front of her. Cristina wasn't wrong that Gwen wanted to avoid answering her questions or giving her any substantive information, especially since Gwen hadn't yet spoken more fully with King Owain. She thought quickly as to what she could say and opted for the essential truth, even if she couldn't give Cristina all of it.

"The body is Tegwen's, as you know, and we are just beginning our inquiry. I can tell you little, even if Prince Hywel hadn't ordered me to say nothing to anyone other than the king." Admittedly, Prince Hywel hadn't said anything of the sort but only because he didn't have to since Gwen already knew it.

Cristina leaned closer to Gwen, which wasn't easy given the size of her belly. "I am your queen."

"Please, Madame, I am well aware of that. Perhaps if you'd like to help us uncover the truth, you could tell me what you knew of Tegwen. I have learned already today that I knew her even less well than I thought I did."

Cristina sat straighter, looking somewhat mollified. "She visited my father's house in Powys, of course."

Gwen nodded. "Mari said as much."

"Her father died when she was twelve, and her mother was not well-born. Still, she was a princess, and my father insisted that I treat her as befitted her station. She was a sweet girl but malleable, and she fell in love with the wrong man."

Gwen waited, but when Cristina didn't continue, she made a small gesture with her hand that fell short of actually touching the queen's arm. "It would be helpful to know the truth of who she was. It will come out eventually. You know how Prince Hywel gets with an investigation."

"He worries at it like a dog with a bone and won't let it go until he's eaten the marrow. I know." Cristina gazed towards the high table, where Cadwaladr remained in close conversation with Cristina's own father, Goronwy. Gwen's father, Meilyr, sat to one side of the dais with Gwalchmai, tuning their instruments in preparation for entertaining the assembled throng.

"It should be I who speaks to this." King Owain sat heavily on the bench on the other side of Gwen. "I don't know anything about the Dane whom we all thought Tegwen ran off with five years ago, but the man she would have married instead of Bran was a man-at-arms in my father's company."

Gwen gaped at the king. She didn't know if she was more surprised to see him sitting on a bench like a commoner or that he was willing to tell her what he knew.

He wagged a finger at her. "I told you to come and find me."

Gwen swallowed. "I am sorry for my lapse, my lord. With one thing and another, I hadn't yet seen my chance."

King Owain accepted her apology with a nod, and Gwen sensed that his chastisement had been no more than a formality. "I wasn't king when she had to forsake her lover for Bran, but I played a part in the decision that she do so. I should have paid more attention to my brother's only child, but I had children of my own and, upon Cadwallon's death, a kingdom to manage for my father."

"But it seems you can tell me something about this man Tegwen loved?" Gwen said.

"He was landless," King Owain said, "with no hope of betterment and not brave, so unlikely to be knighted in battle. It was a hopeless match; everyone but Tegwen knew it at the time, even the man."

"I guessed as much," Gwen said and then paused, worrying that she'd been rude to the king by implying that he was telling her something she already knew. Gwen hurried on, "I'm sorry for speaking so directly, my lord, but we must find him."

Cristina's brow furrowed. "It was my understanding, my lord, that he went to Ceredigion with you after Tegwen and Bran married and didn't return."

"He died?" Gwen said, looking from Cristina to the king.

King Owain kept his eyes on his wife. "You are correct that after Tegwen's marriage to Bran, I made sure that her lover lived far from Rhos. I sent him south to Bala, and then he stayed in Ceredigion after our victory there."

At the mention of Ceredigion, Gwen felt a prickling at the back of her neck, as if someone was watching her. She glanced towards the high table. Cadwaladr was openly glaring at the three of them. She looked away but not before King Owain had seen where her attention had gone. "Gwen," he said, a warning in his voice. "What don't I know?"

"I-I am not the one to discuss this matter with you," Gwen said. "Hywel and Gareth are pursuing the man who brought Tegwen to the beach. I beg that you remain patient. I believe we will have a more complete tale to tell you upon their return."

King Owain didn't look satisfied with that answer. "Don't keep me waiting too long."

"No, my lord."

King Owain rose to his feet, reaching for Cristina's hand, which she took. "I have duties to attend to. Much can change about a man in nine years, especially if those years are hard ones. I suggest you speak to Brychan over there." He indicated a swarthy man on the opposite side of the hall from them. "He should have an interesting tale to tell you."

Gwen glanced over to the man and then quickly up at the king. "Him? Are you saying—"

Cristina's eyes lit as she studied the soldier. He sat alone at the end of a table, shoveling food into his mouth. She leaned down and put her lips to Gwen's ear. The glee in her voice was unmistakable. "He's telling you that Brychan was Tegwen's lover. Aren't you lucky that so many lords have come to Aber for Calan Gaeaf and brought their men with them?"

Gwen's breath caught in her throat, two unspoken thoughts filling her head: A shocked, *really?* And a more triumphant, *finally!*

This was a piece of the puzzle Gwen had been looking for since she'd spoken with Mari, who hadn't known the man's name.

Gwen wasn't sure that Cristina had known it either until this moment.

"If you have any kind of trouble with him, I will require him to speak to you, but I would prefer not to involve myself in this if it isn't necessary," King Owain said. "I admit that sometimes my presence can appear ... heavy-handed."

That was quite an admission coming from the king, for all that he was absolutely correct. It would be far better for Gwen to try to speak to Brychan first, alone, and without undue pressure from his superiors. Being cornered by King Owain might close the man's lips over all but the most basic information.

Cristina and King Owain were already walking away, and Gwen didn't feel she could run after them to ask for a little more to go on or even an introduction. She was going to have to feel her way with Brychan and hope that he would find her less intimidating than talking to Gareth or Hywel.

Gwen continued to be amazed at the way interesting pieces of news could come from such unexpected places. It seemed obvious to Gwen now that while Cristina had sought her out to gossip about Tegwen, she'd been as surprised as Gwen at King Owain's subsequent forthrightness. Gwen watched Cristina smile up at her husband, her expression genuinely joyful. The woman was a potent mix of contradictions. It was Gwen's experience that Cristina never did anything without a reason—and one that ultimately benefited her. Gwen reminded herself to remain wary of what the benefit might be this time. She hoped that it was only that Cristina liked mischief and to stir up trouble for her own amusement. If that was all this was, it would be a blessing.

Meanwhile, Brychan drank deeply from the cup in front of him and rose to his feet, kicking back the bench as he did so such that the couple on the opposite end of the bench were jerked back from the table; they glared at him, but he ignored them and strode towards the door. Gwen followed him from the hall in hopes of catching him before he reached wherever he intended to go. She didn't want to ambush him from outside the latrines if she didn't have to. As she passed through the door to the hall, Brychan was already halfway across the courtyard, heading for the barracks.

Gwen hurried to catch up. "Brychan!"

She put a hand on her belly to stop it from jostling as she hustled down the steps towards him. Though it was just noon, already two servants were trimming the ends of the torches that were set into sconces by the door to the great hall and by the gatehouse, in preparation for lighting the moment it grew dark. One of them raised his eyebrows at Gwen, and she gave him a quick smile. She knew him, as she knew most everyone who worked at Aber. Suddenly, she wondered how many had known Brychan and Tegwen nine years ago when they'd fallen in love and how she might get them to speak to her about it now.

Fortunately, Brychan stopped and turned at Gwen's call. He was close to the barracks, standing in the full sunlight, which continued to shine down on them and which allowed Gwen to get a good first look at his face. When King Owain had pointed him out to her, she'd seen only his profile and hadn't recognized him as someone she knew. Now, she realized that she'd seen him before: he'd been among the men in Cadwaladr's company during the time that Gareth had served him and Gwen's father had sung at Cadwaladr's court at Aberystwyth. Brychan had left Cadwaladr's retinue shortly after Cadwaladr had dismissed Gareth from his service.

As she'd been wallowing in her own misery at the time, she hadn't cared enough about Brychan to learn why he'd left or where he'd gone. To leave a position with a prince unless forced out like Gareth was so rare for a lowly man-at-arms as to be unbelievable. Gwen wondered if loving Tegwen had something to do with his departure, and she hoped that Brychan would tell her if her guess was true. Since he was here at Aber now, he must serve a lord who tithed to King Owain, but that lord couldn't have come often to Aber if up until a few moments ago Cristina thought Brychan was dead.

"Hello, Gwen. May I help you?" Brychan said.

Gwen halted a few paces from him, surprised that he knew her. She put a hand on her chest, trying to slow her breathing. "I was hoping to talk with you a moment."

"Why is that?" Brychan's expression became wary. "We haven't spoken since Ceredigion."

"Seeing you in the hall brought back memories to me of that time. You served Prince Cadwaladr during the year my father sang in his hall."

"You do remember me, then?" Brychan gave a mocking laugh. "I can't say I'm surprised it took you this long to notice me.

I recognized you the moment I set foot in Aber. I hadn't realized before yesterday that you'd returned to Gwynedd too." The corners of his mouth turned down.

Gwen shifted from one foot to the other, more than a little uncomfortable with the direction the conversation had taken. "Yes, well ..." She cleared her throat. "I was hoping you would answer a few questions about Tegwen."

"So that's it, is it?" Brychan took a step backwards, his eyes flicking from left to right as if he was looking for an escape route.

Gwen put out a hand to him. "Please believe me when I say that I mean you no harm. You must have heard that Tegwen's body was left on the beach this morning. What you may not know is that she was murdered."

Brychan had been retreating backwards and now froze, one foot on the bottom step to the barracks behind him. "You're sure?"

Gwen nodded. "Prince Hywel has been charged with uncovering the truth of her death. You knew her well. The more we learn of her last days, the more likely it is that we will discover who killed her."

Brychan scoffed. "I know how royalty think. The king doesn't really want to know who killed his niece. He wants a scapegoat. If I speak to you, I'll lose my position. Again." He backed up the steps, his hand already reaching for the latch to the door that would allow him to enter the barracks. "I have nothing to say to you."

Gwen scurried up the steps after him and reached for his arm to stop him from disappearing through the doorway. Speaking to a man who wasn't her husband was tolerable in the castle's courtyard or hall, but she couldn't follow him into the barracks, even if Tegwen's body was only a few feet away and could provide her an excuse to be there. She could feel the watching eyes of some of the men-at-arms on duty. She needed to stop him here. "You loved her."

Brychan hesitated, halfway through the barracks' door. "I was warned never to speak of it."

"Who warned you?"

Brychan's lips twisted.

"Was it Bran? Or King Owain? Please know that it was King Owain himself who pointed you out to me and suggested that I speak with you."

Brychan stared past Gwen, one hand still on the latch. "I wasn't there for her. She died, and I wasn't there." Then he surprised Gwen by crumpling up right there in a heap on the top step, folding himself in half with his knees up and his face in his hands.

Gwen wavered, uncertain what her response should be. She glanced around the courtyard as those same men-at-arms who'd been watching them with interest a moment ago looked hastily away. Brychan had come undone, and no man wanted to witness his undoing. Gwen was tempted to put a hand on Brychan's shoulder and sit beside him, but his resentful attitude of earlier made her think that he might take offense.

Then Brychan spoke again, his voice choking with grief. "Tegwen is dead, and it's my fault."

Gwen moved down the steps, back to the dirt of the courtyard, in order to stand in front of him. She leaned forward to whisper to him, "How is it your fault?"

"She came to me and begged me to take her away from Gwynedd, but I wouldn't. I couldn't." Brychan put his face back in his hands.

Brychan's tears were making Gwen even more uncomfortable than his earlier frankness about the fact that she hadn't noticed him. She wanted to get him out from under the eyes of everyone else in the courtyard but felt equally awkward about dragging him towards a more private location. Finally, she gave in to instinct and sat beside him on the step, turning resolutely away from the two men crossing the courtyard from the postern gate. They had been heading towards the barracks, but at the sight of Brychan's tears and Gwen patting his shoulder, they abruptly changed direction. She felt like crying too, just witnessing Brychan's despair.

Fortunately, before anyone else could come out of the barracks or enter them, Brychan gathered himself, wiping at his cheeks with the heels of his hands and clearing his throat. "I'd best be off." He stood abruptly.

Gwen rose to her feet with him. "Oh no, you don't. You can't leave it like that."

Brychan's grief had been tumultuous, but now he looked mutinous, with his chin sticking out and defiance in his eyes. Gwen had a moment of panic that he really was going to leave it like that because she didn't know what else she could say to him to convince him to keep talking to her. She understood that he was embarrassed to have been seen crying. Many men would have been, even if Welshmen allowed their emotions to show more than other peoples, like the Normans or Danes. On the other hand, Irishmen, in Gwen's experience, cried openly and often with no compunction about it whatsoever.

Whether he saw the understanding in Gwen's face or simply decided that Gwen was going to hound him until he talked, Brychan's expression softened. As Gwen gazed up at him, he wiped at his cheeks one more time and tipped his head towards the stables, striding away without waiting to see if Gwen would follow. Gwen lifted the hem of her skirt and scuttled after him.

Once inside the door, Brychan stopped. He peered around the darkened stables. What little light to see by filtered through the four open doorways. At night, a man had to bring a lantern inside in order to see, but the danger of fire was ever present, and everyone made do without real light the best they could during the day.

"No one can hear us now," Gwen said.

Brychan grunted his agreement. They did appear to be out of earshot of the handful of stable boys hard at work cleaning out horse stalls, as well as out of sight of anyone in the courtyard. Brychan ran his hands through his hair and then paced three times around the little space by the doorway between a mound of hay and the first stall. "I loved her. I did. And she loved me. She was only fifteen—Christ, I can't believe that was nearly ten years ago—and we had only a few weeks together before her grandfather promised her to another man."

"To Bran, son of the Lord of Rhos," Gwen said.

"Yes," Brychan said. "It was a fine match, of course, appropriate for her station. She should never have even looked at me."

"How did you meet?" Gwen said. "She was a princess—"

"—and I was a lowly man-at-arms?" Brychan nodded. "She was a wild one, that girl. She loved horses, and it always seemed that I was in the stables when she was there. I'd been sent to Dolwyddelan by the king, you see, stationed there as part of Gwynedd's defenses. It's a small castle, and there's not much besides herding sheep to entertain a young girl. I see now that her interest in me was all my fault. I should never have let her know how I felt about her. When I learned that she was to marry Bran—"

"That must have been hard," Gwen said. This was an old story but no less heartbreaking in the telling.

"It split me apart to let her go."

"But you did let her go?" Gwen said.

Brychan nodded. "I told her that I couldn't be with her anymore and that I was leaving so she could marry Bran with honor. We never lay together then; I swear it."

"What did she say in return?"

"When she found out about the wedding and to whom she'd been promised, she asked me to run away with her. But I couldn't, could I? She was fifteen; I was twenty, with no money or land. I was a poor soldier serving King Owain's father and lucky to have the position. It didn't matter that her father had died and that Owain was now the heir to Gwynedd. She was still a princess."

"What happened then?" Gwen found herself hanging on his words, envisioning a stable much like this one and a young girl being told she couldn't have the man she loved. Gwen had been that girl. She knew what Tegwen had felt.

Brychan shrugged. "Nothing happened. She married Bran. I served King Gruffydd as I had since I was fourteen. My life and hers went on apart from one another. I know her grandfather thought he was doing right by her, giving her to Bran."

"It would have seemed a good match," Gwen said.

"Nobody cared that she didn't love him. Nobody expected her to love him when they married. Her grandfather even told her that love was for herders and peasants, not princesses."

"I imagine that everyone else told her she would grow to love him," Gwen said.

Brychan looked down at his feet. "Why wouldn't she have? He was rich and handsome."

"And did she grow to love him?" Gwen said.

"She did, or as much as he would let her."

Mari had said as much, but Gwen was glad to have it confirmed—and since it was Brychan saying it, likely it was true.

"She was full of love, that girl. She forgot me, as I hoped she would, and gave the love she'd had for me to him. But it wasn't returned. He was rich and spoiled as these men often are. When she didn't bear him a son, he lost whatever interest in her he'd had

up until that point. Two daughters in three years she gave him ..."
Brychan's voice faded away.

"When did you find her again?" Gwen said.

"I didn't," Brychan said. "After I left Cadwaladr's service—"
He gave Gwen a sharp look. "You do remember me leaving?"

"I do," Gwen said. "You left not long after Gareth had been
sent off. I didn't ever find out why, though."

Brychan waved a hand. "Ach. It's water under the bridge
now. I was one of the ones who obeyed when Gareth did not, but
every man has a soul, even if it takes him a long while to discover
it. I left Ceredigion and came back to Aber in hopes that I could
serve a different lord, even King Owain, now that his father was
dead. I hoped that enough time had passed that my transgressions
could be forgiven."

"And were they? He found a place for you?" Gwen said.

"He did," Brychan said. "Since Tegwen had been several
years married by then, the past seemed of little importance to
anyone but me."

Gwen eyed him as he stopped his story again. "And
Tegwen, perhaps?" she said.

"She sought me out."

"When was this?" Gwen said.

"Some three years after her marriage? That would have
been after the wars in Ceredigion and the death of the old king.
King Owain sat on the throne. Only a few had known about us the
first time, and we did everything we could not to cause gossip
now."

"Except not see each other," Gwen said.

"Except that," Brychan said.

Gwen had vivid memories of that time. Gareth had been dismissed in early summer of that year, and Brychan had left before winter closed the roads. She had another question to ask but couldn't figure out how to ask it delicately, so she just said, "You became lovers?"

"I never touched her before her marriage. She went to Bran's bed a maiden. But she had grown into a woman, a very unhappy one, and I was weak." He looked away. "We met when we could in a little house to the west of here. Prince Cadwaladr's it was, but as he was in Ceredigion, I didn't much worry that anyone would find us. Cadwaladr used it for his own trysts. I saw no reason not to use it for mine."

Gwen didn't want to interrupt the flow of his conversation, but the mention of the house had her pulse racing. "What house was this?"

Brychan threw out his hand to indicate beyond the Aber River. "It lies to the south of the road to Penrhyn. A strange one, built right into the side of a hill."

"I'm sorry, but did you say that Cadwaladr used it for trysts?" Gwen said.

Brychan lifted one shoulder. "He could be found there in the evenings whenever he left his wife in Ceredigion and came north. It was common knowledge among the men because some of us had to accompany him and then escort the girl home afterwards."

That was more about Cadwaladr's activities than Gwen had ever wanted to know, but she was sure that Hywel and Gareth would be interested to learn of it. Gwen knew the hut in question, though it had belonged to someone else when she was a girl. "Back to Tegwen. When was the last time you saw her?" Gwen said.

"She came to me, two weeks before she disappeared, and told me that she was with child and it was mine," Brychan said. "Her husband had been absent for much of the spring and had sported more with other women than with her. He would know that the child wasn't his."

"She was sure it was yours?" Gwen said.

"We were sure. She asked again for me to take her away. I wanted to." Brychan clenched his hands into fists. "But I was a coward. I needed more time to think about where to go and how we would live. She'd caught me at a bad time for making any decision too. I had come to Aber only because my lord was one of King Owain's captains, and he sent me home with a message for Lord Taran. The war in England was newly started, and King Owain decided to gain himself some territory at the expense of a few Marcher barons he thought needed reining in. I put Tegwen off with excuses and told her that I would come to Rhos before the end of the month. That would have been April."

"But you didn't," Gwen said.

Brychan eyes skated away and didn't return to Gwen's face. "I never intended to, and I never saw Tegwen again. I visited Aber a few months later, but she'd already run off with that Dane."

"What did you think about that?" Gwen said.

"I assumed that since I'd refused her, she'd found another man to take her away," Brychan said. "It made perfect sense. I was happy to believe it because it meant that she had a better man than I or Bran to care for her."

"What about the child?" Gwen said.

"A Dane would have raised her child as his own," Brychan said. "That's the Danish way, and I would have honored him for it."

"Do you think Bran ever suspected that you and Tegwen had renewed your attachment?" Gwen said.

Brychan shook his head forcefully. "Not unless she told him."

Gwen canted her head. "Would she have told him?"

"She might have if she was angry enough or had been drinking enough." Brychan made a mournful face as Gwen's eyes went wide. "The truth is, I knew how unstable she was. It was part of the reason I was reluctant to take her away."

"Which is why you thought her running away with a Dane was well within her character," Gwen said.

Brychan nodded. "But now—I wonder if he ever existed at all."

To Gwen's mind, everybody should have been wondering that by now. Given the condition of the body, she'd been dead a long while. Did it make sense that her new lover would have killed her within days of sailing off with her and then left her body somewhere near Aber? Gwen shook her head. Nothing about this death made sense.

"I have told you the truth." Brychan looked directly into Gwen's face, perhaps confused by Gwen's head shaking and thinking that she didn't believe him.

"Thank you for talking to me. I will make sure that both Prince Hywel and King Owain are aware of your willingness to help."

"I should have taken her away." Brychan's face crumpled, and he pressed his fingers to the corners of his eyes. "I should have protected her."

Gwen put a hand on his arm. "Do you know something about her death beyond what you've already told me? I thought you were in Powys when she disappeared?"

"I was in Powys, but I have no doubt at all who is responsible for her death. Lord Bran must have found out about the baby and killed her."

7

Gareth

As they left Aber, Gareth checked behind them to make sure that Gwen wasn't following them. There was a time when she might have, but as he straightened in his saddle, he acknowledged that her task might well prove more interesting than theirs. Their own quest sounded to him like searching for a particular sheep in a field of sheep. Llelo sat on the horse behind him, confident enough in his seat that he was barely holding on and sure that he had the information they needed.

"She's got herself involved in this one, and you won't be able to convince her to leave it alone," Hywel said.

"I am aware of that, my lord," Gareth said, "and I don't want to. She'll get answers where we can't. "

"She always has." Hywel smirked, and Gareth supposed he had every right to feel self-satisfied. It was Hywel who had asked Gwen to spy for him all those years ago, acknowledging her intelligence and resourcefulness and putting them to work for him. Hywel's pride reminded Gareth of when he'd stood before the community of nuns who'd taken him in, after Cadwaladr had thrown him out of Ceredigion, and for the first time read to them a passage from the Bible. Afterwards, the prioress who'd taught him to read told him that there was no greater satisfaction for a teacher than when her student opened his wings and took flight.

To this day, Gareth had difficulty believing how much his teacher had done for him—and for so little in return—but he could see how Hywel could feel the same great satisfaction about Gwen. Hywel had set her feet on a path that she'd enthusiastically followed. More recently, she'd walked it on Gareth's arm but only because she'd learned to run by herself first.

"There." Llelo pointed to a hut to the north of the road, with a pathway beyond it that led to the beach and the sea. "That's where Ceri lives."

The livelihood of most Welshmen depended upon herding sheep and cattle, but many on the coast lived by and for the sea. Fishermen had plied these waters since before the coming of Cunedda, the great founder of Gwynedd. Oysters, clams, and fish of every stripe and color fed King Owain's people daily. In hard times, when crops failed or in the difficult days before the harvest, food from the sea kept the people alive. Ceri's family was among those who fished.

The hut in which Ceri lived was meager, with thin walls of wattle and daub and a thatched roof that needed repairs if it was to keep out the coming winter. Gareth looked at Hywel with raised eyebrows. Something wasn't right here, and as a steward of this kingdom, it was just as well that Hywel was here today to learn of it. Llelo slid off the back of Gareth's horse, went to the doorway, and rapped on the wall beside the door, since the door consisted only of a leather apron.

A boy of ten swept through the doorway. "Hello," he said at the sight of Llelo, and then his eyes widened to see Gareth and Hywel, both still mounted, behind his friend. "My lords." He pulled on his forelock in obeisance.

"Is your father at home?" Gareth said.

Ceri shook his head. "My father is dead."

"I'm sorry for your loss." Hywel jerked his head at Gareth, who dismounted and approached the boy, agreeing with Hywel that a fatherless child needed a bit more concerned attention while being questioned than one who had a father to stand at his shoulder. Gareth had been such a child once, though he couldn't recall ever being caught up in a murder before he started working for Prince Hywel. "Llelo tells us that you heard a cart pass by here this morning. Can you tell us about it?"

"I heard it and then saw it, my lords," Ceri said.

"Llelo said that you recognized the horse that pulled it?" Hywel said.

Ceri nodded. "The horse stables across the road." He pointed southwest, towards the woods and fields beyond the road. "There's a small steading which you can't see from here because of the trees. We don't go to the house, but when the horse is out to pasture closer to home, I feed him carrots if I have any to spare."

Ceri had moved out of the doorway and was patting the nose of Gareth's horse, a bay named Goch (Red). Gareth felt in his pockets for a bruised apple he'd taken from the stores for just this type of occasion. All men acknowledged the indispensability of horses, but not all men loved them. Ceri seemed to have a knack.

Gareth handed the apple to Ceri, who perched it on his flat palm and held it out to the horse. "Whose house is it?" Gareth said. The sooner they found the owner of the horse, the sooner they could return to Aber.

Ceri shrugged.

Gareth looked at him curiously. "You don't know?"

Again the shrug. Goch had taken the apple, and now Ceri worked his hands nervously in front of him.

Gareth tried again. "You said you don't go to the house. Why not? I would have thought you would range all over these lands when you're not out fishing."

Ceri bit his lip and glanced at Llelo, who'd clasped his hands behind his back and was looking down at his feet, stubbing his bare toe in the dirt. He didn't respond to Ceri's questioning look.

Gareth looked from one boy to the other. "Would one of you please tell me what is troubling you?"

Llelo should have known better than to keep silent when Gareth used that tone of voice, but it was Ceri who finally capitulated. "It's the house. It's ... well ... *haunted*."

Hywel was finally interested enough to dismount. "Say that again, Ceri."

Ceri shrugged for the third time, not obeying Hywel, so the prince lifted the boy's chin with two fingers. "Why do you say the house is haunted?"

As Ceri gave the prince yet another shrug, Gareth had a strong urge to shake him. He restrained himself, however, and Prince Hywel, who had more patience than Gareth, kept his eyes fixed on Ceri's face.

Llelo finally came to Ceri's rescue. "That's what they say. We all avoid it."

Hywel's eyes turned thoughtful.

Meanwhile, Gareth put a hand on Llelo's shoulder. "It seems that what Ceri has told us doesn't surprise you. You knew which house and horse he meant already?"

Llelo ducked his head and nodded.

"So you brought us here, even though you already knew where the horse pastured and could have taken us there directly?"

Llelo nodded again without looking into Gareth's eyes.

"Why would you do that?"

"I don't know." Llelo swallowed hard. "I didn't want you to know that I was afraid to go there."

Gareth contemplated his charge, reminding himself that Llelo had lost his father not long ago. It was a comfort to Gareth to think that those he loved weren't really gone and existed on the other side of a thin veil, but Llelo might not yet have reached that understanding. Still not looking at him, Llelo stubbed his toe again into the dirt.

"Did you think I would be angry with you for being afraid?" Gareth said.

"I just wanted you to learn about it from someone else, and Ceri was the one to see the horse. You needed to talk to him no matter what I told you."

Hywel put one hand on Ceri's shoulder and the other on Llelo's, finally getting him to look up. "I think I understand now. The hut you mean is where the witch lived, isn't it?"

Ceri's expression cleared. "Yes, my lord! They say it's her ghost that haunts the house."

Llelo nodded with equal enthusiasm. "I've *heard* her! If you get close enough, you can hear a moaning sound, and if you open the front door—"

Ceri scoffed. "Not that you've ever done it."

"—the ghost rushes past in a gust of air and disturbs everything in the house," Llelo finished, ignoring his friend's interruption.

"Clearly I've missed an important rite of passage," Gareth said. "What house are we talking about?"

"I should have known which one they meant the moment they said it was haunted." Hywel let go of the boys and stepped back. "If Gwen were here, she would have remembered it too. When we were children, old Wena lived in a house very near to where they describe, which makes me think it might be the same place. I know now that she wasn't any more of a witch than you or I, but we all thought she might be one when we were young." Hywel nudged Ceri's leg with the toe of his boot to get his attention. Now that the boys had confessed the truth, they'd been talking animatedly to one another. "When did Wena die?"

Ceri was back with the shrug. "Years ago, wasn't it?"

"So you never knew Wena?" Gareth said. "Only that she haunts the house?"

"My mam knew her. She might know when she died."

"Where is your mam?" Gareth said.

"In here." Ceri pushed through the door flap.

Hywel and Gareth shared another concerned look before following Ceri inside. They'd been talking outside for too long a time for the mistress of the house not to have given them welcome and offered them food or drink. Hospitality was nearly a holy rite among the Welsh, and Hywel was a prince of Wales.

Once inside the hut, however, it was clear that a haunted house was the least of Ceri's worries. His mother lay on a raised pallet set against the north wall of the house. A fire burned in the central fire pit, and that it flamed well and most of the smoke left through the hole in the roof was testament to how well Ceri was caring for his mother, if not the roof. Hywel sucked on his teeth, taking in the room in a glance, and then went down on one knee beside the pallet.

"You are not well, Ceri's mother," Hywel said as he took her hand.

"Her name's Nan, and she took sick a week ago," Ceri said. "She hasn't been able to rise since yesterday."

"But you've been ill longer than a week, haven't you, Nan?" Hywel stroked Nan's hair back from her face with such gentleness that Gareth had to swallow hard to contain his emotions. It was times like these that Gareth was reminded why he would follow Hywel anywhere, into death if need be.

"Months." Nan's voice cracked over the word. Finding refuge in action, Gareth picked up a pitcher of water from a small table, one of the few pieces of furniture in the room, and poured the water into a wooden cup. He brought it to Hywel, who took it and, lifting Nan's head, helped her to drink. She managed three small sips before falling back, exhausted.

"We were just speaking to your son about old Wena," Hywel said. "Did you know her?"

Nan managed a small smile. "I knew her well."

Hywel waited through several of Nan's rasping breaths for her to speak again.

"She was my aunt."

"When did she die, Nan?" Hywel said.

"A few years back, not long after your father took the throne, my lord." Each word Nan spoke was carefully articulated. Gareth estimated that she had days to live, at most. Her body was nearly wasted, and he suspected that the water Hywel had helped her to drink was all she'd taken in today.

"What has become of her hut, then?" Hywel said. "Whose land is it?"

"Same as it's always been. Wena's house and the paddock belong to Prince Cadwaladr."

Hywel turned to look up at Gareth, who raised his eyebrows, equally confused. "I didn't know he held lands so close to Aber," Gareth said.

"Nor I," Hywel said. "If true, it is something I should have known."

Nan lifted a hand and then dropped it to the bedcovers. "I don't remember how he came by it. Some legacy of your grandmother's that she left to him, I think. Cadwaladr was always her favorite, you know."

"That I did know," Hywel said.

And that fact explained a great deal to Gareth about how Cadwaladr, the youngest of three sons, petted and spoiled for much of his life, had grown to be a man who thought only of himself.

"Wena helped your grandmother deliver him, you see," Nan said. "Wena was an old woman even then, and your grandmother wanted to reward her with something for her long years of service. The hut was hers for the length of her life and then reverted to Cadwaladr on her death."

"Who cares for it now?" Gareth said. "I can't imagine it's Prince Cadwaladr himself."

"Oh no," Nan said. "That would be old Wynn. I heard you speaking to Ceri about a cart and a horse. They're old Wynn's, and he stables them there; he lives in the village with his daughter. She keeps an eye on him since his wife died."

Hywel rose to his feet. "Thank you for seeing us, Nan. I will send someone to help Ceri fix your cottage and make sure you have enough food. You should have let us know sooner of your needs."

"My neighbors take care of us." Nan smiled at Ceri. "And Ceri is a good boy."

"We can do better." Hywel gave Nan a respectful nod and then headed for the door. Once outside, he tipped back his head and breathed deeply. "Christ, I hate to see that."

"From the looks, she suffers from a wasting disease," Gareth said.

"I would say you're right," Hywel said.

"Upon our return to Aber, I will direct workmen from the castle to come here. It shouldn't take long to fix the roof and make the house more secure," Gareth said. "Winter is coming."

"Winter is getting closer with every breath," Hywel said, referring to the celebration of Calan Gaeaf, which marked the end of autumn and the beginning of winter, even if cold weather didn't always show itself exactly on that day. Hywel slapped his gloves into his palm. "At least we have some answers."

Gareth snorted. "And thus more questions than we did before."

Hywel's eyes crinkled at the corners. "We wouldn't want it any other way, would we? Shall we find this haunted house?"

Llelo had followed them outside, and now his eyes grew large; Gareth dropped a hand onto the top of his head. "You don't have to come if you don't want to."

Llelo shook his head. "I'm not afraid."

Gareth just managed not to smile at such a transparently untrue statement. He gave the boy credit for attempting to work through his fear, however. While their Saxon and Norman neighbors might view Welshmen as embarrassingly emotional, a man learned to hide from the world what he didn't want it to see.

"There's no such thing as ghosts, boy." Hywel swung himself into the saddle. "No more than Wena was a witch."

Llelo grabbed at Gareth's arm before he could mount too. "Could be the ghost isn't of Wena but of Tegwen."

Gareth looked up at Hywel, hoping Llelo hadn't offended the prince, but Hywel misread the look, because he said, "Don't tell me Hallowmas is getting to you too, Sir Gareth?"

"Of course not. Even if Tegwen does haunt us, she didn't leave her own body on the beach," Gareth said. "A man did that."

Hywel nodded. "You and I will assume a mortal is at the heart of any wrongdoing until proven otherwise. Men cause quite enough trouble without bringing the world of the spirits into it."

Llelo mumbled from beside Gareth, "It could be her."

Gareth grasped his chin and forced Llelo to look at him. "I have seen enough death to know that it leaves a mark, sometimes on the place the person died but more often on the soul of the man who kills. That is our only concern today." His expression softened. "Tegwen can't hurt you, son."

Hywel chewed on his lower lip as he contemplated the path they would be taking. "Five years ago, a boy such as Llelo could have overheard Tegwen's murder if it happened at the house or near to it. That would have been enough to turn any boy's blood cold and make him and his friends warn others to stay clear ever since. The people need little more than that to start a rumor that Wena's hut is haunted."

Gareth mounted his horse, bringing him level with Hywel. He leaned close and lowered his voice so Llelo, who was occupied with clambering onto the horse's back behind Gareth, couldn't hear. "If Cadwaladr killed Tegwen in that house—"

"Don't say it. Don't even think it," Hywel said. "I know we have his pendant, but as much as I despise my uncle, more treachery from him—another murder by his hand or at his order—will rip Gwynedd and my father apart. I don't want to see that happen today."

Gareth gave way, and they left the road a few hundred yards west of Ceri's house, taking a narrow path that was barely wide enough for a cart. "I didn't even know there was a farmhouse back here or I might have rested in it last winter after Tomos hit me on the head," Gareth said.

Hywel shot him an amused glance. "You were making for Aber and Gwen; you wouldn't have stopped for anything or anyone."

Gareth gave a half-laugh. "You're probably right. Besides, the last thing we needed that day was to find another body, if Tegwen's body was there to be found."

Sooner than Gareth expected, though still well back from the road to Penrhyn, they reached the house in question. It was set back in a hollow, protected from the elements on three sides by hills that stretched north out of the mountains of Snowdonia. Hywel halted at the paddock fence and dismounted, winding his horse's reins around a rail. An old cart horse ambled over to greet him, and Hywel stroked his forehead. "Hey, old fellow." He looked at Gareth. "This looks like the one. What do you think, Llelo?"

Llelo slid off Gareth's horse. "I have been here before, though the horse is usually in the paddock over there." He waved a hand, indicating a fence line that began a hundred feet away, across the clearing to the east of where they were standing.

Gareth dismounted and walked to the rickety barn to their left. He peered inside. It was just big enough for a cart and a single horse stall. For all that it was a lean-to, the roof was well maintained—better than Ceri's house—and the horse's stall had been cleaned recently. Everything smelled of new hay. The old horse had the opportunity to come in out of the rain if he wanted, and judging from the gloss in his coat, somebody obviously groomed him often. Hywel had remained by the horse, and Gareth waved a hand to get his attention. "This fellow has a nice life."

"That's our cart, then?" Hywel peered into the darkness of the barn. "Let's have it out."

Llelo had wandered after Hywel, and now he and Gareth helped Hywel roll the cart out of the lean-to and into the sunshine. With four-foot wheels and a plank bench seat, it was constructed exactly the same as a thousand carts found all over Wales. One such cart had carried Tegwen from the beach only this morning. Scraps of straw lay in the bed, and since the loft above the stall was full of hay, it was easy to guess where they'd come from. The cart contained nothing else.

Hywel clambered up onto the bed and crouched close to the planks, his nose practically to the wood, inspecting each one in turn. Then he spun slowly on the ball of his foot, shaking his head. "Just our luck. Give me a scrap of cloth caught on a nail. Give me something!"

His adamancy caught Gareth by surprise, though it shouldn't have. Guilt and frustration were a potent mix, and Hywel had to be feeling both—and probably had been since he identified the body as Tegwen's. After another full rotation, Hywel jumped down from the cart bed. "We'll do a circuit of the steading later. For now, let's see what the house has to offer us."

Gareth looked across the paddock. From Ceri's brief description, he had expected nothing other than a standard peasant's hut: wattle and daub construction, thatched roof, no windows, with a hole in the roof to let out the smoke and let in the only light when the door was closed, which wouldn't be often.

That wasn't what faced them. The house, built in a mix of stone and wood with a substantial, whole roof, sat on a small rise at the foot of an overhanging cliff. The cliff face formed the back wall of the house and was an outpost of the range from which the Aber River sprang. If Gareth listened hard, he thought he could hear Aber Falls cascading out of sight beyond the eastern ridge. The house faced northeast so was further protected from the weather, which usually blew in from the southwest, and the overhang of the cliff was such that Gareth would have been surprised if a raindrop had ever touched the roof.

A ray of sunlight shot from between the clouds and shone on the nearby neglected garden, which an untamed blackberry bramble had taken over. Though the same sun shone on Llelo's shoulders, he shivered and wrapped his cloak closer around himself. "Are you going to go inside?"

This was a new side of Llelo. When they'd first met at the monastery in England, Llelo had been the less assertive of the two brothers, albeit the elder. He'd felt himself responsible for Dai, though, and as the eldest son, he'd forged a path for them, caring for his younger brother when they were orphaned and reining in Dai's more outrageous exploits. What Gareth hadn't ever seen in Llelo, however, was fear.

"We have to." Gareth gestured to the house. "You have nothing to be afraid of."

Llelo's expression told Gareth he doubted the truth of that statement, but he managed a nod and allowed Gareth to urge him towards the door.

"It's just as I remembered when Wena lived in it." Hywel tapped out the rhythm to an inner song with three fingers on his pant leg as he examined the house. "Serene. Just like Wena."

"Leave it to you to become friends with a witch," Gareth said. "Did Gwen visit her with you?"

"From whom do you think Gwen first learned of herbs and healing?" Hywel said. "This was before her mother died birthing Gwalchmai, mind you. Her girlhood ended that day. After Gwen left Aber with her father, I ceased my visits too. My father was determined that I take my place at his side with Rhun. I had no more time for wandering." Hywel's tone revealed a remembered loneliness. Since Gareth couldn't live without Gwen, he didn't question the effect of her loss on Hywel.

"Someone has maintained the house since Wena died, if not the garden," Hywel said. "Probably old Wynn."

"I wonder why Cadwaladr didn't let the house to someone else," Gareth said.

"Nobody lives here because the house is haunted." Llelo held his shoulders stiff and braced for flight.

"Come along, Llelo." Gareth motioned his young charge forward. "Time to face your fear and see it for what it is."

"A fancy, nothing more." Hywel went to the closed wooden door and unhooked the latch with a flick of his finger. The door swung wide on squeaking hinges.

Llelo started at the sound, his already finely tuned senses telling him to run. "Da—" At least he had the courage to stay put and hadn't actually screamed.

Prince Hywel raised his eyebrows. "By such means are legends made."

"Remember the forest surrounding the farmhouse that belonged to Empress Maud's spies?" Gareth said. "They kept everyone away with wind chimes in the trees. No ghosts walked there any more than they do here."

"Or if they do, they are those of our own making," Hywel said.

Stiff-legged and wary, Llelo kept close to Gareth's side. Being watchful wasn't necessarily a bad thing when walking into an unknown situation, and Gareth reminded himself again that death was very real to the boy. Llelo rarely talked about his parents and certainly hadn't ever said he feared their ghosts. But this would be the first Hallowmas since his father died, and perhaps Tegwen's death was bringing his own loss a little too close for comfort.

Once inside the door, the three companions stood listening to the wind in the trees on the edge of the clearing and the shifting of the horses outside. The house, on the other hand, was completely silent. 'Gravelike', Gareth might have said, if the thought wouldn't have sent Llelo fleeing for the road.

The back wall and the floor were composed of packed earth, and it was dark inside, with the only light coming through the open door. A half-burnt candle sat in a dish on the table. Gareth went to it and lit it with the tools he carried in his scrip. The candle flared, casting their shadows against the wall, and then a sudden gust of wind blew through the room. The candle went out at the same moment that the door slammed shut.

Llelo shrieked into the darkness and scrabbled for the door latch. Gareth found the boy by sound alone and grabbed him around the waist with his left arm. "Hush, Llelo." Feeling for the door with his free hand, Gareth lifted the latch. He pushed the door open, and light streamed into the room once again. Gareth set Llelo on the other side of the threshold. "Stay here and prop the door open with your shoulder."

"Yes, sir." Llelo looked down at his feet.

Gareth put his head close to Llelo's. "I won't mention this to anyone if you don't."

"Thank you, Da." The color slowly returned to Llelo's face.

Hywel shot Gareth a sliver of a smile and tipped his head towards the boy. "Is he all right?"

"He will be," Gareth said, "once he calms down and his courage returns."

Hywel had lit the candle again and now proceeded around the room with it, surveying the contents of the house: a bed in the far corner, a table with two stools tucked underneath it, and a shelf holding platters and cups. A broom leaned against the wall by the cupboard.

"Warm and dry, as I said." Hywel gestured to the beams that supported the plank board ceiling. "Wena hung her herbs here. They never grew mold, not even during the worst of the winter rains."

"How did she manage that?" Gareth said.

Hywel shrugged. "She always said it was in the house's nature, though she did keep a fire burning in that brazier." Hywel pointed to a grate that Gareth hadn't noticed earlier, located in the back of the room at the front of a hollowed-out section of the wall a foot above the ground.

His brow furrowed, Gareth looked around the room for a chimney, but there wasn't one. Nor was there a hole in the roof.

"When the fire was lit, the smoke was sucked right out of the house through that hole. Clever, really." Hywel had always valued cleverness in people more than any other quality.

Gareth found a lantern on the shelf next to the cups. He lit it and brought it over so it could shine into the opening. While the surface of the wall was dirt, he saw now that it was of variable width and backed up by solid rock. This opening was a channel through the rock that went straight up before curving away into the hill. He could feel the breeze on his face as it passed through the house from the door.

"Wena thought that a stream might have run through the rock long ago," Hywel said. "It's why the door slammed shut and the candle blew out. A time or two Gwen and I tried to find the exit point further up the mountain, but we never could."

After one last look into the hole, Gareth moved to the only other feature of the hut that looked interesting: a ladder, the top of which disappeared into the ceiling above them. "Where does that go?"

"There's a second level above us. Sometimes Gwen and I would play among the jars and boxes of herbs that Wena stored there. She always said that they would keep forever because it was so warm and dry and safe from wet."

Holding the lantern with one hand, Gareth climbed the ladder until his head poked through the opening in the ceiling. As wide as the floor below, the loft no longer stored Wena's herbs and in fact held nothing at all. The air was warmer up here, as Hywel had said, and the wooden floor held a layer of dust and dirt that could have been years old, if not decades, but probably wasn't. Wena seemed the type to keep a neat house.

Gareth held up the light. "Someone has been here recently."

"That's good news, I think." Hywel came to the base of the ladder and looked up at Gareth.

"More than one someone, if I'm not mistaken," Gareth added. Many footprints marred the dust. Starting at the ladder, they crossed the floor to a stone retaining wall at the back of the loft and then returned, crisscrossing back and forth as if their owners had made multiple trips. Dirt and footprints marred the ground around the wall too. Gareth climbed all the way up the ladder to get a better look.

Hywel's head appeared through the opening, and he took in the room with a sweeping gaze. "What happened to the retaining wall?"

"I was waiting for you before I found out." Gareth catwalked across the floor, staying to the left of the line of footprints. The wall had been built to a height of six feet. Stones at the top of the wall had come down, such that one section rose only to slightly below Gareth's chest. He peered into the gap, careful not to disturb any more stones.

"Wena had trouble with dirt and rock crumbling off the back wall. She liked things neat," Hywel said.

The builders had piled debris to waist height in the space between the hillside that made up the back wall of the house and the retaining wall. For most of its length, that space was six inches to a foot, but where Gareth stood, a natural curve in the hillside made the gap more like two feet. His brow furrowed. "There's something here."

In a moment, Hywel was beside him. His candle flickered over the scene but didn't go out. The draft in the loft wasn't as strong as downstairs but indicated that more fissures and tunnels besides the large one downstairs wound through the hill.

Gareth reached over the wall and lifted out a deerskin cloak, crumpled as if someone had balled it up and thrown it over the wall. It was heavily stained too, though it was hard to tell with what in this light, and had a Druidic look to it. If it had been Wena's, it was no wonder the children had thought her a witch. Gareth shook it out and held it up to Hywel, who studied it while chewing on his lower lip.

"Is everything all right up there?" Llelo's voice wafted up to them from below in a somewhat higher register than normal.

"We're fine, Llelo," Gareth said.

"I know what you're thinking but not saying," Hywel said, glowering at Gareth.

Gareth stayed where he was, simply looking at his prince.

Hywel sighed. "We have found Tegwen's shroud."

8

Hywel

"You can see it too, can't you? Finding himself with a dead princess on his hands, the killer wrapped Tegwen's body in Wena's deerskin and threw her over the wall," Hywel said.

"It's what I'm thinking," Gareth said. "It's perfect. The wall should have been high enough such that it wasn't possible to see over it. Nobody would ever have looked there if it hadn't come down."

Hywel shook his head. He had both wanted to find Tegwen's grave and not wanted to. But now that they thought they had, he couldn't back away from it. His next step must be to speak to old Wynn. Gareth sent Llelo back to the castle to recover from his ordeal, and he and Hywel entered the village. They stopped first at Wynn's hut, but he wasn't home, and his daughter pointed them to the tavern. They found Wynn seated on a stool at one of the tables, well into his cups.

"How many has he had?" Hywel asked Huw, the tavern-keeper.

"He started early today, my lord," Huw said.

As the sun was still high in the sky, he must have started early indeed. Hywel regarded the old man, who so far hadn't looked up and was gazing into his cup, which was half full of mead. "How early is early?"

"I don't usually see him until mid-afternoon, but he arrived just after the morning meal. I was about to call for his daughter to take him home," Huw said. "I don't want him collapsing on the green and hurting himself."

"Give us some time with him first. We need to talk to him," Hywel said.

"Yes, my lord." Huw touched his forehead with two fingers in a sign of respect, accepting that Hywel's suggestion was actually an order.

Gareth and Hywel dragged stools to either side of Wynn, who looked blearily from one to the other of them over his cup of mead. "What're you looking at?" He didn't seem to recognize Hywel, or at least he gave no obeisance to him as befitted Hywel's station as a prince of Gwynedd.

Hywel didn't take offense. Wynn's befuddlement amused him. He didn't need Wynn's respect, only his attention. Hywel reached out and gently removed Wynn's cup from his hand. "I think you've had enough, my friend."

"You're no friend of mine." Wynn made to grab at the cup but ended up knocking Hywel's arm. Hywel lifted the cup high and managed not to spill what remained of its contents.

"I will give your drink back to you as soon as you answer a few questions." Hywel set the cup two feet away from Wynn on the opposite end of the table.

Wynn peered blearily at Hywel. "Have I seen you before?"

"Many times," Hywel said.

Wynn waggled his finger at Hywel. "I remember now. I've heard you singing up at the castle."

Gareth was trying not to laugh at Wynn's befuddlement. "Our good prince might be singing for us today."

Wynn cupped a hand to his ear. "What's that?"

Gareth leaned in. "We have questions, Wynn."

"Aye." Wynn made another grab for the cup. This time, it was Gareth who whisked it away, though he wasn't as agile as Hywel, and a measure of mead slopped onto his hand.

Hywel tapped his fingers on the table in front of Wynn to regain his attention. "We want to talk to you about where you went today."

"I didn't go anywhere. I've been here." Wynn hunkered down over his elbows, which rested on the table.

"What about before the tavern opened?" Hywel said.

Wynn didn't answer, just shook his head.

Hywel tried again. "Why did you decide to drink breakfast and dinner today?"

Wynn eyed his cup, but Gareth kept an arm across the table to block his access to it. Any more lunges from Wynn and Hywel would return the cup to Huw at the bar.

"That's mine. I paid for it," Wynn said.

"I find that highly unlikely." Hywel glanced at the tavern keeper, who was smirking as he dried a flagon with a cloth. "Shall I ask Huw what you owe him?"

Wynn cleared his throat and sat straighter on his stool. He adjusted his tunic with a look of righteousness on his face. "I can't remember what I did this morning."

"If I ask your daughter where you were, will she tell me you were in bed?" Hywel said.

Wynn couldn't maintain his dignity for more than one sentence. He stuck out his chin. "I was asleep. That's where I was."

Hywel rubbed his jaw. "And before that? At what hour of the night did you find your bed?"

Wynn smiled slyly. "Wouldn't you like to know? But I don't kiss and tell."

Hywel blinked. The image of Wynn sneaking home after carousing with one of the village's widows had his eyeballs burning. Gareth seemed to be having the same problem.

Hywel decided to change tactics. "I understand that you maintain old Wena's hut for Prince Cadwaladr, is that right?"

Wynn nodded, and now he really did look wary. "So?"

"Did you visit the hut yesterday?" Hywel said.

"I always do," Wynn said. "I have to care for my horse, don't I?"

"Did you notice anything unusual there yesterday?" Gareth said.

"No."

"Have you seen Prince Cadwaladr in the last few days?" Gareth said.

"I saw him." Wynn's voice was sullen.

This was as painful as pulling teeth. Hywel glanced at Gareth, who shrugged and said, "What do you think?"

"I think he knows something he's not telling," Hywel said. "I'm not sure we're going to learn what that is until he sobers up."

And then, to prove Hywel correct, Wynn rested his head on his arms and closed his eyes. Within a count of ten, he was snoring gently. Hywel gave a snort of disgust and gestured that Gareth should remove the cup so Wynn wouldn't knock it over if he startled in his sleep.

"We're left with the same questions we had when we left Wena's house," Gareth said.

Hywel scrubbed at his hair with both hands. "At least we can confirm with the daughter that he was in his bed all night."

Gareth handed off Wynn's cup to Huw, promising to inform Wynn's daughter of the state her father was in and ask her to collect him, and the two men strolled back to Wynn's house. Hywel found the back and forth from one informant to another most irritating. They'd already spoken to the daughter, but she hadn't mentioned her father's absence in the night, and they hadn't asked her about it because they'd wanted to speak to Wynn first.

They found her hanging the laundry on a line that stretched between two posts, taking advantage of the rare sunny day to dry her linens. "My lords!" She dropped the cloth she was holding into the basket of wet items. "Is my father—?"

"He's fine, Elen." Hywel put out a calming hand. "Drunk and sleeping it off at one of Huw's tables. Huw asks that you collect him at your convenience."

Elen let out a sigh. "I worry about him ever since my mother died."

"Was he out last night?" Gareth said.

A wary look came into Elen's eyes. "What do you mean?"

"Was your father absent from his bed at any time in the night?" Hywel said.

"He left to use the latrine at one point," Elen said.

"Was he gone long?" Hywel watched Elen's face carefully for any sign of deception.

"I-I don't know." Elen looked away. "I fell back asleep, and when I awoke, it was morning, and he was snoring in his bed."

"Huw says that your father doesn't usually visit the tavern until later in the day. Do you know why he is drinking so heavily today?" Gareth said.

"No," Elen said. "Can you tell me what this is about?" When Hywel and Gareth didn't answer immediately, she added, "Has my father done something wrong?"

"We won't know until we find out where he was before dawn," Gareth said.

"Is this about the body on the beach? My father couldn't have had anything to do with that. He couldn't!"

"We are making inquiries at this point, that is all," Hywel said. "Calm yourself."

Elen had taken several steps towards them, but she subsided, the wary look returning. "I'll finish up here and go to him."

"That would be best," Gareth said.

Then Hywel bent towards Elen. "If your father can tell us where he was last night, if he went anywhere besides the latrine, we would be grateful. We aren't accusing him of any wrongdoing. We simply need to know what he knows."

Elen swallowed hard. "Yes, my lord."

Hywel nodded at Elen. "We'll take our leave."

"Ceri thought he may have seen two men with the cart," Gareth said as they walked back to where they'd tied the horses.

"If Uncle Cadwaladr was one, it makes sense that Wynn was the other," Hywel said. "Let's check in with Gwen, and then I'm afraid it's time to speak to my father."

Hywel wished he could avoid that conversation, but it seemed he had no choice. "We may have to pretend we know for certain that Cadwaladr is a part of this."

"He is a part of this," Gareth said.

Hywel shot Gareth a quelling look. "I am certain my uncle was on the beach this morning, but we have no evidence of his further involvement."

"If he didn't murder Tegwen himself," Gareth said, "he can at least confirm that her body was found in Wena's hut."

"True," Hywel said. "If we're very convincing, he will be anxious to absolve himself of any other crime and will have seen something or know something else that will help us. We must get whatever that is out of him."

Hywel wasn't sure how he was going to do that. Cadwaladr was an accomplished liar. In fact, he lied as well as Hywel himself did. Hywel was grateful that if Gareth had the same thought, he chose to keep his observation to himself.

9

Gareth

Gwen greeted them at the gatehouse upon their return to the castle. It appeared she'd been waiting for them. Gareth could tell at once by her expression that something was wrong.

"It's not good news, is it?" he said.

Gwen's look was apologetic. "I thought it might be better to talk here where we can't be overheard. Your father is sitting at the high table with Cadwaladr even now, waiting for your return."

"Does he know that we suspect Cadwaladr of something?" Hywel said.

Gwen nodded. "I'm sorry. I couldn't help it. Your uncle was glaring at me, and King Owain saw him."

Hywel grimaced. "Tell me quickly what you've learned."

Gwen obeyed. Both Hywel and Gareth knew Brychan— Gareth better than Hywel, since he'd been among the garrison in Ceredigion all those years ago. Neither had known that he'd been Tegwen's lover, however. That bit of news, and that Tegwen and Brychan had met at Wena's hut, left Gareth shaking his head and staring at his boots. Then Hywel told Gwen what they'd found.

"Old Wena." Gwen sighed. "I asked about her when I returned here a year ago and was sad to learn that she'd died. I never thought to wonder what had become of that marvelous house of hers."

"It's still there," Hywel said, "but now the children say that it's haunted."

"I find that fitting," she said. "Could be what they've heard is the wind moving through the mountain. In bad weather, it could scare anyone away."

"It scared Llelo," Gareth said.

It had occurred to Gareth also that the squeaky door and the moaning of the wind through the tunnel wouldn't have been the only sounds that the boys could have misconstrued as the result of ghosts. To come upon the house at a time when Brychan, Cadwaladr, or who knows what other man had brought a woman to it could frighten any innocent boy. He bit his lip and looked down at his feet, suppressing his amusement.

"Where is Llelo, by the way?" Gwen looked past Gareth, her eyes searching. "I didn't see him come in."

"We sent him home before we visited Wynn in the village," Gareth said. "I hope he's licking his wounds in the kitchen."

Gwen smiled. "Dai was upset to have missed all the excitement. That will teach him to be such a lay-about when intrigue is afoot." Then she sobered. "I don't mean to make light of Tegwen's death, my lord."

"I know," Hywel said. "Our grief at her loss was tempered by the thought that she had gone of her own will. None of us who loved her are having an easy time of it today."

"There *is* something I don't understand, my lord," Gwen said.

Hywel had been about to head off across the courtyard but turned back to Gwen.

"Why didn't Tegwen's murderer remove her necklace and cloak?" Gwen said.

"Where would he have taken them?" Hywel said. "He must have thought it more prudent to leave them with her."

"Or he was squeamish," Gareth said.

"I wondered that too," Gwen said.

Hywel tipped his chin towards the front door to the hall. "We can't put off my father any longer."

The walk across the courtyard felt like a march to the gallows. Hywel kept his head high, however, so Gareth squared his own shoulders and strode after him, Gwen in tow. The guard standing at the top of the steps to the hall opened the door for them, and a wave of warmth hit Gareth's face.

The hall was packed with people, every bench filled, but at the sight of the three of them walking through the door, the babble cut off abruptly. By now, everyone from Aberffraw to Rhuddlan knew that when Gareth, Gwen, and Hywel were seen consulting together the way they had been today, an investigation was underway. The crowd had been waiting to see them together in the hall ever since Tegwen's body had arrived at Aber, and everyone was anxious to learn what they knew.

King Owain nodded at Hywel, who saluted his father while Gareth and Gwen bowed. King Owain gestured them forward. As they paced between the tables the length of the hall, Gareth tried very hard not to look at anyone or anything other than the back of Hywel's head.

"We've been here before, haven't we?" Gwen said.

"I can't say that's a comforting thought," Gareth said.

"I can safely say that you won't be thrown into a cell at the back of the stables this afternoon," Hywel said.

It was nice to see that Hywel still had his sense of humor, though Gareth's incarceration in August of last year for a murder he didn't commit hadn't been at all amusing at the time.

As they passed through the hall, murmured conversation broke out around them, a thrill of expectation rising among the diners at the prospect of news. Dinner wouldn't be served until sunset, but Aber was full of people, and there was nothing like a dead body to bring out the curious. Even if Tegwen hadn't been a princess, the word of anyone's remains on the beach on the day before Hallowmas would have been enough to set tongues wagging.

King Owain fixed his gaze on the trio as they approached the dais. Gareth tried not to look at Cadwaladr, but he instinctively glanced at him out of the corner of his eye. Cadwaladr wasn't looking at him, fortunately, but was in close conversation with his neighbor, a minor lord from southern Gwynedd. Gareth couldn't help but think his detachment was feigned and that his ears were as attuned as anyone's to what Hywel had to say to King Owain. Gareth's would have been if he'd been wearing Cadwaladr's boots.

Hywel stepped onto the dais to stand opposite his father's seat, put his heels together, and bowed. "Father, may I speak to you in private?"

"Is that truly necessary?" King Owain put a hand to his breast bone, touching the thick cross strung on a chain around his neck. Gareth couldn't help but think he was wearing it as if it were armor, or a talisman, but it wouldn't protect him from the news Hywel was bringing him.

Gareth's eyes flicked again to Cadwaladr, who still wasn't looking in his direction. Hywel may have done the same, because the muscles around his father's mouth tightened, whether in concern or suppressed anger Gareth couldn't tell. With King Owain, the latter was always a likely response.

"We will speak in your chambers." Without a word to anyone who shared the table with him, the King stood and headed towards the side door.

The moment he passed into the corridor, the buzz of conversation in the hall rose behind him. To approach him so publicly had been a mistake. After this, the king would have to say *something* to his people, if only to ward off the wilder and more imaginative rumors.

Once everyone was inside Hywel's office, Gareth closed the door. King Owain had paced to Hywel's chair, but the instant he sat in it, he was on his feet again, unable to stay still. He went to the window and looked out of it, his back to the room. "What have you found?"

Gareth had no wish to sit himself, but he escorted Gwen to the bench against the wall. Hywel clasped his hands behind his back and stiffened his legs. He looked like he was bracing for a strong wind that, as it happened, bore a remarkable resemblance to King Owain's temper.

"We think we have found the place where Tegwen has lain all these years," Hywel said.

King Owain turned to look at his son, his expression clearing. "That was quick work."

"One of the fisher boys heard and saw a cart pass by his house in the early hours of the morning, before low tide and the clammers were out. He recognized the horse pulling it, though he couldn't make out the driver. After we questioned him, we found the horse and cart at a homestead close to Aber village. It was old Wena's place."

"I haven't thought of her in years." Now that they'd started talking, King Owain seemed to relax. He went to Hywel's chair and sat.

"No one lives there now, but I understand that the house and the land it's on belong to Uncle Cadwaladr," Hywel said.

King Owain rocked back in the chair, the front legs lifting off the floor. "Cadwaladr was not in Gwynedd when Tegwen disappeared. None of us were."

"I know that, Father," Hywel said. "We were fighting in Powys, Cadwaladr at your side, and as it turns out, Tegwen's lover,

Brychan, fought there too. I have no mind to accuse my uncle of anything so perverse as the murder of his niece."

"But you suspect your uncle of something." King Owain tapped a finger to his lips. "Gwen implied as much to me earlier."

"I believe it was he who left Tegwen on the beach." Hywel signaled to Gareth, who stepped forward.

Gareth would rather have faced down a wild boar without a spear than pull the pendant coin from his scrip. But he did as Hywel bid him and held it out to King Owain.

"This was found near her body this morning," Hywel said. "It belongs to Uncle Cadwaladr."

"I see." King Owain eyed the pendant. "Is that all? He could have dropped it on the beach at any time. Weeks ago, for that matter."

"Father—" Hywel was struggling to keep impatience out of his face.

King Owain brought the legs of his chair back to the floor with a *thud*. "Let me see if I am understanding you correctly. You think that someone killed Tegwen five years ago and left the body in old Wena's hut, but your uncle discovered it and decided—instead of informing me, or you, or Rhun—that he should deposit her on Aber's beach this morning."

"Yes," Hywel said.

King Owain scrubbed at his hair with both hands, cursing under his breath.

"Father, I would like your permission to speak to Uncle Cadwaladr," Hywel said.

King Owain took in a deep breath through his nose and let it out. "I accept the need. Cadwaladr should come here now so we can get this over with." Then he hesitated as he contemplated the three of them. "But I can't send any of you to fetch him."

Gareth looked at Gwen. Because he knew her so well, he recognized the light in her eyes and that she was trying to constrain her mirth. The king was right: if any one of the three of them walked up to Cadwaladr as he sat on the dais in the great hall, he would refuse to accompany them. Even if he didn't have half of Gwynedd watching his every move, he would still have viewed his brother's choice to summon him by means of Gareth, Gwen, or Hywel as an insult.

The animosity among them ran deep: Cadwaladr had dismissed Gareth from his service six years ago; he'd abducted Gwen last year, spiriting her away to Ireland, after which Hywel had burned his castle at Aberystwyth and then taken over his lands in Ceredigion. If Cadwaladr were to name the residents of Aber Castle he hated the most, their names would top the list.

King Owain gave a snort of disgust and rose to his feet. "Just as I thought. None of you can disagree."

"Perhaps I could fetch Lord Taran," Gwen said. "He could then ask Prince Cadwaladr to join us?"

"More to the point, my lord, perhaps meeting in this space is not advisable," Gareth said.

King Owain opened the door to Hywel's office. "I agree. I will speak to Cadwaladr in my chambers."

"But Father—"

King Owain made a dismissive gesture. "Son, the presence of you and Gareth will only inflame matters. Gwen alone can attend to us."

Gwen opened her mouth to protest too, but Gareth put an arm around her shoulders and spoke for them both. "Surely, my lord—"

"Unless you don't think you're capable, my dear?" King Owain said, baiting her.

"I am perfectly able, my lord," Gwen said.

The king blithely ignored her glare. "Good. I will see you there shortly." He strode away.

The three of them stared after him. Hywel muttered something indistinguishable under his breath. It sounded like he was cursing Cadwaladr, possibly his father, and circumstances all at the same time.

"Why does he want me there?" Gwen said. "I didn't find the pendant and didn't even go to Wena's house. I know what you saw only because you told me about it."

"Gareth raises my uncle's hackles by his very presence," Hywel said. "I took his castle and his lands. You, on the other hand, merely annoy him."

Gwen choked down a laugh. "I can safely say that the feeling is mutual."

"You're my secret weapon." Hywel went to the door. "You can do this."

Gareth and Gwen stood together for a moment after Hywel left, looking at each other with the same surprise at Hywel's candor.

Gwen lifted one shoulder. "I suppose I shouldn't keep King Owain waiting."

The pair hastened to catch up with Hywel, detouring into the courtyard by a side door and coming back inside through a different door on the other side of the keep to avoid the great hall.

"No matter how long the interview lasts, I will be waiting for you outside," Gareth said.

Gwen's morose expression didn't change.

Hywel grinned to see it. "We both will."

10

Gwen

In general, whenever she was forced to occupy the same room as Cadwaladr, Gwen avoided him: she didn't look at him, she didn't talk to him, and she looked for any excuse to leave the room before she had to do either of those things. Thus, the idea of questioning him about his recent whereabouts had her stomach in knots, and she clenched her hands together to stop them from trembling. Cadwaladr was a snake in human form. He had abducted her. It wasn't something she could forgive. Not today. Maybe not ever.

Gareth stayed beside her until King Owain and Cadwaladr passed through the doorway from the great hall into the corridor that led to King Owain's rooms. Then he kissed her cheek, squeezed her hand, and departed. Gwen tried to slow her pounding heart. She opened her hands wide and placed them flat at her sides against her skirt. She was glad she had taken off the plain homespun she'd worn to the beach and replaced it with one of her two finer dresses, this one green with a white underskirt. It was a kind of armor against the unpleasantness to come.

"What is this all about, Owain?" Cadwaladr's voice echoed down the corridor towards her. "I was just about to—" He pulled up short as he spied Gwen standing outside King Owain's door.

King Owain took his brother's elbow and urged him forward.

Cadwaladr's face screwed up in disdain. "What is she doing here?"

At times, King Owain wasn't as good a judge of people and situations as Hywel, but he'd been right in this instance. If Gwen's presence sent Cadwaladr into sputtering protests, the presence of Gareth and Hywel would have thrown him into apoplexy. Even if they had remained silent and allowed King Owain to question him, Cadwaladr would have hated to have them witness his interrogation.

"We have identified some ... irregularities regarding the finding of Tegwen's body and hoped that you could help us with the investigation," King Owain said. "It seemed preferable to have this conversation in my chambers rather than under the watching eyes of everyone in the hall."

"I didn't kill Tegwen." Cadwaladr came to a full stop.

"We know that," Gwen said, daring to speak. It wasn't strictly true. They didn't *know* anything of the sort, but it seemed politic to appease the prince on the chance this admission might encourage him to be more helpful. "But someone killed her, and we were hoping that you could help us discover who that might have been."

The pinched look remained in Cadwaladr's face. "I have been on the receiving end of another of your *investigations*, girl, and it wasn't pleasant. Why should I help you now?"

"You should help because *I* am asking, not Gwen. This way, Cadwaladr." King Owain practically shoved his brother into his receiving room. "As Gwen said, we aren't accusing you of Tegwen's murder. We know already that you didn't kill her."

Cadwaladr straightened his tunic with a jerk. "I should hope so."

Gwen followed, closing the door behind her. She felt rage boiling up inside her and was afraid that if she opened her mouth, it would come out. That wouldn't be good for anyone. Needlessly antagonizing Cadwaladr—and King Owain—with Cadwaladr's past sins wouldn't help them find Tegwen's killer. When Gareth had shown her the coin pendant, she'd had a moment of wild hope that Cadwaladr was the murderer, but even between the pendant and his ownership of Wena's hut, she couldn't construct an argument to hang him for it yet.

"You know more than you're telling," King Owain said. "I realize that the body just came to light this morning, but to clarify your role in these events would allow us to pursue more profitable leads."

Gwen looked down at her feet, trying not to laugh at how easily King Owain had adopted Hywel's way of speaking. *Profitable leads,* indeed.

Cadwaladr put his nose into the air. "More profitable leads than what? Than dragging me in here? I can guarantee you that I had no role—"

"You own the farmhouse where Wena used to live," King Owain said.

"What of it?"

Gwen sighed. "We found where Tegwen's body has been hidden all these years, in the loft, concealed behind the retaining wall."

Cadwaladr's face went completely blank. Then his expression hardened, and he glared at Gwen. "I have no idea what you're talking about."

King Owain shot Gwen a warning look and put a hand on his brother's arm. "The cart that delivered Tegwen's body to the beach this morning was seen and recognized as the one stabled at Wena's former steading to the west of the village. The cart and horse belong to old Wynn, who maintains the house and lands for you. Brother, you are familiar with the house. Don't deny it."

King Owain didn't remind Cadwaladr that he brought his women there. It turned Gwen's stomach to think about the prince with any woman, even his wife, who had to be a saint to put up with him. Under Welsh law, Alice could divorce Cadwaladr if she caught him with another woman three times. Alice was Norman, however, and might not feel the option was truly hers. If she left Cadwaladr, she would have to return to her family in England. The English Church would never accept her divorce as legitimate nor allow her to remarry. Still, Gwen would have accepted that shame over having to live with Cadwaladr for the rest of her life.

"Do you think that I would ever have entered the house if I had known that Tegwen's body was hidden there?" Cadwaladr said. "What do you take me for?"

Cadwaladr was putting on a very good show of ignorance. Could it be that he knew nothing about this? Gwen shot King Owain a worried look, but he was observing his brother with an amused expression.

"I know you wouldn't have," King Owain said. "When did you find the body? Only yesterday? Or was it old Wynn who found it and ran to tell you of it?"

Cadwaladr still had his nose in the air. "You should be speaking to Wynn, not me. I have had nothing to do with the place for years."

King Owain's expression was one of complete disbelief. Gwen took out the coin pendant, which Gareth had given to her before he left, and showed it to Cadwaladr. "We would believe that if this hadn't been found on the beach this morning. It is yours."

"We? Who's we? Hywel and that ... that bastard husband of yours?" Cadwaladr said. Facing a question he didn't want to answer, Cadwaladr had gone on the attack. It was typical behavior for a cornered man. Or dog.

Gwen didn't flinch and fought back the image of Cadwaladr as a wolfhound, barking and gnashing his teeth at her, having surged to the end of his leash. But it was a leash that King Owain still held. The king lifted the pendant from Gwen's palm by its leather thong. "The girl is right, Cadwaladr. This *is* yours."

Cadwaladr took a step back, his hands reaching for the table behind him. He leaned against it. "I haven't seen that coin in years."

"From all the to and fro that occurs daily on the beach, it couldn't have been lying in the pathway longer than a few hours. It was sitting up in the sand and was picked up by one of the village boys on his way to clamming," King Owain said. "It would have been obvious to anyone walking by."

"It has nothing to do with me," Cadwaladr said.

"Cadwaladr, how came it to the beach?" his brother said.

"I have no idea." Cadwaladr snatched the pendant from King Owain's hand. "The man who stole it from me must have dropped it."

King Owain heaved a sigh. He gazed at his brother through several heartbeats. Cadwaladr set his jaw and glared defiantly back. The king walked to his chair and sat in it, leaning back and resting his elbows on the arms. Cadwaladr was forced to turn around and now stood before the table like a supplicant while King Owain observed him over hands steepled together in front of his lips.

Gwen recognized that silence was the best option for her, and she backed away slowly towards the side wall to sit on a bench underneath the lone window.

"This might go better if I told you what I think happened," King Owain said and continued without waiting for agreement from Cadwaladr. "I think your man, Wynn, discovered the body recently—maybe as recently as yesterday."

Cadwaladr sputtered, spittle flying from his lips in his anger, but King Owain held up one finger to stop him from speaking. To Gwen's amazement, Cadwaladr subsided. King Owain had power over him. Gwen felt a little better to see it.

"He informed you of its existence," King Owain said, "and you decided that with Hallowmas so close, you had to get rid of it. You couldn't have a dead body in a house to which you brought your women. So, in the middle of the night, you loaded the body into the cart and drove to the beach at Aber, where you left her in the sand. Are you going to stand there and tell me I'm wrong?"

Cadwaladr's hands were clenched into fists at his sides like Gwen's had been earlier. "I didn't kill her."

"Nobody said you did." King Owain's voice turned soothing. "We merely want to know what you did do, so we can look to others for the actual deed." King Owain kept his eyes fixed on his brother's face. Cadwaladr looked down so he wouldn't have to meet the king's gaze, chewing on his lower lip and staring at the floor.

Cadwaladr remained that way for a long count of ten before he gave a sudden laugh and threw up his hands. "Fine. You caught me out." Cadwaladr pulled up a chair that had been set at an angle to the table and plopped himself into it, still laughing. He shook his head as if he was mocking himself instead of capitulating completely.

"I should have known better than to expect I could remain anonymous in this. Just as you said, old Wynn found the body and told me of it. God knows what he was doing up in that loft, the old fool. *Seeing to things*, he told me. Meddling, more like. Once he'd found it, though, I couldn't have a dead body in my house, so I took it to the beach this morning. I must have dropped my pendant when Wynn and I lifted her from the cart."

King Owain leaned forward. "I'm trying to understand how you could find the body of your niece—"

"I didn't know who it was! What little I saw of the body told me it was a woman, but it was all—" Here, Cadwaladr waved his hand back and forth, his face contorted in disgust, "—wrinkled and brown. To my eyes, it was a body wrapped in a cloak. Nothing more or less. I didn't look closely other than to make sure she was dead. Long dead, by my reckoning."

King Owain sat back in his chair again, contemplating his brother. "You didn't notice the lions embroidered into the hem of the cloak or her garnet necklace?"

"I didn't look at her closely," Cadwaladr said, "and even if I had noticed, I wouldn't have linked those items to Tegwen. I barely knew the girl. What would I know of her jewelry or clothing?"

Cadwaladr's assertion was completely in keeping with his character. King Owain knew it too. He heaved a sigh and fingered a stack of papers on his desk. "God knows why, but I believe you."

Cadwaladr sat straighter in his seat. "Well, you should."

Neither Gwen nor King Owain jeered, though they could have. King Owain cleared his throat. "Nevertheless, your first impulse when you came upon a dead body in your house was not to tell me or to bring it to the attention of my son—"

Cadwaladr made a disgusted face.

"—who has years of experience dealing with such matters. Instead, your next move was to leave her on Aber's beach?"

"I could have buried her in the garden, couldn't I? I knew someone would have missed her, even if her death occurred a long time ago, but I didn't want to involve myself." Cadwaladr glared at his brother. "Given our history, I knew that Hywel's first thought would be that she was one of my women and that I'd killed her. What reason I could possibly have had to do that, I don't know, but under the circumstances, it seemed better to remain anonymous."

Gwen bit the inside of her lip to keep herself from speaking. Cadwaladr was right about that, startling as it was for her to admit. If the body hadn't been Tegwen's and Cadwaladr had come to Hywel with the news of its appearance in his wall, Hywel would have suspected Cadwaladr's hand in her death. In fact, if the body had belonged to anyone but Tegwen, the list of suspects would have been hugely long.

"Except, of course, you didn't remain anonymous," King Owain said. "You were seen, and since you were seen, we traced the body back to your property and wasted most of a day chasing after evidence that you could have told us yesterday!" His last words were accompanied by a raised voice and the thump of his fist on the table. "You left your niece's body on the beach!"

Cadwaladr's chin jutted out defiantly. "I did what I thought was best."

Then Cadwaladr stood abruptly, the chair protesting as he shoved it back. He adjusted his long burgundy robe, made of finely woven wool embroidered at the hem, much like Tegwen's. Like all of Cadwaladr's clothes, it couldn't have come cheap, and for the first time ever, Gwen wondered how Cadwaladr afforded it. With his reduced lands and the huge expense he'd incurred in paying off the Danes he'd hired to kill King Anarawd, she would have thought he wouldn't have had the wherewithal to buy himself expensive clothes. And then she wondered what he could be doing to gather wealth to himself—and if it was something King Owain wouldn't like if he knew about it.

"You did what you thought was best for you," King Owain said. "You always do."

"I will return to the hall." Cadwaladr turned on his heel and paced towards the door, his shoulders back and his dignity—at least on the surface—intact. He even closed the door gently behind him.

King Owain's last comment had been the truest thing Gwen had ever heard him say about his brother. She closed her eyes, struggling to contain her own emotions. She hated Cadwaladr and wanted to see him humiliated—but the actual seeing of him humiliated hadn't made her feel good at all. The sickness in her stomach returned, and she rubbed her belly, comforting herself when her child did a somersault under her hand.

"That went well," King Owain said.

Gwen opened her eyes to find the king tipped back in his chair with his boots on the table and his hands clasped behind his head. The top rung of the chair hit the wall, and the king smiled up at the ceiling.

"My brother is a sanctimonious bastard, and I can't believe he sprang from the same loins as I did. Where's his honor?" He spread his arms wide. "He cares only for himself."

Gwen decided that the correct response was to make no response. A silence fell between them as the king continued to look up at the ceiling. Then he swung his feet off the table and let the front legs of his chair hit the floor. He pointed a finger at Gwen. "Don't tell anyone I said that."

"No, my lord. Of course not."

Then King Owain allowed himself a laugh, sounding a great deal like his brother. "What am I saying? You'll run and tell my son and Gareth as you always do." He waved a hand at Gwen, sweeping her from the room. "Go on. What are you waiting for? Find me Tegwen's killer."

"Yes, my lord." Gwen couldn't get to her feet fast enough. She curtseyed to the king and left the room. Once outside, however, she hesitated. King Owain's bellow of laughter had followed her into the corridor.

11

Hywel

"That's that, then," Hywel said after Gwen recounted the conversation with Cadwaladr to him and Gareth. "My father seemed pleased with the result of the interview? Actually pleased?"

"He was angry at your uncle," Gwen said, "but then he wasn't. You know how he is—quick to anger and equally quick to laugh. I think he was relieved to know that his brother didn't kill Tegwen. So he laughed. I don't know how your father sleeps at night."

"He has learned to manage the worry," Hywel said. "Kings have far less power than everyone thinks."

The trio had chosen to stand outside the kitchen to talk, for lack of a more private location. The family that would be housed in Hywel's rooms had arrived while Gwen had been speaking with Cadwaladr; every noble soul was doubling or tripling up for the next few days, even Hywel and Mari. Though Gareth and Gwen weren't noble, Gareth was Hywel's captain, and to share a room with Mari and Hywel meant Gareth and Gwen wouldn't have to sleep in the hall. Even Rhun, Hywel's elder brother, had found a bunk in the barracks. Depending on how the rest of the day went, some of them might not be sleeping at all anyway.

Gwen had found a sunny spot on one of the stumps used for chopping the wood that kept the fires going in the kitchen. A boy worked with a pile of cuttings a few yards away, the satisfying *thunk* of his axe into the next block of wood punctuating their conversation.

"What if Brychan is right and Bran murdered Tegwen?" Gareth said.

"An entire investigation completed in one day?" Hywel clapped his hands together before making a rueful face. "I don't think so."

"I think we need a great deal more evidence before we can conclude who killed Tegwen," Gwen said. "We can't hang a man based upon the opinion of the dead woman's lover. So what if Bran didn't love Tegwen? That's not a crime."

"It is a crime in my eyes," Hywel said, "but even our knowledge of the poor state of their marriage is based on nothing but hearsay."

"So where do we go from here?" Gareth said. "I admit to being surprised that we have discovered as much as we have, but Cadwaladr's activities happened only this morning. We're looking now for answers about a death that may have occurred five years ago."

"Two deaths, actually," Hywel said.

"Two?" Gwen said.

"Bran was murdered two years later," Hywel said. "That changes everything."

Gareth glanced at him before looking down at his feet, clearly wanting to say something but choosing to hold his tongue. Thus, Hywel hesitated before continuing. Gareth had wanted the murderer to be Cadwaladr, which Hywel understood completely, but that desire was affecting his judgment and preventing him from seeing the whole situation as clearly as he sometimes did.

"What if the same man murdered them both?" Hywel said. "I admit it's a long shot, since their deaths were two years apart, but it's worth considering, especially since Tegwen told Mari she knew a secret about her husband. What if it was a secret her husband shared with someone else?"

"I'm wondering how Tegwen got from Rhos to Aber without anybody knowing about it," Gwen said. "Did the Dane she ran off with bring her here, or someone else? Where was Bran at the time?"

"In Powys with everyone else," Hywel said.

"Did you see him there?" Gwen said. "You always know everything about everyone."

Hywel scoffed. "This was five years ago, and I was hardly paying attention to where any specific man was during the campaign. We had periods of inactivity. Who's to notice who slipped away?"

"Cadwaladr could have slipped away," Gwen said.

"Perhaps," Hywel said.

Gareth raised his head. "I'm reluctant to admit this, but Cadwaladr *is* a prince of Wales. If he'd been gone long enough to return to Aber and murder Tegwen, someone would have noticed."

"Besides, she was his niece," Hywel said. "I find it unlikely, even as repugnant as I find my uncle, that he would have had cause to murder her. A romantic liaison with Tegwen would have been beyond even him."

"Who knew of the house?" Gareth said. "Riding hard through a night and a day during a lull in the fighting, any man could have returned to Aber."

"Many of Cadwaladr's men knew about it too," Gwen said, "not to mention all of the women he brought there and whomever they told about it."

"My lord," Gareth said, "only Gwen has spoken with either Brychan or Cadwaladr. Bran is clearly out of reach, but Brychan is here. I think it's time we asked him some more questions." Gareth put out a hand to Gwen. "Have you seen him since you talked to him?"

Gwen took in a surprised breath. "I didn't think to keep an eye on him or ask anyone else to. Have I been a fool?" She put her hand to her mouth. "He was distraught enough after our conversation that he might have thought twice about staying at Aber."

"If you have been a fool, we all have. Let's just see if we can find him," Hywel said. "Brychan should know better than to think I would arrest him just because it's convenient."

"You, yes," Gwen said, "but your father?"

"I see your point." Hywel's mouth twitched. "Still, my father has behaved reasonably up until now, and we still have another full day before the sun sets tomorrow night and Hallowmas begins."

"Even for us, solving Tegwen's murder by then would be quick work." Gwen shivered. "This isn't like our usual investigations. Years have passed since any of these events took place."

"And yet, we've had at least one murderer running loose in Gwynedd, maybe two, between Tegwen and Bran," Hywel said. "By now, he must have thought it would never come to light. We can use that to our advantage."

"Gwen, if you could look for Brychan in the hall while Prince Hywel and I—" Gareth cut off his sentence as a wail of pain and grief went up from the entrance to the castle.

"Go! Go!" Gwen said.

Gareth and Hywel raced around the corner of the keep, pulling up when they saw that the cries were coming from a woman who had buried her face in King Owain's chest. The king, looking extremely uncomfortable indeed, held her and patted her back. The begging look his father gave him was one Hywel had never seen in his eyes before.

Gruffydd, the castellan of Dolwyddelan Castle, stood nearby, and it was his wife, Sioned, in King Owain's arms. Although Hywel knew Sioned to be in her early fifties, she had the dark hair and smooth skin of a much younger woman. Perhaps to match his wife's youthfulness, Gruffydd retained the straight posture and flat stomach of a man ten years younger too. The couple was accompanied by a matron holding the hands of two girls who had to be Tegwen's daughters.

Fortunately, before his father could foist Sioned off on Hywel, Gwen appeared. Sioned raised her head to look into the king's face, tears streaming down her cheeks, and then at the king's urging, collapsed in grief onto Gwen's shoulder instead. Hywel hadn't realized until that moment what a tall woman Sioned was. Although she wasn't overweight, she was well muscled, and the much smaller Gwen struggled not to bow beneath the older woman's weight. Noticing his wife's distress, Gareth took Sioned's elbow, turning her towards him. "I'm so sorry for your loss."

King Owain cleared his throat. "Tegwen's grandparents have just learned of the events of the morning."

"I need to see my baby." Sioned's head remained bowed.

"What happened to her?" Gruffydd said.

"We're doing all we can to discover exactly that," King Owain said. "It will take some time."

Gruffydd clenched his jaw. "Hallowmas is tomorrow night. We must put her in the ground before then."

Hywel stirred. "We can't complete our investigation that quickly."

Gruffydd turned on him. "My granddaughter deserves to rest in peace!"

"We will see to her burial by then, regardless of how much we've learned," King Owain said appeasingly. "To do otherwise would be unseemly."

Hywel bowed his own head, his jaw clenched tightly, and didn't contradict his father. He recognized a command when he heard one.

While Calan Gaeaf was the day to celebrate the harvest and the first day of winter, the night before, Nos Galan Gaeaf—or Hallowmas—was the day the spirits of the dead walked abroad. Hywel knew why Tegwen's grandfather wanted Tegwen buried before then. Nobody wanted to think about her body lying in a room in the barracks—within the castle walls—on such a night. Although burning the body upon death like the pagans of old would have deprived them of material evidence, Hywel could understand the impulse to put the dead beyond reach forever.

"I will bring you to her." Gareth still held Sioned's arm, and now he moved away with her. Before they reached the barracks, Gareth glanced over his shoulder at Gwen and mouthed the words *find Brychan.*

Gwen threw up her hands in frustration.

Hywel leaned in to appease her. "Get Evan to help you. He was on the wall-walk earlier."

"What are you going to do?" Gwen said.

"Investigate." Hywel nodded towards the barracks. Tegwen's grandparents had just disappeared inside with Gareth.

"If the murderer is at all clever, and he must be to have come this far undetected, he'll know that we're looking for him now," Gwen said.

"Don't worry, Gwen," Hywel said. "I've got Gareth's back."

"As he has yours, my lord."

Hywel didn't know what he'd ever done to deserve such staunch companions as Gareth and Gwen, but it was one of the blessings of his life to know that what Gwen said was true.

12

Gareth

The room in the barracks to which they'd brought Tegwen's body was one that could hardly be spared, given the crush in Aber, but Gareth had no concerns that anyone would begrudge it to her either. He hadn't known Tegwen—had never even met her—but from the accounting of her that he'd heard since he stood over her body on the beach, he'd come to think of her as a sweet girl, but lost. The news that she drank more wine than was good for her had surprised him at first, but given the tragedies of her short life, whether of her own making or another's, the desire to lose herself in drink was one he understood.

And was one he had known well, once.

When Cadwaladr had dismissed Gareth from his service, Gareth had left his entire life behind him. In one day, he'd lost both his position and Gwen, and the humiliation of one and the pain of the other had brought him to his knees—at first only figuratively and then in fact as he'd been rescued by a convent of women and found a place as its protector. They'd give him a job and a purpose.

He'd gone back to them once, after he'd joined Prince Hywel's retinue, to show them what he'd made of himself. The prioress had greeted him, holding his arms and kissing each cheek. When he told her that he'd found a position in Prince Hywel's retinue, instead of congratulating him, she'd asked if he was being of service. As was a habit with the wise, she'd ignored his material possessions—his new sword and fine armor—and gone straight to the only issue that mattered.

Tegwen, for all that she was a princess, had walked a hard road not entirely of her own making. And yet Gareth couldn't look at Gruffydd's wife, who'd found a stool in the corner and was bent over her knees, her arms wrapped around her waist, sobbing, and judge her for her part in it. Tegwen's grandparents had done what they thought was best for her. She was dead today not because she was unhappy but because a man had killed her. Gareth's service to Tegwen, to his lord, and to God would be to unravel the why and the who.

While Gruffydd ignored his wife and stared down at his granddaughter's body, rubbing at his jaw, his face completely expressionless, Hywel was looking distinctly uncomfortable with the raw emotion pouring from Sioned. Tegwen was his cousin, and Gareth believed that he'd loved her, but Gareth also knew what was going on in his prince's mind without him speaking: *Tegwen is dead, and the longer you stand over her body and keep me from my work, the longer it is going to take to find out who killed her.*

"Do you think it's Tegwen?" Gareth said.

"My baby!" Sioned sobbed into her hands. "My baby is dead."

Gruffydd's glance towards his wife seemed to be without sympathy, but then he cleared his throat, and his voice was thick with emotion as he answered. "I have no doubt."

Hywel put a hand on Gruffydd's shoulder. "I recognized her as soon as I saw her too. I am so very sorry."

While Gareth wasn't a parent yet, he did sympathize with their grief: the wound caused by Tegwen's loss had scabbed over in the years after her disappearance, but in the time it took for them to ride under Aber's gatehouse, that scab had been ripped off. The situation was made particularly difficult because Tegwen's grandparents hadn't been expecting anything more this afternoon than a few days of camaraderie and feasting with their friends and relations. Now they had the funeral of their granddaughter ahead of them.

"I'm sorry also to have to speak about her death at a time like this," Gareth said, moving to stand beside Gruffydd at the foot of the table on which Tegwen lay, "but we need to ask some questions about Tegwen's last days."

"You mean the same questions you should have asked five years ago when she disappeared? After her husband killed her?" Gruffydd was no longer the affable castellan of Dolwyddelan but an angry, grieving grandfather.

"Why do you say that her husband killed her?"

"He beat her, didn't he?" Gruffydd said. "It was only a matter of time."

Gareth blinked. Gruffydd's certainty that Bran was at fault was the same as Brychan's, though Brychan hadn't mentioned physical abuse and neither had Mari. "If so, why didn't you do something about it?" In Wales, a woman could leave her husband if he physically harmed her, and her family would support her. Tegwen could have left Bran if she was afraid of his fists.

"She refused to admit that he hurt her," Gruffydd said.

Gareth looked at Hywel, who raised his eyebrows and nodded to indicate that he should leave it for now.

"When did you last see Tegwen?" Gareth said.

"We were with her for most of Epiphany," Gruffydd said, "through the funeral of the old king and the ascension of Bran to rule of the cantref. But once the winter thaw set in, travel became difficult. It's twenty-five miles from Dolwyddelan to Bryn Euryn. We wanted to see her—"

At these words, Sioned cried all the louder, her shoulders shaking.

Gruffydd glanced at his wife and finished, "—but whenever we visited, Bran made us as uncomfortable as he could."

"What do you mean by that?" Gareth said.

"He would complain about the expense of housing us and our men or indicate that our chamber would be needed shortly for a more important guest," Gruffydd said.

Sioned took in great hiccups of air and wiped at her eyes.

"We didn't want to appeal to Tegwen," Gruffydd said, "since it would put her in the difficult situation of having to choose between her husband and us, so we never stayed long. And Bran made it difficult for her to visit us too."

"Tegwen—wouldn't leave—the girls at Bryn Euryn," Sioned said, speaking through gasping breaths as she tried to control her tears, "and Bran claimed the journey would be too taxing for them, being so young."

Gruffydd finally bent to Sioned, holding her hands and whispering words Gareth couldn't hear.

"Bran sounds like a delightful fellow," Gareth said in an aside to Hywel.

"Two have named him now," Hywel said. "We will have to look at him more closely."

"How?" Gareth said. "He's dead."

"So is Tegwen—and look what we've learned of her in a day," Hywel said.

Gareth gave a slight cough to regain Gruffydd's attention. "When did you first learn of your granddaughter's disappearance?"

"Ten days afterwards!" Gruffydd spun around, his face once again flushed red with anger. "She disappeared at the Feast of St. Bueno, and we didn't know of it until the first of May."

"Bran didn't send for you when it happened?" Gareth said.

"He did not!"

"Is that why you accuse him of her murder?" Gareth said.

Gruffydd glared at Gareth and didn't address his question. "The trail was cold before we even started looking."

"It does seem odd that Bran didn't tell you of her disappearance," Hywel said. "All the same, how can you accuse Bran of murder when he was in Powys at the time with the king and most of the lords of Gwynedd?"

"Come to think on it, why weren't you in Powys too?" Gareth said.

Gruffydd snorted his disgust. "I'd broken my leg." He pointed at Gareth with his chin. "You remember—I was still recovering when you came to Dolwyddelan that summer."

"I remember," Gareth said.

"Damn knee has never been right since," Gruffydd said.

"So you couldn't personally have searched for her, regardless of when you heard the news," Gareth said. "Did Bran know of your injury?"

"Know of it?" Gruffydd said. "He was riding right behind me when it happened. I was on my way to Aber for the gathering of the troops for the march on Powys. The horse stepped into a hole. My boot was caught in the stirrup, and I went down under the horse."

Gareth winced. "You were lucky to live."

Gruffydd ran a hand through his hair, still thick with almost no gray at all in the brown. "After Tegwen disappeared, I almost didn't want to. It was only Sioned—" He gestured to his wife, "—who kept me going. And then after Bran's death, we took in Tegwen's daughters."

If the girls had been boys, Ifon might have kept them in Rhos, but a girl was of little interest beyond diplomacy. Tegwen's marriage to Bran had been intended to further an already well-established relationship with Rhos. Ultimately, if he'd lived, Bran would have arranged for a similar marriage for his daughters.

"I loved her." Sioned spoke again, renewed sobs choking her throat. "I miss her every day."

Gruffydd rested a hand on his wife's shoulder. "Come, *cariad*. She is gone from us. Let's leave her to these men, who will see to her."

The pair departed. Hywel gazed after them for a moment. "What if I have a daughter?" He shook his head. "You and I are in for it, aren't we?"

"Is everything all right between you and Mari?" Gareth said, not looking at his lord—and not sure he should be asking this in the first place.

"I didn't mean that. You know my feelings for Mari."

It was Hywel's desire to see his wife that had prompted him to ride north in August for a three-day visit because he couldn't bear to be parted from her any longer. Gareth had ridden with him and been glad to see Gwen too. Before he left again, Gwen had begged to come south with him, though they both knew her condition prevented it. Gareth wouldn't have wanted her to be a part of what he'd had to do anyway. When Hywel had returned to Ceredigion, he'd burned Cardigan Castle to the ground.

Gareth didn't want to think about the death he'd seen on that day or its possible repercussions, so he drew back the cloak that covered Tegwen. He restrained his instinctive recoil at the sight of her mummified remains. Tegwen's body hadn't so much rotted as dried out. Wena's cottage, with its constantly moving dry air, had provided an unusual environment for a corpse. Gareth glanced at Hywel, who was standing in his usual position with his hands on his hips, studying her.

"If she was pregnant when she died, we have no way to tell," Hywel said.

"She might not have been far enough along to show," Gareth said. "I suppose if her tissues had disappeared, the baby's bones might have remained among her own. Impossible now to know."

"How did she get from Rhos to Wena's cottage?" Hywel said. "Gwen was right to see that as the most pressing question."

"That's because you're looking at this all wrong." The door to the room swung open. Cadwaladr's wife, Alice, stood in the doorway. "It disturbs me that you are trusted by your father to see to this when you have no idea how go about to investigating wrongful deaths."

Gwen, who'd come through the door after Alice, closed it gently. Behind Alice's back, Gwen put a finger to her lips. Hywel had been opening his mouth to protest Alice's slight and now snapped it shut. He rubbed his chin, his eyes flicking from Alice to Gwen, who remained a pace behind the older woman. Gareth focused on covering Tegwen's body with the cloak. Although Alice had already received an eyeful, none of them needed to see Tegwen's remains while they talked.

"Alice has some important information for us regarding the circumstances surrounding Tegwen before her disappearance," Gwen said.

"Anything you have to say might be helpful," Gareth said into the silence that nobody else was filling.

"Right." Alice marched to the stool upon which Sioned had been sitting and sat herself down. "First of all, I know that I can rely on you not to let anything I say leave this room. My husband must never hear that I spoke to you. I will deny all rumor of it."

"Certainly," Hywel said.

"You may not tell your father either," Alice said.

Hywel looked at her carefully. "If it must be kept so secret, are you sure you want to tell us at all, Aunt?"

"My husband is under suspicion for yet another crime. He has committed enough on his own without adding false accusations," she said. "I could not bear it if he lost his lands in Merionydd. My children must have some inheritance."

Gareth could accept that.

As the lord who had taken Ceredigion from Cadwaladr and who had fought all summer to maintain his grip on it, that was something Hywel could understand too. "You have my word," Hywel said. "Please tell us what you know."

"My father died eight years ago, ambushed during a return journey to Ceredigion. Upon his death, Cadwaladr and Owain took the lands my father had carved out for himself. My family lost all of our lands in Wales, and my mother retreated to England. After his wife died in childbirth two years later, Cadwaladr came to

England to ask my mother for my hand in marriage, to make peace from war. My mother accepted on my behalf, and I returned to Ceredigion as Cadwaladr's wife."

Gareth had to give credit to Alice for treating Cadfan, the son of Cadwaladr's first wife, as her own. For the rest, Alice hadn't said enough as yet to know where this was leading. Hywel was watching Alice, a finger to his lips. He didn't interrupt or ask what this was about either.

Alice continued, "Cadwaladr spent the spring of Tegwen's disappearance in the east, having been called upon by his brother to fight. He left me at Aber with Gwladys, King Owain's wife."

"I remember," Hywel said.

"Lord Bran was often with us as well." Alice primly folded her hands in her lap, looking pleased with herself.

Silence fell among the companions. Gareth was lost but didn't want to say so. Then Gwen stepped forward. "You can't leave it there, my lady. As you said, we aren't as clever as you and need more to understand what was going on five years ago."

Alice sighed, irritation crossing her face. Gareth had admired Alice's fortitude when he'd encountered her in Ceredigion, but she'd been the lady of her own castle then, even if Hywel soon burned it down. This Alice seemed pettier and angrier. Maybe she always had been. But then, she was the Norman wife of a dishonored Welsh prince, living in exile in Gwynedd—not the refined Norman life she was born to. He could see how that could wear on her.

"Gwladys and Bran were lovers, of course," Alice said.

"No!" Hywel gaped at his aunt. "They can't have been. Gwladys never would have betrayed my father."

"She could have and she did," Alice said primly. "I was the only one who knew. She confided in me, loath to send Bran away but terrified of the king and sure that he would discover all when he returned from the east."

"Wait a moment," Gareth said. "All along we've been saying that Bran was fighting in Powys with everyone else. Are you saying that he wasn't?"

Alice sent him a look of disdain. "I wasn't in Powys, of course, but I heard about that little war. It was chaos: lords fighting here and there, practically at each other's throats as much as at the Earl of Chester's, raids from Shrewsbury all the way up to Chester itself, and nobody was ever where he said he would be." Her brow furrowed. "Didn't you know?"

Gareth looked from Gwen to Hywel, both of whom seemed stunned speechless by the revelation about Gwladys. Gareth had been guarding his convent during that 'little war' and had been on the receiving end, so to speak, of the fighting. He rubbed his forehead. "You're saying that Bran wasn't reliably in Powys that spring?"

"That is it exactly."

"How is that possible? Surely the residents of Aber would have noticed if Bran returned frequently to consort with their queen," Gareth said.

"She didn't meet him at Aber. They held their trysts at that little house where Cadwaladr says you found Tegwen's body," Alice said.

Satisfaction flooded through Gareth. Since Hywel's tongue appeared frozen to the roof of his mouth, he spoke for him. "How long did the affair last, do you know?"

"A few months, no more. She broke it off—before Tegwen's disappearance, mind you."

Finally, Hywel pulled up a second stool to sit beside his aunt; he took her hand. "You're sure about this?"

"I'm sure."

Gwen stepped to Gareth's side. "I don't remember Gwladys having such a compelling character that she would attract someone like Bran. She was a mouse, especially in comparison to Cristina."

Alice had overheard Gwen's comment. "He didn't woo her for her looks."

Hywel looked up at Gwen. "Though I know little of Bran, his desire was probably less for Gwladys herself than for what he thought he could gain from her."

"You mean he wanted a good word from Gwladys in King Owain's ear?" Gwen said. "Why would he need that? He'd already married Tegwen, a princess, and ruled Rhos."

"A man can never have enough land, Gwen," Hywel said.

"I assume I'm not the only who's noticed that nearly everyone involved in Tegwen's disappearance is already dead themselves. Is that a little too convenient?" Gwen said.

"I am *not* investigating Gwladys's death," Hywel said. "She died of a fever just before Christmas that year. My father was distraught."

"That was a momentous year for Gwynedd," Gwen said. "Tegwen disappeared, Gwladys died, war in England and the March—"

"I came to Gwynedd that summer. Clearly the most momentous event of all," Gareth said, trying to lighten the atmosphere in the room.

"But what does Bran's affair with Gwladys have to do with Tegwen's disappearance and death?" Gwen said, not acknowledging his jest. Gareth wasn't sure that she or Hywel had even heard it. "Why does telling us this clear Cadwaladr of wrongdoing?"

"Bran was very angry when Gwladys wouldn't see him anymore," Alice said. "One night, he snuck into her room through the window and asked Gwladys what she would do if Tegwen and King Owain were no longer among us."

Hywel surged to his feet so quickly that he knocked over his stool. "He threatened the life of the king? You can't be serious?"

"I am." Alice looked like she was biting back a smile, enjoying the effect she was having on Hywel.

"Why would you wait five years to tell us this?" Gareth said. "King Owain's life could have been in danger; Tegwen's clearly was."

"I admit that when Tegwen disappeared shortly after that incident, I had some concerns," Alice said. "I kept an eye on Bran, but since Tegwen wasn't dead—and he was still married to her—I thought she was out of his reach. Then when everyone returned from Powys, Cadwaladr took me away to Ceredigion. By the time we returned a full year later, Gwladys was dead, and I saw no reason to tarnish her memory with accusations of infidelity."

Alice finished this last sentence, still looking pleased with herself. Gareth had seen the same look on Cristina's face when she'd come to them with information. He understood it. Who didn't feel satisfaction at airing a long-kept secret? Perhaps she was also relieved to be rid of it.

"Thank you for your assistance, Aunt." Hywel held out his hand to Alice to help her to her feet. He escorted her to the door, bowed her out of it, and then shut it with a gentle click, after which he rested his forehead against the wooden slats for a long count of ten.

13

Hywel

"You must know that I'm not happy about any of this." Hywel paced to the table upon which Tegwen's body lay, flicked back the cloak, gazed at her body, and then covered her up again. Every time he looked at her, he was torn between the knowledge that he was among those who'd failed her and the wish that they could all go back to a day ago when they were blissfully ignorant of her death. "All we have so far is hearsay after hearsay and no hard evidence of any kind other than Tegwen's body." He spun around to look at Gwen. "Where's Brychan?"

"Lady Alice approached me the instant I entered the hall. I didn't have a chance to look for him."

Hywel took in a long breath through his nose. "Lady Alice—" He shook his head. "That woman is as much of a menace as Cristina. Do we believe any of what she told us? I certainly don't want to."

"Why would she lie?" Gareth said.

"Alice has been married to a consummate liar for years," Hywel said. "You tell me."

"She was straightforward with us about wanting to protect Cadwaladr," Gwen said, "but to go so far as to defame Queen Gwladys..."

"It was a bold move whether or not it was the truth," Hywel said. "Gwladys wasn't my mother, but she was kind to me and didn't seem to mind that her sons would inherit Gwynedd after Rhun and me."

"What is important about Alice's information," Gareth said, "is where it leaves us."

Hywel pressed both hands to the sides of his head, trying to force his thoughts into some kind of order. He'd been caught off guard by the appearance of Tegwen's body and been distracted by the disparate evidence ever since. He knew—and wasn't too proud to admit—that the presence of Cadwaladr in the middle of this had diverted his attention and clouded rational thought.

Hywel had always prided himself on *not* having inherited his father's temper, but this investigation had him seeing red. Under normal circumstances, when he tried to find a murderer, everyone lied to him as a matter of course. He expected it and didn't take it personally. He'd taught himself not to care a long time ago. In this investigation, however, the only person he could be sure was not lying to him was his hated Uncle Cadwaladr. It was just too much.

What the three of them needed to do now was clarify among themselves what they knew and create a plan for moving forward from there.

"Let's assume that everything we've learned so far is at least partially true," Hywel said. "What do we know?"

"We know from the condition of the body that Tegwen has been dead a long while," Gwen said. "We also know that she was estranged from her husband and that she had a lover, Brychan, whom she asked to run away with her."

"But he refused." Hywel nodded. "What else?"

"According to the legend, five years ago, a maid and a guard reported—to whom, I have never heard—that they'd seen her get into a boat with a Dane," Gareth said.

"Cadwaladr, Bran, *and* Brychan used Wena's hut for trysts," Gwen said.

"When Wynn found Tegwen's body yesterday, he and Cadwaladr arranged to leave it on the beach this morning," Gareth said.

"It stuns me to say it, but I am grateful to my uncle for that last point," Hywel said. "At least I don't have to go trailing around to determine if he was in his bed last night."

"That would be embarrassing," Gareth said with a straight face.

Hywel rolled his eyes at his captain. If Cadwaladr had been upset at being questioned by Gwen, he would have been furious to know they were tracking his whereabouts.

"Cadwaladr openly admitted his involvement, and since he's never covered up for anyone else in his life, we can take him at his word." Gwen laughed. "Did I just say that?"

"So where does that leave us?" Gareth said.

"It leaves me going to Rhos," Hywel said.

Gareth and Gwen gaped at him.

Hywel snorted laughter. "What? That surprises you? The people of Rhos will not be coming to Aber to celebrate Calan Gaeaf. They have their own festival at Bryn Euryn. If I am to discover more about these events, I have to go there."

"I don't object to the need to go to Rhos," Gwen said. "Of course someone has to. But that you would leave Aber the day before Hallowmas ..."

"All the more reason to start now," Hywel said.

"I will come with you—" Gareth said.

Hywel held up one finger. "No, you won't."

"But my lord—"

"You will stay with Gwen. The bulk of the investigation is here," Hywel said. "This is a little journey. I can see to it myself."

Gwen tried again. "What about Mari—"

"Not now, Gwen." Hywel turned on her. "I will attempt to return in time for Tegwen's funeral tomorrow or, at the very least, for the feast at Hallowmas. I can't miss it. My father would have my head. Meanwhile, you two should see if you can track down Brychan and anyone else who might be able to tell us something about Tegwen's death."

"Or Bran's," Gwen reminded him.

"Or Bran's," Hywel agreed.

Gareth folded his arms across his chest. "It is odd, my lord, this situation with Bran."

"How so?" Hywel said.

"He died in an ambush," Gareth said.

"Alice's father was killed in an ambush on the way home to Ceredigion," Gwen said. "And Cadwaladr paid Danes to ambush Anarawd near Dolwyddelan last summer."

Hywel frowned. "What are you getting at?"

"Nothing in particular," Gareth said, "except that the ambush that resulted in Bran's death seems very sketchy. He was the king of Rhos, it's true, but that's not a position that normally puts a lord in danger, not in Gwynedd. He tithes to your father, after all, and doesn't have the power to wage war or expand his lands."

"While you're in Rhos, it might be a good idea to speak to someone who rode with him and was there when it happened," Gwen said.

"That was my thinking too," Hywel said.

"You really should take me with you," Gareth said.

"And me!" Gwen said. "Though I admit if I rode with Gareth, Mari would want to come with us too."

"None of you are coming with me." Hywel's thoughts returned to his wife. A knot formed in his stomach.

"My lord?" Gareth peered at him.

Hywel schooled his expression; he'd wandered in his mind in the middle of a conversation and given himself away. He didn't often do that, not even in the presence of his two closest companions.

Gwen put a hand on his forearm. "Mari will be fine. She's just having a baby."

Hywel glared at her. "No reading my mind. I won't have it."

Gwen didn't cease with the knowing look.

Laughing to himself, Hywel ran a hand through his hair. Lately, he'd allowed it to grow long, so it now stuck straight up in the air. "I admit the idea of becoming a father has shaken me. I worry for her; I worry for all of us."

"I'll keep her company, my lord," Gwen said.

"Would you mind seeing to her right now?" Hywel said. "Gareth and I will finish up here before I go."

"Of course, my lord." Gwen curtseyed and left the room.

Gareth wasn't as easily put off. He didn't move to the body to continue their examination of it, just stood looking at Hywel. Hywel laughed again, dismissing his need to hide his true self from Gareth, who knew him all too well. "Murder I can handle. I can even understand it much of the time. But to lose Mari—"

"Mari will be fine. Gwen is going to be fine."

"You don't know that," Hywel said.

Gareth set his jaw. "I have to believe it."

"Now, that it is the truth. You and I—" Hywel's eyes flicked to the door through which Gwen had gone, "—we go into battle confident. We train for it all our lives. I have come to see childbirth as similar for women. Each woman tells herself that she's going to come out alive. But some don't: Gwen's mother. Mine. Eira and her babe."

The ache of that loss settled on Hywel's shoulders, though he'd not allowed himself to feel it for several years. He'd had many lovers, but Eira had been Hywel's first real love. She'd died birthing their child. The pain wasn't as raw as it had been, but it was waiting to rise up and threaten him with Mari's death.

"You're right, of course," Gareth said. "But we can't stop living, can we? And Mari needs you as Gwen needs me, because she's afraid too."

Hywel let out a breath. "I know that."

"Tegwen, at least, didn't die in childbirth," Gareth said. "Which is why we have to find her killer."

Hywel looked down at his boots, though he wasn't seeing them. He knew he couldn't bargain with God, but he found himself doing it anyway: *find Tegwen's killer and in return, Mari's life will be spared.* Hywel straightened the cloak covering Tegwen's body with a quick tug. "Let's get some air."

Hywel found Gwen and Mari in their temporary chambers in the manor house. Mari was asleep; Gwen had found a christening gown to embroider and was cursing over it.

Hywel poked his head into the room. "I know I'm not fooling anyone, least of all you."

"I have no idea what you mean." Gwen broke off a length of thread with her teeth. "Mari just fell asleep, but I'll wake her if you like."

Hywel warred with himself. Mari would be upset to know that he'd gone without saying goodbye, but sleep was so precious to her these days he couldn't bear to wake her. "No. Let her sleep." Hywel rested a hand briefly on Gwen's shoulder. "Stay out of mischief while I'm gone, will you?"

Gwen smiled.

His next port of call was the great hall and his father, whom Hywel found holding court by the fire. Rhun was with him. At a gesture from Hywel, Rhun detached himself from the group.

"I was wondering when you would come to find me," Rhun said. "What have you discovered?"

Rhun was Hywel's level-headed older brother. Where Hywel was dark-haired, Rhun took after their father, with his shock of blonde hair and burly frame. He had the ability to wield a sword for hours on end. Hywel had never yet beaten his brother in a mock battle, even by trickery. Rhun was going to make a fine king one day. Hywel wasn't jealous to have been born second. He knew his own strengths and happily left the diplomacy and long meetings to his father and brother.

"Not enough, I can tell you that much," Hywel said. "Gareth and Gwen will pursue the investigation from Aber, and I'd like you to give them whatever support you can."

Rhun laughed. "You mean you want me to protect them from Father."

Hywel smirked. "Better you than me." Then he sobered. "Mari was sleeping, so I left her with Gwen. Please reassure her that I will return tomorrow afternoon at the latest."

"Where are you going?"

"To Rhos."

Rhun raised his eyebrows. "Tonight?" And at Hywel's nod, Rhun added, "Is that really necessary?"

"I think so," Hywel said. "I must speak to Ifon myself."

"You could wait until after Hallowmas and the harvest festival," Rhun said. "It's only two days. The trail has been cold for five years."

"But it's warm now, isn't it?" Hywel said and then amended, "at least it is here. People are thinking and talking about those days again, and I'm hoping that someone will remember something important, which is why Gareth and Gwen are staying here."

"Father won't like it," Rhun said.

"He'll have to let me go when I remind him that Tegwen was a lady of Rhos too," Hywel said. "It would be unseemly for the news of her death to arrive there before I do."

Rhun nodded. "Perhaps I should come with you. Ifon and I were friends of a sort when we were younger."

"Father needs you here."

Rhun scoffed. "No, he doesn't, and besides, Cristina is due in the hall at any moment, and I would prefer to be far away when she arrives."

"Is she matchmaking again?" Hywel said with sympathy. "You would do well to find yourself a wife all on your own, rather than reject the one our stepmother chooses for you."

"Darling Rhun!" Cristina's penetrating voice echoed off the rafters; Rhun couldn't pretend he hadn't heard her. He grimaced at Hywel as Cristina glided up to him and took his elbow.

"I'm so glad you're here," she said. "I *must* introduce you to my cousin."

"My lady—" Rhun tried to tug away.

Cristina held his arm in a tight grip. "Surely you can spare a moment—"

"I was just leaving for Rhos with Hywel," Rhun said through gritted teeth.

"My dear, that's impossible." Cristina's lower lip stuck out in an artful pout. It made Hywel uncomfortable to see that look on his very pregnant stepmother. "I will speak to your father. It would be so unfair for you to leave us now."

Hywel took a step back, grinning, intending to beat a hasty retreat. As he turned around, however, his father dismissed his courtiers with a gesture and summoned his two sons and his wife to him.

"Do you have something to tell me?" the king said.

"Rhun tells me that he and Hywel are riding to Rhos tonight, and they won't be here for the feast of Hallowmas tomorrow," Cristina said before Hywel or Rhun could speak. "I was so hoping he could sit with my cousin, Anna. She has never been to Aber before and needs an escort. I've been so busy ..." Her voice trailed off as she batted her eyelashes at Owain.

Hywel couldn't believe his father could fall for this act, but he did—yet again. "Hywel can go to Rhos, Rhun. I need you here," King Owain said.

"But—" Rhun swallowed down his protest. His father's words had been decisive. Both brothers knew better than to argue when he used that tone of voice.

Hywel put a hand on Rhun's arm. "Good luck."

Rhun growled back. "You too, you dog."

Hywel gave Rhun a cheery salute and left the hall, in a better mood than when he'd entered it. There was something to be said for being the second son. Outside, Evan had gathered ten of Hywel's men-at-arms, and they stood waiting for him by the gate.

Gareth stood with them, giving last minute instructions to Evan. They both greeted Hywel, and then Gareth held the horse's bridle while Hywel mounted. "I should be riding with you."

"No," Hywel said. "You should stay here."

"We have so many questions—"

"And I shall ask them," Hywel said. "Don't be an old granny. I will be fine, and when I return, we will pool our knowledge and solve this." He leaned down. "You might rescue Rhun from my stepmother."

"It would be my pleasure, my lord." Gareth stepped back.

As Hywel turned his horse and rode out of Aber, he felt his whole body relax. It was good to be moving and to have a plan. With Uncle Cadwaladr no longer on the list of possible suspects, he needed to know who else to put on it. The answers might lie in Rhos.

And whatever his father's hopes in keeping Cadwaladr close, Hywel knew as surely as he knew that the sun would rise tomorrow that his uncle would betray Gwynedd again. Hywel intended to be there to catch him—and stop him—when he did.

14

Gareth

Gareth wanted to be riding with Hywel—with Gwen too, of course—because movement was better than no movement, and it was difficult to be left behind. He could understand just a bit of what Gwen must feel every time she watched him ride away.

"Mari is asleep and her maid is watching over her, so can I at least walk if I can't ride?" Gwen slipped her hand into his.

He looked down at her upturned face. "What do you mean?"

"We're going back to Wena's hut, right?" she said. "I know you're itching to see if you can find any evidence there that you missed the first time."

"You aren't going anywhere today," Gareth said. "The sun will set within the hour."

Gwen's face fell. "I suppose you're right."

Gareth looked carefully at her. That capitulation came way too easily. "Have you seen Rhun?"

"I passed through the hall on my way to find you. He was being introduced by Cristina to a very pretty girl," Gwen said, "one of her many cousins, I believe."

"Hywel described him as in need of rescue," Gareth said. "Perhaps he'd like to accompany me to Wena's hut."

Gwen laughed. "Then we'd better see to it. If we didn't have Tegwen's funeral tomorrow, Cristina would have him married off by All Saints' Day."

It was nice to laugh with Gwen. Gareth felt some of his tension leave him. Then a call went up from the gatehouse tower.

"Danes!"

Gareth swung around. The guard was pointing towards Aber's beach. Shouting at the men to close the gate, even though they were already doing it, Gareth took the steps up to the wall-walk two at a time and came out at the top. Skidding to a halt beside the sentry, he looked to where the guard pointed: three longboats were approaching Aber's beach, not far from where Tegwen's body had been found.

Gwen stood in the courtyard below. Other guests had clustered around her. "How many come?" she said.

Gareth squinted through the late-afternoon sunshine, his heart racing—and then he laughed out loud. A beefy, fair-haired Dane had raised a long pole with a white flag on it. He waved it back and forth above his head in broad sweeping motions. The white flag wasn't a traditional symbol of peace among the Danes, not that they ever surrendered and so would have had no cause to use it anyway, but they knew what it meant. Their leader had known the peril inherent in approaching a Welsh beach. Too many Danes had raided Welsh shores for too many years for any Welshman to look upon a Danish longship with anything but dismay.

As the boats approached the shore, Gareth grinned again as certainty grew within him about who was leading them. Danes were blonde and large as a matter of course, but none were quite as blonde and large as the man with the white flag.

Gareth leapt down the steps from the battlement at the same moment that King Owain, Rhun, and the majority of the inhabitants of Aber surged out of the great hall. Gareth jogged across the courtyard to greet the king and went down on one knee before him. "Three Danish ships approach Aber beach, my lord, but I believe Godfrid son of Torcall leads them. He raises the white flag of peace."

King Owain made an impatient gesture indicating that Gareth should rise and then waved Rhun closer too. He put one hand on Rhun's shoulder and the other on Gareth's. "How many men, Gareth?"

"Two dozen, my lord. No more."

"Do you believe their intentions are truly peaceful?" the king said.

"If it is truly Godfrid who comes, then yes, my lord," Gareth said. It had been Godfrid who'd kept Gwen safe after Cadwaladr had abducted her and stolen her away to Dublin. Gareth would trust the man with his life. "Godfrid is not here to raid Gwynedd's shores."

King Owain gave him a quick nod. "Take a strong force and ride to the beach. Rhun will lead a second company around the dunes to the east. If these Danes mean us harm, the two of you will have the men to stop them."

Rhun grinned at Gareth. "Try not to start a war before I get there."

"Sire, if I may ask," Gareth said, "you don't seem surprised to learn of their approach."

"I invited an embassage from Torcall months ago." King Owain waved a hand carelessly, as if he communicated with the Danes of Dublin on a daily basis. "Given the time that has passed, I didn't expect him to take me up on my invitation. The situation must be dire indeed in Dublin for him to send his son to me." Then he grinned broadly and wheeled around, waving at his people. "Back to the hall! The wind grows chill. We will wait for our guests inside."

Gareth tugged his cloak tighter around his shoulders and wished for a scarf. He hadn't noticed the change in the weather until the king mentioned it. Rhun clapped a hand on Gareth's shoulder. "Kings do as they please, do they not?"

"It seems so," Gareth said.

In all the hubbub, Gareth had lost track of Gwen, but he spied her near the gatehouse and reached her in a few strides. "I must ride to the beach." He pulled her hood up to cover her ears. "Go inside with the king so you don't become chilled."

"Yes, my lord," Gwen said, holding her cloak closed at the throat with a gloved hand. "Has Godfrid truly arrived?"

"I told the king he had, so it better be he." Gareth glared at his wife in mock severity. "You will stay well away from him."

Gwen leaned forward and pecked Gareth on the cheek. "Don't be silly, husband. I chose you."

Gareth smirked, and Gwen patted him on the chest in reassurance before departing for the hall as he'd asked. Stable boys were already working to saddle the many horses they'd need for their short ride to the beach. With so many noblemen at Aber, there was no lack of men-at-arms from whom to choose. He would meet Godfrid with the same number Godfrid himself was bringing, while Rhun would ride with two dozen more.

Gareth mounted his horse, which pranced at the head of his company, impatient to get started. Gareth patted his mount's neck, controlling him with his knees while waiting for the rest of the troop to form up behind him.

"Hywel would have liked to have been here," Rhun said. "He finds the Danes amusing."

"Most Welshmen wouldn't agree," Gareth said.

"Oh, but they're big and loud and full of themselves," Rhun said. "You have to admire them."

Rhun's grandfather had been born in Dublin because his great-grandmother, Ragnhild, had been the daughter of Olaf of Dublin, son of King Sigtrygg Silkbeard. That kinship connected the kingdoms of Gwynedd and Dublin and meant that the raids from Dublin on Wales had been far fewer in the last forty years than in the previous hundred. It also meant that King Owain's invitation to Godfrid to come to Aber was not without precedent.

"Do the Danes celebrate Calan Gaeaf?" Gareth said.

"Godfrid isn't here for the holy day," Rhun said. "He wants our help in his fight against Ottar. That's what he wanted last year, and that's what he wants now."

"Is your father going to give it?" Gareth said.

"We'll see," Rhun said, "but I think not yet."

Rhun's contingent rode away first. His company would turn right at the bottom of the hill upon which Aber perched, galloping east down the road towards a track to the beach different from the one Gareth's company would take. Gareth signaled to his men to follow on his heels. It was Gareth's second journey to the beach that day. It seemed weeks since the finding of Tegwen's body. That morning, he'd stood on the sand and watched the sun come up over the mountains to the east, and now he would stand at the same spot and see it sinking into the western hills.

The track upon which Gareth's company rode petered out at the dunes. High tide had come and gone and washed away all traces of their footprints from the morning. At low tide, the Lavan Sands would stretch out across the Menai Strait, creating a dangerous but passable footpath to Anglesey. With several hours to go until that moment, however, the shallowly built Danish ships had found a passage through them and now floated a few feet off shore. As a courtesy to King Owain, Godfrid hadn't ordered his men to pull up to the beach until given permission to do so.

Gareth looked to the west, noting the clouds gathering on the horizon and the chop on the water as it lapped at the Danish boats.

Poor weather was more normal than not for Wales this time of year, but after a beautiful day, it looked like they were in for a change in the weather with the onset of evening. Only a fisherman could tell him if the rain would last through tomorrow. Rain at Hallowmas would be a disappointment, though perhaps appropriate for Tegwen's funeral.

Gareth signaled to his men to stop and rode alone the last yards to the water's edge. He dismounted, dropping his horse's reins to the sand, and held out his hand in greeting to Godfrid, who leapt from his boat. Godfrid covered the distance between them in three strides, and instead of taking Gareth's arm, he caught him in a tremendous hug, lifting him off his feet. Gareth tried to speak, but Godfrid was squeezing the wind out of him. He coughed as Godfrid set him down.

"Good man! Good man!" Godfrid pounded Gareth on the back.

Gareth laughed, getting his breath back, and clasped Godfrid's forearm in a more decorous greeting. Rhun was right that it was hard to resist the outrageousness of this prince of Dublin. As they stood grinning at each other, Rhun and his company appeared on the beach to the east and galloped across the sand towards them.

"What is this? Didn't you trust me?" Godfrid said in mock dismay.

"I did."

Godfrid bellowed his good humor and clapped his hand on Gareth's shoulder yet again, pounding him a few inches further into the sand. "But when Danes arrive on a Welsh beach, it's better to be cautious about their intentions, is that it?"

"You have to admit, your people have not always been friendly," Gareth said.

"Those were the days, eh?" Godfrid rubbed his hands together as if relishing the memory. Then he strode away to catch the bridle of Rhun's horse, and when Rhun dismounted, he gave him the same treatment he'd given Gareth. The two princes then stepped back and bowed to each other, after which Godfrid waved his men out of their boats. "We are all friends, yes?"

"Yes," Rhun said. "My father awaits you in his hall. You are just in time for the evening meal."

Godfrid's eyes lit at that, and Gareth suspected that he'd timed his arrival to coincide with sunset for that very purpose. "That would be most welcome. Our boat was swamped within hours of leaving Dublin, and we've eaten nothing but salted meat and stale water since then. That is no food for warriors."

At Rhun's raised eyebrows, Godfrid guffawed and added, "Though I assure you, we are not looking for war today."

Rhun waved his men off their mounts, and the Welsh and Danish parties converged, communicating with each other in a mix of languages and unconcerned by whose accent was more atrocious. Godfrid's Welsh had somehow improved since Gareth had last seen him. Gareth wished he could say the same for his Danish.

"Where is Prince Hywel?" Godfrid said as the men began walking up the beach towards the main path that would take them back to Aber Castle.

"He is not here," Gareth said.

"The body of a royal cousin was found on the beach this morning," Rhun said.

Godfrid frowned. "I am sorry to hear that."

"She was murdered," Rhun said, more bluntly than was usual for him. "Prince Hywel has departed on a quest for information regarding her disappearance and death."

Godfrid halted abruptly in the middle of the path, and it was fortunate that the men behind them had kept their distance or one of them might have bumped his nose into Godfrid's back. "You're not serious?"

"Sadly, Prince Rhun is perfectly serious, and in fact—" Gareth's brow furrowed as he considered the possibilities, "You might even be able to help us clear up a point or two."

"How is that?" Godfrid said.

"The body was of our beloved princess, Tegwen. She was the daughter of Cadwallon, King Owain's older brother, who died twelve years ago."

"I have heard tales of Cadwallon. He was a mighty man." Godfrid thumped his chest with his fist. "Much in the manner of a Dane." Then he sobered. "Again, I am sorry for your losses."

"Thank you," Rhun said, "but it is the circumstances of her death and its discovery that concern us now."

"If she was murdered as you say," Godfrid started walking again, "then this is no time for guests such as I. We should greet your father and take our leave."

"That won't be necessary," Rhun said. "We lost her a long time ago."

Godfrid canted his head. "Now you've lost me."

"Our pardon, Godfrid," Gareth said. "Prince Rhun and I began the story at the end. You see, all these years we'd thought she'd run off with a Dane."

By the time Godfrid, Rhun, and Gareth reached Aber Castle, they had explained the situation with Tegwen to him as fully as they could, given their imperfect understanding of each other's languages. Godfrid seemed to be growling under his breath in Danish as he contemplated what they'd told him. While Rhun entered the great hall to make sure his father was ready to greet his guests, Godfrid put his annoyance aside to greet Gwen.

Or rather, he went to greet her but then held back at the sight of her burgeoning belly. Taking her by each of her arms, he said, "You are so beautiful."

"Now, now." Gareth stepped between them.

"Well done, old friend." Godfrid clapped Gareth on the shoulder. Another few wallops from Godfrid and Gareth was going to need to see the healer.

"It is good to see you too, Godfrid," Gwen said.

Godfrid stretched his arms out wide, taking in the bustling courtyard of the castle. "It is good to be seen and good to be here."

Then he looked down at Gwen. "But I hear we have a murder to solve."

"I was hoping that Godfrid could help us identify this Dane who may have run off with Tegwen," Gareth said.

Gwen looked hopefully towards Godfrid. "We are wondering now if he ever existed."

"Five years ago, you say?" Godfrid tapped a finger to his lower lip. "I don't know of any of my father's men, or Ottar's for that matter, who appeared with a Welshwoman at his side. He would have been a brave man to have stolen away a princess of Gwynedd, even if her father was dead and would never claim the throne."

"He could have sailed east, I suppose," Gwen said.

"Certainly, I have many relations back in Denmark," Godfrid said. "Many favor marriage to foreign women."

"Why would that be?" Gwen said.

Godfrid laughed. "Until they learn Danish, they don't talk back."

Gwen's eyes narrowed at Godfrid. Seeing her expression, he hastily turned to Gareth. "If there was no Dane, where does that leave you?"

Gareth sighed. "With more questions than answers, dare I say as usual."

"I am sorry that I could not have been more of a help," Godfrid said. "My memory of five years ago might also be imperfect."

"It was a long shot at best," Gareth said. "The man could have been Irish or Norse besides."

"We still have a murderer loose in Gwynedd," Gwen said.

For the first time since he arrived, Godfrid sobered completely. "We are all murderers, Gwen, at one time or another."

"The story grows more complicated when you add in that Bran, Tegwen's husband, was also murdered," Gwen said.

Godfrid's brows lifted. "I am liking your tale less and less."

"He died not far from where the Danes bought by Cadwaladr ambushed Anarawd," Gareth said.

"We're not accusing you or your people of anything," Gwen hastened to add. "Bran died by an arrow."

"Ah." Godfrid nodded. "Not a Danish weapon."

"My lord." Rhun approached the three companions. "My father would welcome you and your men."

"Of course. Lead on." Godfrid gestured that Rhun should precede him.

Gwen and Gareth fell into step on either side of the huge Dane.

"The last time I was here, the king's brother, this Cadwaladr you spoke of, was the one causing all the trouble," Godfrid said. "What has become of him?"

"You will see him in a moment and can judge for yourself; he sits at the high table next to King Owain," Gareth said.

Instead of scowling as Gareth felt like doing, a smile twitched at the corner of Godfrid's mouth. "Such is the way of kings, eh? Ottar and my father dine together while secretly plotting to do each other in."

"How is your father?" Gwen said.

"Ottar is in the ascendancy at the moment," Godfrid said, "so my father is not very well. He broods in his hall over what might have been, and I worry for his health."

"That's why you're here, isn't it," Gareth said, "to ask King Owain to go to war with you?"

"Oh no, my friend." Godfrid put a hand on Gareth's shoulder, more gently than before, Gareth was glad to say. "I came to see you."

15

Hywel

Bryn Euryn, the seat of the Lord of Rhos, lay a little over ten miles to the east of Aber but fifteen miles by the high road through the standing stones at Bwlch y Ddeufaen and the fort of Caerhun. With his father and two older brothers dead, the third son, Ifon, had inherited the cantref. After Hywel's grandfather had taken the throne of Gwynedd for the third time forty years ago, defeating the last of the Norman invaders, he'd reduced the kingdom of Rhos to a lordship. The Lord of Rhos tithed now to the King of Gwynedd. Even so, Ifon ruled over extensive lands stretching east from the Conwy River all the way to Rhuddlan.

Despite Gwen's warning about a killer still roaming free, Hywel wasn't worried about reaching Rhos safely, even in the dark. Any action on the part of the murderer, particularly Hywel's death, would result in more scrutiny, not less. The killer hadn't been quiet all these years only to panic now.

They reached Caerhun two hours after sunset, stopping briefly to rest the horses and confer with the commander, and then rode on nearly another hour before they finally picked their way up the slope to the castle of Bryn Euryn. Built below the ancient ruins that took up the crest of the hill, rising some four hundred feet above the valley floor, it was a well-fortified palace, not unlike Aber Castle, though built entirely in wood and surrounded by a wooden palisade.

Hywel hadn't been here in years. Usually, if the Lord of Rhos and the King of Gwynedd needed to speak to one another, the Lord of Rhos came to Aber and not the other way around. But Calan Gaeaf was upon them, and while the people who lived to the west of the Conwy River flocked to Aber, Ifon had called his own people to his seat. Hywel's small company was admitted through the main gate, prompting a flurry of activity in the courtyard. Ifon himself came out of the hall to greet Hywel.

"My lord." Ifon bowed from the waist. "To what do I owe this honor, especially this day, with Hallowmas so close?"

"I would speak to you in private, if I may," Hywel said. "I leave it to you how much of my news you wish to share with your people."

"Of course," Ifon said, "but surely you would like to refresh yourself first after your journey?"

"This is urgent," Hywel said, "and cannot wait."

"This way." Ifon gestured that Hywel and his men should dismount.

"We need shelter for only one night as we must return to Aber by tomorrow afternoon," Hywel said. "We won't trouble you for longer than that."

"It is no trouble, as you well know." Ifon's expression showed no irony or resentment. Hywel peered at him carefully, but it seemed as if he meant what he'd said.

Hywel had hoped Ifon's involvement in Tegwen's death, or in Bran's for that matter, would be immediately obvious in his manner. It wasn't, and now Hywel had to admit to himself that it had been ridiculous to have expected it. Her loss was clearly making Hywel soft in the head. Ifon didn't know why Hywel had come to see him, and years had passed since either murder.

Hywel had arranged in advance with Evan that he should not only see to the men but should also take on his own investigations on Hywel's behalf, as Gareth would have done if he were here. Hywel needed Evan to question Ifon's men, from the lowest stable boy to his first captains. If Gwen were here too, she would have been responsible for inquiring of the women of the castle. But for now, between Evan and Hywel, they would have to make do with what they could manage themselves. Hywel was a married man, but that didn't mean he couldn't smile at a pretty girl if he needed information from her.

Ifon led the way to the keep, and as he walked beside him, Hywel studied Ifon's profile. Ifon was older than Hywel; he was older than Rhun too, for all that Rhun had known him reasonably well as a boy. As a youth, Hywel had never had more than a handful of conversations with any of the brothers of Rhos. Bran had always struck Hywel as too full of himself and had thought himself the smartest person in any room he entered, which naturally raised Hywel's hackles. Ifon had faded into the background, letting his brother speak first and sometimes never speaking at all.

Hywel reminded himself that if he'd had a different brother that could have been his fate too: always in his brother's shadow and never allowed an opinion or action of his own but expected to follow Rhun's lead. Hywel was the second son, but he knew both his brother and his father loved and trusted him. He couldn't say the same for Ifon, which made the irony of his elevation to the throne all the greater. With Ifon's father and both older brothers dead, he was all that had been left to rule Rhos.

"I apologize for adding to the size of your gathering by ten," Hywel said. "It is not my intent to put you out."

"I say again that you honor us with your presence, my lord," Ifon said.

Hywel decided to take Ifon at his word and not mention it again. Ifon's courtesy towards Hywel was slightly shaming, in fact, considering what Hywel had come here to task him with.

"I have more apologies," Hywel said as Ifon led him to an exterior staircase that took them to the floor above the great hall. As at Aber, Bryn Euryn consisted of a great hall, stables, craft halls, barracks, and a small chapel, but on a smaller scale. In particular, the hall didn't have wings built off of it or an adjacent manor house in which to put Bryn Euryn's residents, much less its guests. With the inhabitants quadrupled for the holy day, Hywel might be sleeping in the stables with his men.

Ifon's office was among the four rooms that took up the floor above the hall. Two of the other doors were open as they passed them, revealing a bedchamber and a narrow room housing stacked trunks and crates of household goods. Weapons and armor would be stored in the barracks or armory near the gatehouse. Turning into Ifon's chamber, Hywel seated himself where Ifon indicated.

Ifon then walked around a table and sat behind it, folding his hands and resting them in front of him. He kept himself stiff, his shoulders tight and his back straight. "You have me worried now."

Hywel had known his appearance would cause consternation in his host. No minor lord ever wanted his prince to appear unheralded and ask for a private audience, and for Hywel to appear so close to Hallowmas had to be even more disconcerting.

"I have been searching my mind for what disaster could have brought you here on such a night," Ifon said when Hywel didn't immediately begin to explain. "It isn't—it couldn't be your father—?"

Hywel put up a hand, wanting to put Ifon at his ease. "No. It is a matter that is far less urgent and at the same time far more so." Hywel forced his own shoulders to relax. "We have found the body of Tegwen, your brother's wife."

Across the table, Ifon sat frozen. The silence between them stretched out for ten heartbeats before he said, "Please explain."

Hywel gave a brief summary of the finding of Tegwen, leaving his uncle's involvement out of it for the moment. "From the condition of the body, it seems that she has been dead for many years."

"If that is so, why do you think the body is Tegwen's?" Ifon eased back in his chair, recovering from his initial surprise and allowing his intellect to begin to work.

"It is a complicated matter, and to tell you all would give you more details than you might want to know, but suffice to say, the king has seen her, as have her grandparents, Gruffydd and Sioned. We have no doubt that the body is that of my cousin."

"Well—" Ifon let out a *whuf* of expelled breath and sat still for another moment, thinking. "Of all the things you could have told me, I would never have expected this."

"I'm sorry," Hywel said.

Ifon tapped three fingers on the table in front of him. "What I don't understand is why you, of all people, came here to tell me this, especially the night before Hallowmas? While Tegwen was a lady of Rhos, she disappeared a long time ago. You could have sent a message through someone of lesser stature."

"I needed to come," Hywel said.

Ifon canted his head, his attention focusing more closely on Hywel's face. "There must be something about Tegwen's body—or perhaps the manner of her death—that is troubling."

Hywel sighed. "Tegwen was murdered."

Ifon leaned closer. "You're sure?"

"There can be no doubt," Hywel said.

"How did she die? When did she die?" Ifon said.

With every sentence Ifon spoke, Hywel revised his estimation of Ifon's intelligence, which seemed to have developed since Hywel had seen him last. Ifon must have been hiding it all these years when he was in Bran's shadow. In fact, thinking back, Hywel was sure of it.

"She was bashed on the head, though from the condition of the body, it happened a long time ago, perhaps years. Perhaps even within a day or two of her disappearance." Hywel didn't like imparting such crucial information to potential suspects, but Ifon was hardly a suspect in Tegwen's murder, and his cooperation was vital if Hywel was going to get anywhere in Rhos.

Ifon expression showed distaste. "Hell."

Hywel nodded. "The finding of her remains has complicated my life considerably."

"As it will mine." Ifon slapped his palm onto the table in front of him. "Tell me, what do you want from me?"

"I need permission to speak to your people," Hywel said. "Everyone at Aber believed that Tegwen had run away with a Dane. I need to talk to whoever reported that event."

"That would be her maid and a guard," Ifon said. "The maid is dead, but the guard still lives. I will arrange a meeting for you tomorrow."

"I have other questions too," Hywel said. "Who was this Dane? When did she meet with him? And what about her children? By all accounts, she was devoted to them. How could she have left them so precipitously?"

"All good questions. I always thought that part strange too," Ifon said. "I spent very little time at Bryn Euryn during those years, but I was aware that Tegwen wouldn't visit her parents without them, and of course, my brother wouldn't permit the girls to leave Bryn Euryn."

Hywel was glad to have that bit of information confirmed straight away. When Gruffydd had spoken to him of it, Hywel had thought it in keeping with Bran's character. "How well did you know Tegwen?" Hywel wanted to ask as many questions as he could while he had Ifon's full attention. Given the upcoming festivities and the demands on Ifon's time, Hywel might not get another chance as private as this.

Ifon raised one shoulder. "Not as well as you might think for a woman who was married to my brother for four years." He waggled his hand back and forth at the wrist. "Admittedly, I spent most of those years overseeing my own estates, and once my father died and my brother assumed the mantle of Lord of Rhos—"

"—that was shortly before Tegwen's disappearance, wasn't it?"

"Yes," Ifon said. "At Epiphany. After my father's funeral, I made myself particularly scarce."

"And why was that?"

Ifon eyed Hywel. "You know why." But when Hywel didn't help him with his explanation, Ifon folded his arms across his chest and leaned back in his chair, his chin sticking out. "My brother was a tyrant. I became a man in his shadow, made worse after my eldest brother died and my father turned to Bran as his heir. He could never see Bran's flaws—or at least he couldn't admit to them."

Within Welsh law, lands and wealth were split among all sons upon a man's death, but when lordships were at stake, usually it wasn't quite that simple. Only one man could wear the mantle of Lord of Rhos. "Where are your lands?"

"To the east. I kept them and have defended them with my own men, despite my brother's insistence that all of Rhos should belong to him." Ifon tipped his chin towards Hywel. "Your father came to my assistance before my brother and I came to actual blows."

Hywel was glad to hear it. He was liking this third son of Rhos more and more but told himself to remain wary. Ifon was looking like a better candidate for the hand behind Bran's death with every word he spoke. "When did you last see Tegwen?" Hywel said.

Ifon rubbed at his jaw with thumb and forefinger. "I wasn't here when she disappeared. I'd have to say it was when we marshaled our forces to march on Powys."

Hywel sat up straighter. "You were in Powys with the fighting?"

Ifon snorted in apparent disgust. "I was, though my brother did everything in his power to ensure that I was kept to the rear. Again, it was your father who intervened and gave me command of a small force he used to scout for enemy locations around the River Dee. My brother didn't want me anywhere near him." He shrugged. "Your father trusted me, but I am able to admit that while I have a knack for managing men, my hand with a sword—" Ifon shook his head. "Let's just say that I am not a fearsome sight."

That must have been yet another strike against Ifon in Bran's eyes, but Ifon's ability to admit his flaw elevated him in Hywel's. "Where was Bran?"

"I couldn't tell you," Ifon said. "I didn't see him more than once or twice that entire spring. He was with the main body of your father's army."

"After Tegwen disappeared, did he return to Bryn Euryn?" Hywel said.

"I suppose he did. I couldn't tell you when or how he heard the news, though come to think on it, it must have been fairly immediately afterwards since he was involved in organizing a party of searchers."

"Can you tell me anything about that day? Anything about where Tegwen went and what she did?" Hywel said.

Ifon shook his head regretfully. "I can tell you only what I was told. She was here over breakfast. Nobody saw what she did or where she went afterwards until she sailed off with that Dane. That's all I know."

"Was that unusual?" Hywel said. "Bran wasn't at home. Surely she had the run of the place. Someone must have seen her."

"You can't be unaware of her—" Ifon stopped with a wary look at Hywel.

"Her what?" Although Hywel thought he knew what Ifon was implying, he wasn't going to help him out in this either.

"She was a very unhappy woman and left most of the raising of her children to the maids and nannies. That's not unusual, of course. Many women of her station do, but those mothers have other tasks to see to. Tegwen did not manage Bryn Euryn. She drank wine."

"I had heard that," Hywel said without apologizing for not saying so earlier. "You're telling me that she kept to herself?"

"Most days, from what I understand, she wandered the beaches and the woods around the castle. Frankly, when the maid and guard said she'd run off with a Dane, we thought she'd met him on the beach and went off with him on a whim. If she was drunk enough, she could have."

"There's a piece missing here," Hywel said. "Don't you see it?"

"What do you mean?"

"No Danish longship could close in on Aber's beach without the castle marshaling its forces to meet it. How could one approach Bryn Euryn without raising an alarm?"

"I-I don't know. I guess I never thought about it. And of course, I wasn't here when it happened." Ifon hesitated.

"What?" Hywel said.

"I confess that I wanted the story to be true because I knew Tegwen was unhappy and ... my brother was not good to her," Ifon concluded in a rush.

"I'd heard that too. How was he not good to her? Did he beat her?" Hywel said, looking for confirmation of Gruffydd's version of events.

Ifon pursed his lips. "No. Not that I heard or saw, but then, I didn't spend much time here, as I said. It was more a matter of disregard. Certainly, he wasn't faithful to her."

Hywel nodded. Tegwen's grandfather had said that he beat her, but so far he was the only one to make that accusation. "Do you have any thoughts regarding how her body ended up half a mile from Aber?"

Ifon looked down at the table in front of him. Hywel let the silence draw out, trying to be respectful of Ifon's own emotions but sensing for the first time that what might come next out of Ifon's mouth would be something less than the truth.

"I have no idea," Ifon said.

"Is there anybody I can talk to this evening?" Hywel said. "Why can't I speak to this guard now?"

"He is elderly and has already retired for the night. In addition, he is hard of hearing. He may have trouble understanding what you say to him."

"Then I will take whomever you can find me," Hywel said.

Ifon bit his lip. "There's no one, my lord."

Hywel's brow furrowed. "What do you mean *no one?*"

"No one lives at Bryn Euryn, other than the guard, who lived here when Tegwen was its lady."

A wave of unease rose in Hywel. "How is that possible? Surely not everyone from that time is dead?"

"Some are dead. Many have relocated to other areas of Rhos," Ifon said. "I hadn't ever given it much thought, but my brother made some changes when he returned from the fighting in the east that summer. He said he wanted to distinguish his rule from our father's. In truth, I felt the same after my brother died. I didn't want to be surrounded by his former men."

Hywel bowed to Ifon's greater knowledge of his cantref, but whatever the current strength of Ifon's rule, he couldn't help thinking that all had not been well in Rhos in the year Tegwen disappeared.

16

Gwen

The revelry among the diners was waning, and many of the guests had begun to disperse to their crowded bed chambers. The barracks were full to bursting with men, and twice that number would sleep on the floor of the hall. Tomorrow evening would bring Hallowmas. Tegwen would be put into the ground before then. Gwen wasn't looking forward to the ceremony, not with the grief so fresh and close to the surface. Earlier, when the king had finally stood at the high table and announced Tegwen's death (though not that she was murdered) and then when Gwalchmai sang a lament without accompaniment, the outpouring of emotion had left Gwen stricken along with everyone else.

She had told Mari that she pitied Tegwen and was trying not to judge her. But Gwen wished Tegwen had shown a little more spine. Gwen understood that Tegwen loved Bran—or had at one time—but love should have set her free, rather than cowing her as it seemed to have done.

"Why me?" Gareth said, bringing Gwen's attention back to the table where she was sitting with him and Godfrid.

"You are good at finding things," Godfrid said.

Gareth leaned forward. "You want something found?"

"The Book of Kells."

Gwen's mouth dropped open. "The Book of Kells is missing?" The Book of Kells was a three-hundred-year-old manuscript containing the first four gospels of the New Testament. The monks had so beautifully illuminated it that the book was treasured by all the peoples of Ireland, regardless of what kingdom they lived in.

"It has been stolen," Godfrid said, "by Ottar's son, Thorfin. I believe he brought it to Wales."

"You'd better start at the beginning," Gareth said.

"Like you did with your story?" Godfrid said and then pursed his lips, his eyes raised to the ceiling as he thought. "You are aware of the troubles in my country?"

"I am aware of the conflicts between the kingdom of Dublin and the four kingdoms of Ireland," Gareth said. "It seems to me that with your people holding only Dublin and all the kings of Ireland after it like a prize, you are in a precarious situation."

"They eye us like dogs with only one bone among them," Godfrid said.

"I gather that things have grown more difficult in the year since we were there?" Gwen said.

"My father maintained a tenuous peace, and he was happy to allow the Irish kings to fight among themselves for the high kingship," Godfrid said. "In turn, they did not actively object to his rule of Dublin." He made a motion as if to spit on the ground. "Since last year, however, we have grown weaker under Ottar."

"Ottar?" Gwen said. "I hear you speak of your father as if he is no longer king. I thought Ottar and Torcall shared power."

"Not anymore. My father is unwell, and my brother and I have been unable to win over to our side enough of the men who once supported my father and now support Ottar. They see my father's illness and call him weak."

That was a sin of the greatest magnitude—for any king, though more for the Danes than for some.

"It is Ottar who threatens our very existence," Godfrid said.

"How so?" Gareth said.

"He fails to strategize and use our men and resources wisely. He fights when he should run and retreats when he should stand."

While Godfrid's body remained relaxed in his seat, his words belied his external calmness. This was important to him. In fact, there might not be anything more important to him than this. He'd been born a Prince of Dublin, raised to believe that the throne would one day be his, and now found himself to be a grown man without a kingdom.

Despite his denials, Gwen hoped he hadn't come to Wales expecting King Owain to give him an army to lead against Ottar. The king had his hands full as it was with the wars to the east and south, among the Normans, the lords of the March, and lesser barons in Powys. In addition, King Owain was cousin to the same Irish kings that threatened Dublin. He would have to see a huge advantage in angering them by taking the side of the Dublin Danes.

"How does the Book of Kells come into it?" Gareth said.

"Ottar's son, Thorfin, sacked Kells and burned it as part of a summer campaign to expand our territory and create a buffer around Dublin," Godfrid said. "In the course of the fighting, he stole the Book of Kells."

"He meant to hold it hostage?" Gwen couldn't think of another reason to take it. It wasn't a person, but the Irish of Leinster might be willing to move heaven and earth to get it back.

"As a bribe," Godfrid said.

"I don't understand," Gareth said.

"Thorfin took the book intending to use it as a partial payment to Gilbert de Clare to convince him to help us in our fight against the Irish," Godfrid said.

Gareth kept his eyes fixed on Godfrid's face. "Clare. The Earl of Pembroke."

"Indeed," Godfrid said.

"Clare has been fully embroiled in the fighting in England," Gareth said. "He's switched sides almost as many times as the Earl of Chester."

Given how many times the Earl of Chester had switched sides, that was saying something. Gwen had never given any thought to the Earl of Pembroke's allegiances, but she reminded herself that Gareth had just spent three months in the south, in lands bordering on Clare's. He was Hywel's right hand man and was more aware of political alliances than she was. When they were alone, politics weren't something they often discussed—especially when the hours they'd had together were few enough as it was.

"Exactly," Godfrid said, "which is why Ottar has turned to him. Clare has lands in Wales, but his hold on them is as tenuous as King Stephen's hold on his kingdom. Clare has lost men and resources on a war that at the moment cannot be won, and if he did have lands in Ireland, they would make him that much more powerful and influential. Land equals wealth equals power, as you well know."

"And the Normans can never have enough," Gwen said.

Godfrid snorted. "No man can ever have enough, Gwen."

Godfrid's tale was the last thing Gwen had expected to hear. She could understand how desperate Ottar must feel to have his kingdom slipping away from him, but to bring in the Normans was folly. "Ottar should know better than to invite the Normans in. Once they achieve a foothold on Irish soil, it will be all but impossible to get them to leave."

"That is my fear," Godfrid said.

"What do you believe to be Ottar's plan?" Gareth said.

"Leinster, the kingdom to the south of Dublin, is ruled by the weakest of the Irish kings," Godfrid said. "Ottar would welcome Clare's army into Dublin and use his men to fight outward from there."

"The Book of Kells is a strange sort of pledge," Gwen said. "Is Ottar even a Christian?"

"We are all Christian, of one kind or another," Godfrid said.

Gwen supposed that King Stephen was too, and Empress Maud, and that hadn't stopped them from tearing each other and England apart. Gwen had seen the consequences of their struggle for the English throne firsthand and wanted no part in it.

Godfrid continued, "But from what I understand, it wasn't Ottar's idea to take the book. Clare wanted Ottar to attack Kells, which is northwest of Dublin and outside our current range, and burn it as proof that he has the wherewithal to use Clare's men effectively if he is given them. Clare wants to come into the middle of a war, not arrive in Dublin to discover that Ottar expects him to do all the work."

"It sounds like a foolish idea to me," Gwen said. "The people of Ireland, of whatever kingdom, treasure that book. All Ottar may have done is arouse the anger of the four kingdoms of Ireland. When and if Clare arrives in Dublin, he might find them fully arrayed against him."

"That could be Clare's plan," Gareth said. "He wouldn't be the first lord to incite his opponents to do battle against each other and then swoop in afterwards to find neither has the strength left to fight him."

Godfrid growled low in his chest. "You do not comfort me."

"I apologize, old friend," Gareth said, "but my words weren't meant to."

"Do the Irish kings know of Ottar's plans for Clare?" Gwen said.

Godfrid shook his head and shrugged at the same time. "I do not know. I only know that my father wants me to find the book and return with it to Ireland. He would stop this war before it starts."

"What if Clare could help Dublin regain its former glory?" Gwen said.

"Ottar is headstrong and reckless," Godfrid said. "He might lead us into battle, but I don't believe he can lead us out again. Remember, it was he who allowed himself to be tricked by Prince Cadwaladr into coming to Wales. The man sees only what is in front of him. A king needs to see many steps ahead."

"Getting back to Thorfin," Gareth said, "if he has already given the book to Clare, I don't see how I can be of help."

"That's just it," Godfrid said. "It doesn't appear that Thorfin has succeeded in his quest. We know that he sailed for Wales, but we have heard nothing from him since."

"Would you know?" Gwen said. "Are you in Ottar's confidence?"

"I have shamed myself by standing at his side of late. I would never have done it if my father hadn't ordered me to so that I might spy for him in Ottar's court." Godfrid made a face as if he'd tasted something bitter. "I begged Ottar to allow me to come here to search for the book, though I didn't tell him that I wanted the task because the bile in my stomach threatens to undo me."

"What of your brother?" Gareth said.

"He obeys my father too. Ottar believes him to be outspoken at times against aspects of his plan but loyal to his cause."

"Clare isn't going to be happy to discover that Thorfin sailed for Wales but has not brought him the book. Depending on his own plans, he will have to choose between supporting Ottar anyway or giving up the plan entirely," Gwen said.

"The two men Clare sent as ambassadors to Ottar's court sailed with Thorfin and are also missing," Godfrid said.

"Could they have had a better offer?" Gwen said. "If so, the book could be anywhere by now."

"That's unlikely, surely," Gareth said. "I can see Thorfin changing his mind and using the book for his own ends, whatever they might be, but I can't see him working with Clare's men to betray his father."

"Ottar agrees," Godfrid said, "which is why I'm here."

"I can't believe that Ottar actually sent you," Gwen said. "You are the son of his rival! What's to prevent you from finding the book and presenting it to Clare yourself, to gain his help in overthrowing Ottar?"

Godfrid threw back his head and laughed. "I like how your wife thinks, Sir Gareth!" Then he shook his head. "Ottar sent his own men to Pembroke to confer with Clare. Ottar sent me here, which he hopes will keep me far away from his allies and out of trouble." He took a long drink from the cup in front of him and wiped his mouth on the edge of his cloak. "He doesn't know the extent of my friendship with Gwynedd."

"How you managed to escape suspicion after the events at Abermenai is beyond me," Gareth said, "but I am glad that you did."

"Ottar got rich off Cadwaladr's cattle," Godfrid said. "He even gave me some credit for making it happen."

"You are a crafty devil," Gareth said.

"As are you." Godfrid clapped a hand on Gareth's shoulder and shook him. "I have long thought that you are the man to come to if trouble strikes. I have seen it with my own eyes."

"I would like to help you, Godfrid. I would. But I do have the matter of Tegwen's murder to clear up first," Gareth said, "and I must speak to Prince Hywel before I could even begin such a quest."

"Of course, of course," Godfrid said. "I am also an ambassador from my father to the court of King Owain, come to celebrate Calan Gaeaf with his people."

"And perhaps gain his help in overthrowing Ottar," Gareth said.

Godfrid smirked. "That too."

17

Hywel

Hywel debated whether or not to allow Ifon to offer up his own chamber to him but in the end decided to bed down in the stables with his men. He'd slept in worse places, and the stables had been cleaned in preparation for the festival. A cloak thrown over sweet-smelling fresh straw and Hywel could sleep like a baby. He missed Mari beside him, but there were times when a change of scenery did a man good.

In addition, bedding down with men-at-arms and more common men could offer Hywel a glimpse of what kind of a lord Ifon really made. Even if this trip didn't prove fruitful in terms of his investigation of Tegwen's murder, his father would want to know what passed for stewardship in Rhos.

A whisper of unease curled in Hywel's stomach as he dared to wonder what his father would think of his own stewardship of Ceredigion. The two lords he'd left in charge had been deposed from their lands by Normans and regained them only at Hywel's hand. His departure was a kind of test for them, but Hywel feared that it might prove more of a test for him and of his judgment instead. Ifon had admitted Hywel to Bryn Euryn with more welcome than Hywel would have given his father had he come to inspect Aberystwyth.

Still, Hywel couldn't help but think Ifon was hiding something, and he wished he'd been able to speak to the guard. But Hywel could hardly have forced Ifon to wake him when the morning should do well enough. What disturbed Hywel most was the lack of others to ask about Tegwen. Even if the residents of the castle were all new to Bryn Euryn, half the people of the cantref had come to celebrate the harvest festival with their lord. One of them had to have lived here five years ago. Surely.

But Ifon hadn't given Hywel a single name, and Evan hadn't found anyone to speak to either. Ruminating on the problem kept Hywel awake until most of the men in the stables were sound asleep. Somehow, he must not be asking the right questions yet.

The next morning, after a simple breakfast of mutton and bread at the high table, Ifon at last sent his steward to find the guard, a man named Madog. Hywel was using his crust to soak up the last of his gravy when the steward came rushing back, his agitation evident. He threw himself to his knees in front of Ifon and Hywel. "My lords! I have just come from the barracks. Old Madog is dead!"

Ifon had risen to his feet at the steward's approach and now stared blankly at the steward's downturned head.

Hywel leaned across the table to look down at the steward. "Tell us what you know." This was Ifon's castle, but Hywel was a prince of Gwynedd, and he was tired of being stymied at every turn.

The steward lifted his head, though he remained kneeling before them. "I don't know anything more than I've said, my lords. Madog didn't appear at breakfast, but with this crowd I didn't notice. When Lord Ifon sent me to fetch him, I found him lying in his bunk. I went to roust him, but—he's dead." The steward said the last two words in a small voice.

"He must have died sometime in the night." Ifon's face was completely expressionless.

Hywel was having trouble deciding what exactly he should do or say. His inclination was to think that Ifon had something to do with the guard's death, but he could hardly accuse the man of murder in his own hall. It would be dramatic certainly but not worth risking if the death truly was natural, as unlikely as that seemed at this moment.

Ifon bent toward Hywel. "My lord, I am terribly afraid that Tegwen's killer is belatedly tying up loose ends."

"It was my first thought," Hywel admitted.

"This is my fault." Ifon straightened to his full height, his jaw rigid. "He was your one witness, and now he's dead."

"We should not assume anything until we see him." Hywel found it odd that he was comforting Ifon instead of accusing him of murder.

"Of course, my lord. I will come with you. Perhaps I will learn something." Ifon turned back to the steward. "Did you leave Madog where you found him?"

"Yes, my lord," the steward said, wide-eyed. At Ifon's gesture, he clambered to his feet on creaking knees and led the way from the hall.

Before leaving with Hywel, Ifon lifted a hand to gain the attention of his people. Many had risen to their feet to watch the exchange on the dais. Even if those in the rear hadn't been able to hear Ifon's conversation with the steward, the news of Madog's death had flown around the hall with the speed of a trapped sparrow.

"Please continue with the meal," Ifon said. "Our old companion, Madog, has died; we will bury him before the sun sets."

As with Tegwen, the need for Madog's burial was pressing. Hywel had never known anyone to actually die on the day of Hallowmas, and to have matching funerals for Tegwen at Aber and Madog at Bryn Euryn was disconcerting. "The more superstitious among our people will be fearful tonight," Hywel said to Ifon as they crossed the courtyard to the barracks.

"Will you be here or at Aber for the feast?" Ifon said.

"I must leave for Aber by noon," Hywel said.

"You would be welcome to stay," Ifon said.

Hywel tried to discern a sense of relief in Ifon's voice, but all he heard was the straightforward questions of a lord who had people to see to.

"We bury our dead near the chapel at the base of the mountain," Ifon added. "If you would consent to stay until we see

Madog in the ground, I would be grateful. The grave diggers will begin work immediately."

"Of course," Hywel said, not sure what he was agreeing to— if anything beyond respect for an old man who had the misfortune to die at Hallowmas.

Madog had been sleeping in the barracks with dozens of other men, but while twenty had lain on the floor last night, Madog had been given a bottom bunk. He lay on his side, facing the wall. Ifon approached the body first and put a hand on his shoulder. The old guard didn't move, not that Hywel expected him to, and after a respectful pause, Hywel moved closer and helped Ifon roll Madog onto his back.

Madog's eyes were closed as if he were still sleeping. Hywel lifted one eyelid. The man's eyes were rheumy, but neither bloodshot nor bulging. Nor did his face show signs that he'd been smothered in the night, which had been Hywel's first thought. An overdose of poppy juice was his second, and Hywel leaned forward, sniffing for the sweet aroma that often lingered around the face after death. He straightened, not finding it, his eyes narrowing as he scrutinized the body.

"He liked his mead," Ifon said, indicating a splotch staining Madog's shirt.

"Who doesn't?" Hywel sucked on his teeth. "He seems to have died in his sleep."

"Soldiers claim to want to die in battle with their boots on, but I would choose this if I could," Ifon said.

"Was he ill?" Hywel said.

Ifon lifted one shoulder. "He had an old man's ailments, but none that I thought were pressing, though over the last few days, he had developed a nasty cough."

"Would your healer have given him something to help him sleep?" Hywel said.

Ifon looked Hywel speculatively. "Are you thinking that he took—or was given—too much poppy juice?"

Hywel kept his gaze steady on Ifon's face.

Ifon expelled a sudden snort of laughter. "You think *I* ordered his death? For what purpose could I possibly have done so?"

"To prevent me from questioning Madog about what he saw five years ago," Hywel said.

"Do you think me that foolish—or desperate?"

"The thought had crossed my mind." Though when Ifon put it that way, it made less sense than it had in Hywel's head.

"I suppose you wouldn't be the man I know you to be if you didn't think I could have had a hand in Madog's sudden death," Ifon said, his surprise and amusement subsiding. "But surely you don't think I killed Tegwen?"

"Did you?"

"No." Ifon's answer was immediate and without equivocation. He gestured towards the door of the barracks. "Please come with me. I have something to show you."

Hywel nodded, as curious about Ifon now as he'd ever been about another man's thoughts. All these years, Ifon had been hiding here at Bryn Euryn in obscurity, guiding his people and managing his estates with little oversight and no expectation of raising his standing. Provided Ifon had nothing to do with Tegwen's death, after today that should change. Hywel was going to have a talk with his father. Men with Ifon's intellect were few and far enough between; it would be a waste to allow Ifon to languish another day in obscurity in his backwater cantref. Gwynedd could *use* him.

Ifon and Hywel climbed the ladder to the wall-walk above the gatehouse. The sun put in a brief appearance, playing hide and seek with the clouds that mostly covered the sky. It had rained in the night, so the ground was wet and soft, which the gravediggers would appreciate, though Hywel hoped for a dry ride home to Aber.

The tips of the wooden palisade were at chin height for both of them. Ifon pointed east over the top of them. "What do you see?"

"The sea," Hywel said.

"Yes, my lord, the sea. But can you see the beach?"

Hywel squinted into the morning sun, holding up one hand to block the light from shining directly into his eyes. "No." He turned to look up at the mountain behind him. "What about from the summit?"

"In good weather, you can see the beach from up there, but you can't see individual people. Madog's story was that he was on duty and saw the Danish boat come in to take Tegwen on board." Ifon nodded his head at Hywel's unasked question. "Yes, obviously someone should have wondered why he didn't raise the alarm from the first."

Hywel gazed over the rampart. His eyesight was excellent, but five years ago, Madog had already been an old man. Hywel would have been surprised if Madog could have distinguished individual trees two hundred yards away, much less spied a longboat out on the water.

"What about the maid who said she witnessed Tegwen's departure?" Hywel said.

"She claimed to have seen what Madog saw, but from the village," Ifon said.

"Would that have been possible?" Hywel said.

"Possibly." Ifon scanned the land around Bryn Euryn, not looking at Hywel. "But I think now that my sister-in-law no more ran off with a Dane than she joined that convent." Ifon waved a hand towards a cluster of buildings tucked together along a river winding to the northwest of Bryn Euryn. Hywel could just make out a bell tower poking above the trees.

"Then what do you think happened?" Hywel said. "If Madog's story wasn't true, why did he tell it?"

"It could only be because someone made him or even that he had a hand in her disappearance," Ifon said. "Until today, I told myself that Tegwen ran off with another man because my brother was a fool not to see what he had. Madog's story was full of holes, but I wanted to believe it."

"And now?"

Ifon let out a long breath through his nose. "Now I question if Madog died by chance or was murdered, and I wonder where my brother was when Tegwen died."

Ifon gave Hywel a deep bow and turned away, stepping down the ladder first. Once at the bottom Hywel turned to face Ifon, who'd waited for him. "You didn't have to tell me the truth. You could have sent me on my way with all my questions unanswered."

"But you would have come back with even more, my lord," Ifon said. "Your reputation precedes you."

"How do you mean?"

"All of Gwynedd knows that you always catch your man," Ifon said.

Hywel just managed to hide his smirk. That was a reputation he would gladly embrace.

"My lord! My lord!" A squat man with a full beard came around the corner of the keep. He puffed up to Ifon and bowed deeply. "I am so sorry, my lord. I just heard the news."

Ifon raised the man up. "Of Madog's death, you mean?"

"Yes, my lord," he said. "It's all my fault."

"I'm listening." Ifon's voice had turned cold.

Nobody could miss Ifon's tone, and the healer put out a trembling hand towards his lord before bringing it back to his side an instant later. "Madog had been coughing, with great pains in his chest. I had given him poppy juice three nights running to quiet it."

"You're the castle's healer," Hywel said.

"Yes, my lord." The man ducked his head, not looking into either lord's eyes.

"You gave him some last night?" Ifon said. "At what hour?"

"It must have been close to midnight," the healer said.

Ifon sent a sharp glance at Hywel. That was hours after Ifon had told Hywel that Madog was already asleep. And well after Ifon had informed the hall of Tegwen's death.

"That's not all." The healer hurried on as if anxious to get the full story into the open as quickly as possible, which he probably was. "I checked my stores just now and the larger vial from which I'd poured his smaller dose is missing." He wrung his hands in front of him. "I slept in the herb hut all night. I don't see how anyone could have come in and taken it."

"Then what's your explanation for its absence?" Hywel said.

"I think—I think Madog took the vial himself before he left, in a moment when I'd turned away and wouldn't see him."

Comprehension was dawning on Hywel. He glanced at Ifon, who pointed at one of his men. "Check around Madog's bed— I'm guessing under it—for a vial. It would have held poppy juice."

The man ran off.

Ifon turned to Hywel. "If he took it—"

"If he took his own life rather than submit to my questions—"

Ifon put a hand on Hywel's arm. "Please, don't say any more, my lord."

Then the soldier Ifon had sent into the barracks returned, bringing with him the vial in question. Ifon sniffed it and gave it to the healer, who took it, nodding. "This is it." He peered inside. "It's empty. No man could survive such a dose."

Ifon caught the healer's upper arm in a strong grip. "Not a word of this to anyone."

They stared at each other through several heartbeats, and then the healer nodded. "Of course, my lord. The original dose I gave him must have confused him. He was an old man and must have taken the rest by mistake."

Hywel clasped his hands behind his back. His throat was thick around all the words he wasn't going to say.

"Exactly." Ifon dismissed the healer, gave Hywel a long look, and then took a step towards the great hall. "Come, my lord."

But Hywel put out a hand to stop him. "I'm sorry, Ifon, but I have yet another question I must ask you."

Ifon stiffened, but he turned back. "There's more?"

"Regarding your brother's death," Hywel said. "Please tell me what you know of it."

Ifon opened his mouth, closed it, and then said, "Do you think Tegwen's death and Bran's could be related?" Relief crossed his face. "If that were true, then Bran could be absolved of Tegwen's death."

"I can't know until I start asking questions," Hywel said. "As far as I am aware, nobody investigated the ambush that killed your brother."

"He died two years after Tegwen ran off—" Ifon stopped and then gave Hywel a rueful smile. "I'm used to saying that." He gazed over Hywel's shoulder towards the gatehouse, but Hywel didn't think he was seeing it. "For what reason might someone have killed both of them?"

"I can't answer that yet, but I have to consider it," Hywel said. "At the very least, knowing who killed Bran could lead me to who killed Tegwen and vice versa. Obviously, Bran didn't shoot himself. What of his enemies?"

Ifon gave a tsk of disgust. "My brother was a hard man, as you know. He angered many a man from here to Powys. It could have been anyone who held a grudge. We are all archers here."

"Even you?" Hywel held his breath. There couldn't be a greater violation of the law of hospitality than to accuse a man of murder in his own castle—for the second time within the hour.

Ifon regarded Hywel for a moment. "I didn't kill my brother." He made a broad gesture to include all of Bryn Euryn. "I wouldn't be the first man to envy his brother's holdings, but I have my own lands and my own people in eastern Rhos. As the third son, I would have had to kill three people—my father and my two elder brothers—to inherit. I never dreamed of it; I never wanted it."

Cadwaladr could lie with a sincerity to which Hywel had grown accustomed over the years, but Ifon's frankness and steady gaze had Hywel believing him despite his misgivings. "Then who did?"

Ifon shook his head. "I just don't know."

Both silent, they walked side by side across the courtyard until, out of the corner of his eye, Hywel saw Evan appear in the doorway to the stables and lift one finger.

"Excuse me," Hywel said.

Ifon nodded and continued towards the hall door, which a guard opened for him.

"I apologize, my lord, but I didn't want to shout to gain your attention." Evan's face colored as Hywel approached him. Hywel knew he was referring to the lifted finger, though he should have known better by now than to think that Hywel would be bothered by the gesture. Hywel demanded that his men treat him with respect, but he didn't have patience for obeisance for its own sake.

"Never mind that. What is it?" Hywel said.

"I have been inquiring of Ifon's men—gently, I assure you— as to their knowledge and feelings about their former lord, Bran," Evan said.

"I'm glad to know you're working on our second murder," Hywel said. "I just accused Ifon of murdering not only the guard but his brother too—and he still treated me with courtesy. I don't know if I can ask him for more. Not today."

"What of the guard?" Evan said.

"He is dead, possibly by his own hand. Whether it was by accident or to avoid my questions, I can't tell you," Hywel said.

"The former would be a strange coincidence," Evan said.

Hywel jaw tightened. "I have no further avenue to pursue in this regard, and I have no interest in preventing a long-suffering servant to be refused burial in consecrated ground."

Evan took in a breath. "The men here tell me that Bran was not a pleasant man to work for. But that word is still mostly hearsay."

"Like every other piece of evidence," Hywel said. "How so in this instance?"

"Of the twenty men in Bran's *teulu*, only three remain at Bryn Euryn."

Hywel rubbed his chin. "Ifon said something about that to me last night. Discomfort in being guarded by another man's former men, I think."

"The transition from Lord Cynan to Bran was troubled, or so two of the fellows tell it," Evan said. "Bran found places for most of his father's men elsewhere, as did Ifon when he assumed the lordship. From what those here tell me, the men who served Bran are scattered about Wales, some as far south as Gwent."

"What of the remaining three?" Hywel said.

"Two were no more than boys at the time, sons of lesser lords who joined Bran's ranks a few weeks before he died. The third is an older fellow who begged to remain at Bryn Euryn," Hywel said.

"You spoke with all three of them?" Hywel said.

Evan nodded. "Do you want me to find them for you?"

"Not right now," Hywel said. "I trust that you learned what you could from them."

"Thank you, my lord." Evan stood a little straighter.

Hywel was itching to talk to Bran's men, but Evan was coming along as a lieutenant, and Hywel didn't want to dampen his enthusiasm or make him think he didn't trust him. "I want to know about Bran's visits home to Bryn Euryn and Aber that spring and about the ambush two years later. Did you ask them about those times?"

"I did, my lord," Evan said. "The two boys were present only for the ambush, and all they could do was describe to me the flurry of rearing horses and frightened men. Half of Bran's men charged into the forest after the archer while the two boys were among those who stayed in the road, huddled over Bran's body."

"Was that the first time either of them had been under any kind of assault?" Hywel said.

"So I understand, my lord." Evan's lips twitched. "From the shame in their eyes, I imagine they lost their breakfast in the process."

Hywel heaved a sigh. "And the old man?"

"He was reluctant to speak ill of the dead, as he put it, but Bran was not faithful to his wife, nor a dedicated captain to King Owain in Powys."

"That is what we expected to hear, isn't it?" Hywel said.

"Yes, my lord."

Hywel hadn't told Evan about Bran's liaison with Gwladys, but his information upheld Lady Alice's story.

"We still must wonder: how did Tegwen get to Aber with nobody noticing?"

Evan shook his head.

"What's more, although the head wound makes me think her murderer killed her in anger, the burial and the subsequent cover-up seem more calculated. *Why* did she die when she did?"

"Could the murderer have been afraid of something Tegwen knew—or something she'd seen?" Evan said.

"I don't know." Hywel shook his head. "Why do I get the feeling that with every hour that passes we are getting further from Tegwen's killer?"

"Further sounds better to me." Evan gave an involuntary shiver. "The murderer has remained hidden for five years. But with Tegwen's body coming to light, and Madog's death besides, what is to prevent him from killing again in order to keep his secrets?"

18

Gareth

Gareth lay on the pallet he shared with Gwen, listening to her easy breathing. His mind churned with all the pieces of the puzzle they were trying to put together. It was only now that he remembered that he had neither returned to Wena's hut to look for more clues nor had made a concerted effort to find Brychan among the crowd at Aber. Godfrid's arrival and his story of the Book of Kells had put both concerns completely from his mind.

Dawn was still some time off, but Gareth rose from the pallet, unable to lie still any longer. He glanced up at the big bed to make sure Mari remained asleep and tiptoed to the door. Gwen rolled onto her side, murmuring in her sleep. He thought he saw a gleam which could have been her eyes opening, but then she closed them again, and he went out the door.

The manor house in which they were staying consisted of four rooms on two floors, each built around a central stair that was more of a ladder. The sole purpose of the manor was to accommodate the overflow of visitors from the castle. Since the manor was built outside the castle walls, it was vulnerable if an opposing army was ever to attack Aber, so it was unadorned, consisting of nothing more than the eight rooms. Gareth didn't think he had a war to worry about today. The border with Powys was quiet, and the Earl of Chester had his hands full maintaining his own lands without trying to push into Gwynedd.

Coming down stairs from the front door, Gareth almost stumbled over the turnips piled on the steps. With Hallowmas that night, the people had been getting ready for days. Before sunset, the turnips would be hollowed out and candles lit within them to guide the souls of the dead who had trouble finding their way to the next world. From the furor in the hall yesterday, it seemed many feared that Tegwen would be among them.

She would be buried in a few hours, which King Owain hoped would ease the people's anxiety. Gareth wasn't sure King Owain would even wait for Hywel to return. The needs of the dead today superseded those of the living. Hywel hated funerals anyway, and even if the investigation hadn't been urgent, Gareth wouldn't have put it past Hywel to visit Bryn Euryn simply to avoid Tegwen's interment.

Gareth hated funerals too, though what was there to enjoy about them, really? This was one he couldn't avoid attending, but he could occupy himself in the meantime. The sooner he figured out who had murdered Tegwen and Bran, the sooner he could begin the search for the Book of Kells. While far too many of the people who had known Tegwen were already dead, he had a castle full of people to talk to today. He needed to find the one man who might know more than he was currently saying: maybe not because he was deliberately hiding something, but because he might not realize that bits of what he did know could be important.

King Owain's longtime friend and steward, Taran, bobbed to the top of Gareth's list.

The king himself would still be asleep, presumably with Cristina, though one never knew, but Taran was an early riser. He was often up with the dawn even in the summer. He'd been awake when Gwen had come to him the previous morning; he would be awake now. Gareth found him, as he thought he might, hard at work in King Owain's office off the great hall, going over the castle accounts.

Gareth knocked on the doorframe, since the door itself was halfway ajar, and Taran looked up. The smile that flashed across his face at the sight of Gareth turned wary within a single heartbeat. "Hello, Gareth. Please tell me you aren't here to inform me of another death."

"No, sir," Gareth said.

"I'm delighted to see you then." Taran pointed to the chair opposite his own on the other side of his table. "How may I help you?"

"I want to tell you everything that I know so far about Tegwen's disappearance and death—and Bran's for that matter, which is very little—and ask that you speak to me of what you remember of that time."

"We do have ourselves a puzzle, don't we?" Taran rested his elbows on the arms of his chair and clasped his hands in front of his lips. "King Owain is greatly troubled by his niece's death. I will help you in any way I can."

Gareth took a moment to collect his thoughts and then said, "It is my understanding that you were here and not in Powys at the time of Tegwen's disappearance."

A distant look came into Taran's eyes. "That is correct. The King had gathered his nobles to him, and though I rode with him in the first forays, I returned to Aber after only a few weeks."

"Why was that?"

Taran coughed, his expression reluctant. "He was having ... domestic troubles and needed someone he trusted here at Aber."

"He wanted you to keep an eye on Gwladys," Gareth said.

Taran's expression cleared. "How did you know?"

"I would prefer not to reveal that," Gareth said, "not unless I must."

"Of course, of course." Taran rubbed at his forehead with the heel of his hand. "Well, if it helps, I was here when Tegwen ran away—died, I suppose—but I don't know how that helps you."

Gareth looked curiously at the old steward. "You loved Tegwen." Gwen had told him of Taran's emotional reaction to her death. "I can hear it in your voice when you say her name."

"She was a sweet little thing, growing up," Taran said.

"Were you in support of her marriage to Bran?" Gareth said, not that it mattered now, but he was curious, given what they'd learned of Tegwen's husband.

"He was a second son but a lord of Rhos nonetheless. He wasn't my first choice, but I didn't know what I know now—or what I learned of him after her marriage." Taran's jaw firmed at the memory.

"He didn't love her," Gareth said. "Did he hurt her?"

Taran pointed a finger at Gareth. "I never saw bruises, which is why I didn't intervene in their relationship. He ignored her, certainly, and as a result, she retreated to her own world. She wouldn't leave him; she denied any wrongdoing on his part. She was a simple girl at heart. I know that she married him under duress, having fallen in love with that man-at-arms, Brychan, but it was my impression that she grew to love her husband and turned to drink because he didn't share her love." Taran's shoulders lifted and then fell in resignation. "It's not an uncommon story."

"When was the last time you saw Bran?" Gareth said.

Taran raised his brows. "Why do you ask?"

Now it was Gareth's turn to shrug. "It may be that he had something to do with her death."

"Really?" Taran said. "I'm disappointed, then, that I can't tell you when I saw him. Not before Tegwen disappeared, certainly."

"My informant believes that Bran and Gwladys met each other in Wena's hut during their affair, which ended before Tegwen's disappearance. Bran knew this area well enough to know about the hut, and given that Tegwen's body was found at the hut ..." Gareth's voice trailed off at the look of astonishment on Taran's face. "What?"

"*Bran* was Gwladys's lover?"

"You didn't know?" Gareth said, suddenly confused himself. He'd thought he and Taran had been in accord.

"No, I didn't know it was he!" Taran said. "I thought it was Gruffydd, Tegwen's grandfather."

Gareth almost choked on his own saliva. "That's not what I was told."

Taran sat back. "It would make more sense if it was Bran. Gruffydd has always been a friend, and that spring he'd broken his leg, which was why I felt I was wasting my time at Aber when I could have been serving Owain in the field."

"So you never saw Bran at Aber?" Gareth said.

"All these years and I never harbored a suspicion against him." Taran shook his head. "I would apologize to Gruffydd for misreading him, but Gwladys's affair was not common knowledge. Or so I believed until now." He glared at Gareth.

Gareth put up both hands, palms out. "I will tell no one. I only brought it up because it seemed you already knew."

Taran subsided, still looking disgruntled. "I will have to speak to the king."

Gareth was glad that task would not be his. "So, if I may ask again, when did you last see Bran?"

"I was about to repeat that I didn't, but—" Taran put up his finger again. "Give me a moment." He pushed to his feet, went to a shelf on the wall, lifted out a heavy book, and began flipping through the ancient pages. Gareth had seen the book before, though he'd never been given the opportunity to read it: it was an account of important events in Aber since its founding, all the way back to Rhodri Mawr. "Here it is. It was the twenty-second of April. *Bran ap Cynan, Lord of Rhos, rode to Aber to tell of the disappearance of his wife, Tegwen ferch Cadwallon.*"

"May I see that?" Gareth rounded the table and read where Taran pointed. "I don't understand."

Taran spread his hand wide. "What's there to understand?"

"Tegwen's grandfather, Gruffydd, told us that Tegwen disappeared on the Feast of St. Bueno, which I believe is only two days earlier."

Taran closed the book and looked at Gareth. "Bryn Euryn is only ten miles from Aber. He could have easily ridden this far in a day."

"Except that he was supposed to be fighting in the east; I wouldn't have thought that he could have known of her disappearance yet, much less reach Aber so quickly."

"Perhaps when Prince Hywel returns, he can shed light on these events." Taran put the book back on the shelf.

"Why didn't you send word to Gruffydd that his granddaughter was missing?" Gareth said.

Taran shook his head. "Now that I've seen the writing and the date, I remember Bran's visit but little about it other than the fact of Tegwen's disappearance." His brow furrowed. "I do believe he told me that he had already informed Gruffydd that she was gone."

"Gruffydd claims otherwise," Gareth said.

"I can't tell you any more than I've said." Taran pinned Gareth with a sharp look. "Where is this going in your head?"

"Gruffydd and Brychan both accused Bran of killing Tegwen," Gareth said. "I have no other suspects at the moment."

"Given that he's dead, he is certainly a convenient one," Taran said.

"You don't believe he could have done it?" Gareth said.

"Wouldn't it have been smarter to murder her near Rhos?" Taran said. "And if he wanted to hide the body, there are smarter things he could have done with it. Why bring her all the way here?"

"Perhaps because he was already here," Gareth said. "Are you sure that he couldn't have met Gwladys during that same time period?"

Taran lowered himself back into his chair. "I do sleep, you know."

"Maybe he was smart enough to kill her far away from Bryn Euryn where nobody would suspect him if the body was eventually found," Gareth said. "Did Bran get along with Cadwaladr?"

Taran snorted laughter. "No. They hated each other."

"Do you know why?" Gareth said.

Taran's eyes narrowed as he thought. "In truth, I couldn't say. Bran was a good ten years younger than Cadwaladr, so it must have been something that happened once they reached manhood."

"Maybe they were too much alike," Gareth said.

Taran eyed Gareth, his lips twisting in a wry smile. "Thinking always of themselves and nobody else? You may be right."

Gareth left Taran to his work. Walking away from Taran's office, he reflected on how much he was growing to despise this investigation. He had never been one to gossip, and he didn't enjoy accumulating other people's secrets the way Hywel did. Had he wanted to know that Gwladys was unfaithful to King Owain? No, he had not. And at this point, he didn't know if her activities had any bearing on Tegwen's disappearance and death beyond informing him that something wasn't right in Bran's relationship with Tegwen. It occurred to him that nobody had yet told him if Bran himself had wanted something different in a wife and had married Tegwen only because his father made him.

At times like this, Gareth was glad he wasn't born a nobleman.

The great hall was filled with sleeping guests, and Gareth paused to listen to the chapel bell toll for prime. Many would be rising now that the sun was up, and Gareth might not have a single quiet moment for the rest of the day. He turned on his heel and left the hall.

Standing on the top step, Gareth beheld the courtyard, which was already filling with villagers coming into Aber to spend the day, anticipating rich meals, gossip, and entertainment. Meilyr and Gwalchmai had sung for everyone last evening and had even coaxed Gwen up on the dais for one song at the end. They would play on and off for much of the day. King Owain had also arranged for jugglers and storytellers, some who would sing and some who would not. The most important event of the day, however, would be Tegwen's funeral.

Gareth had some time before then, so he pointed himself towards the stables, thinking that he would saddle his horse and roust one of the castle's men-at-arms to ride with him to Wena's hut. When he arrived at the entrance, however, Godfrid and his Danes blocked the way inside, in the midst of a heated discussion.

Gareth stopped a few feet away. He'd picked up some Danish over the years but not enough to make out more than one word in three when they were speaking so quickly. After a moment, Godfrid spotted him and sliced his hand through the air, cutting off all discussion. Gareth took that to mean that he should approach. "What's wrong?"

"One of my men is missing," Godfrid said.

Gareth raised his hands and dropped them in a gesture of disbelief. "I don't know what to say."

Then Godfrid's eyes focused on something behind Gareth; he turned to see four gravediggers with heavy shovels on their shoulders depart through the main gate.

"When is it to be?" Godfrid said.

"Before the evening meal." Gareth turned back to Godfrid. "There's plenty of time for a thorough search. What is your man's name, where have you looked, and why would he have gone?"

19

Hywel

Gwen had once told Hywel that he should have the words *never assume* inscribed above his door, and right now, as he waited for Madog's funeral train to pass him, he reminded himself of the reason why. He had thought that his main purpose in coming to Rhos was to pin Ifon down about Tegwen's last days. And he'd done it, but he felt now as if he'd learned too much information about the wrong things. If Bran had done something so terrible that both he and his wife had died over it, Hywel almost didn't want to know what it was.

Almost.

As Ifon had promised, it wasn't quite noon and Madog would be in the ground within the hour. The preparations for Hallowmas could then go forward as planned. Tegwen might have been dead for five years and Madog for only few hours, but from the buzz of conversation around Hywel, most everyone was focused on Tegwen. Her death had been violent, and everyone knew that it was those spirits who were the most restless.

Hywel and Evan stood to one side of the path leading out of Bryn Euryn as four mourners carried Madog's body towards them in its temporary coffin, inside which the body lay, washed and shrouded. As was the custom in Gwynedd for all burials other than noble ones, Madog would be laid in the grave in just his shroud, and the coffin would be reused. The priest led the procession, followed by Ifon, his family, and Madog's family.

Hywel hated funerals. He understood the need for them and the importance of easing the soul into the next life. It was supposed to cleanse the grief of those left behind. But Hywel had attended too many funerals of loved ones to have any interest in witnessing the last journey of someone who may have feared death less than speaking to Hywel about Tegwen's disappearance.

Evan shifted beside Hywel, restless too, and Hywel canted his head to indicate that he should move through the crowd. Hywel's other men-at-arms had spread themselves out among the mourners, acting as Hywel's eyes and ears the best they knew how.

Hywel brought his attention back to the procession, and as the body passed his position, he felt the pressure of a hand in his, followed by a low hiss and the words, "Tegwen met with a man the morning she disappeared."

Hywel licked his lips, his eyes flicking among the crowd to make sure nobody was looking at him, and took a step back. His fellow mourners shifted to fill in where he'd been standing. An ancient yew tree arched over the pathway a few feet away, and he and the woman who had come to find him stepped behind it, allowing Hywel to get a good look at his informant for the first time. She was perhaps ten years older than he was, blonde and blue-eyed, and if he hadn't been a happily married man he would have regretted not meeting her the previous evening.

"What can you tell me?" Hywel said.

"You have to understand that when the story of how Tegwen ran off with a Dane came out, I assumed I'd been mistaken in what I'd seen. Madog was so sure that he saw her getting into that boat. But now that Tegwen died instead, I knew I needed to come forward."

With *never assume* echoing in Hywel's head, he pressed the woman's hand. "With whom did Tegwen meet?"

"His name was Erik, a half-Dane in Bran's company," the woman said. "Tegwen met him over in the trees not far from here. She wandered, you know."

Hywel tried to keep his impatience in check. "So I've heard."

"I know she came back to the castle after she met him, but my duties as wet nurse for her younger girl prevented me from asking her what Erik had wanted. I never saw her again."

"You never told anyone about this?" Hywel said.

The woman shook her head uncertainly.

"Not Lord Bran?" Hywel said, trying to keep his voice gentle. What he wanted to do was shake the answers out of her.

"No." The woman's eyes went wide. "When Lord Bran was told that Tegwen had gone, his anger was terrifying! I stayed out of his way, and since Erik was his man, I didn't think it was my place to say anything."

"What about this Erik?" Hywel said. "Did you ever talk to him about it?"

The woman sniffed and wiped at her nose. Hywel was reconsidering his initial attraction. "No. He left Bran's service that summer, and by then I'd decided I was mistaken. He was half-Dane, and since Tegwen had run off with a Dane, perhaps I'd confused one man for the other and it hadn't been Erik I saw."

"Thank you for telling me."

The woman gave him a coy smile. *Had he actually fallen for this sort of thing in the past?* Hywel decided he must be growing more discerning with age. He patted her hand and dismissed her. By now, the funeral procession had reached the bottom of the hill, and Hywel walked along the edge of the road, passing some stragglers, until he could see the chapel and the circular graveyard with its freshly dug grave. The pallbearers had removed Madog from his coffin and were lowering him into the ground.

Evan stood at the back of the mourners, and Hywel moved to his side. They were standing to the left of the priest who raised his hands and began a prayer. "Is everything all right, my lord?"

Hywel settled back on his heels. He'd walked up to Evan with a spring in his step, but to be so bright-eyed at a funeral was unseemly, and he should have known better. "I was just given helpful information and a real lead. I'll tell you when this is over."

Hywel waited impatiently for the funeral rites to end and for Ifon to greet each person who'd attended. Ifon had made himself into a fine lord, even if he hadn't been born to it. If things had fallen out differently, Ifon might have been pledged to the church, though it was rare enough in Hywel's experience for a lord with only three sons to think that he had any to spare. Hywel's father, King Owain, had fathered ten sons already: Rhun and Hywel as the eldest, both in their twenties, sons of an Irishwoman their father had loved but never married; and Iorwerth and Maelgwn, born to his first wife Gwladys.

Of the six remaining sons, Hywel had met only three: Cynan, who was three years younger than Hywel himself; Cadell; and Madoc, all of whom lived in Powys, serving lords who would train them as warriors the way Hywel himself had been trained. The Norman church would have had Iorwerth as his father's heir, but fortunately for Hywel, in Wales, all acknowledged sons could inherit. In another world, Iorwerth might have made a fine King of Gwynedd, but Hywel knew that Rhun would make a better one than all of them.

"Lord Ifon, if I may have one more word before I go." Hywel touched Ifon's elbow as the last of his people bowed before him and departed.

Ifon's eyes flicked to Hywel and then back to the crowd of mourners heading up the hill to the castle.

"I know you have people to see to," Hywel said. "This won't take but a moment, and my men and I will be on our way."

Ifon let out a breath and turned to face Hywel directly. "Of course. How may I serve you?"

"It is my understanding that after Bran's death you found places for his men all over Wales," Hywel said. "I would like to know why."

Ifon gave a snort. "Isn't it obvious? It's as I told you last night. They were loyal to my brother."

"In many households, that loyalty transfers to the man next in line," Hywel said, "which would be you."

"I did not trust them," Ifon said. "I had my own men, and Bran's men deserved the opportunity to serve a lord who would use them well. That lord was not I."

Hywel bent his head once in acknowledgement of Ifon's reasoning. "I'd like to inquire in particular about one man, Erik. He would have been half-Welsh, half-Danish."

Ifon was nodding before Hywel finished his sentence. "Bran got rid of him before my time. He sent him home, I believe."

"Home, as in ... Dublin?"

"Yes," Ifon said.

"You say *got rid of him*. Do you know why?" Hywel said.

"It was during the transition from my father's rule to Bran's," Ifon said. "Bran arranged for most of our father's men to find posts with other lords."

"Thank you." Hywel stepped back. "And thank you for your hospitality. I won't keep you from your people any longer."

Ifon bowed, his hands clasped before him, and then strode past Hywel and up the road to Bryn Euryn, the aforementioned people crowding around him as he went.

Evan and the other men from Aber, meanwhile, converged on Hywel. "Do we have a lead?" Evan said.

Hywel's eyes brightened. "Any of you fancy a journey to Dublin?"

20

Gwen

Too many mornings since she'd become pregnant, Gwen would wake so tired she could barely lift her head from her pillow, and after last night's late conversation with Godfrid, this morning was no exception. She lay with her arm across her eyes, listening to Mari throwing up into the basin and knowing she should stop pretending to sleep and help her friend. Gareth, lucky for him, had woken hours before while it was still dark and gone off. He hadn't returned. There was a time when Gwen would have been irritated with him for continuing the investigation without her, but this morning she was too tired to care.

Growing a baby was far more work than she had anticipated. And she thought she'd been paying attention.

She knew about the dangers of childbirth itself. Her own mother had died birthing Gwalchmai, and Gwen had been a witness until the very end when the midwife and pushed her out the door before a last effort to save her mother. Gwen had been left to sob alone in the corridor. She'd realized much later that her father had known hours earlier that her mother was going to die, which was why he was well into his cups by then and no use at all to Gwen. The midwife had opened the door to hand Gwalchmai to Gwen instead of Meilyr. She'd stood there, bereft, tears on her cheeks and unable to wipe at them because of the squirming bundle in her arms.

And here she was, pregnant herself and joyful about it, despite the terrors ahead. She supposed she was naïvely hopeful, but she couldn't be anything else.

Gathering her strength as if she were about to climb a mountain instead of get out of bed, Gwen pushed up from her pallet and staggered to Mari's side. Mari knelt on the floor beside the basin, her head resting against the wall. Her face was very pale. Gwen put a hand to her forehead, but she wasn't feverish. This was simply the sickness that many pregnant women experienced—often in the morning—but in Mari's case it afflicted her all the time.

"Will you be all right for a moment if I ask the maid to empty this?" Gwen said.

Mari nodded, barely moving her head and keeping her eyes closed. "There's nothing left inside me anyway."

Too often that wasn't quite true. Holding her nose, Gwen hastened to the door. Mari's maid was just coming through the front door of the manor house with a serving girl. Gwen handed the basin to Hafwen, who passed it immediately to the girl, who ran off with it.

"I have some herbs that might help her," Hafwen said. A widow with grown children, she was fifteen years older than Mari and Gwen and refreshingly no-nonsense about pregnancy and everything else. Hafwen picked up a tray containing Mari's breakfast, still warm from the kitchen, which she'd left by the door earlier.

"Perhaps you can get Mari to eat something too," Gwen said. "She often feels better when she does."

"What about you, madam?" Hafwen said.

"I'll dress and then eat breakfast in the hall," Gwen said. "Don't worry about me."

As Gwen re-entered the bedroom, she made for the lone window. The shutter had been closed for the night, but she opened it to let the fresh air compete with the smell of sickness. Gwen kissed Mari's cheek. "I love you dearly, but—"

"Get out of here." Mari waved her hand at Gwen. "I'm in good hands with Hafwen. Go before you end up sick too."

Gwen didn't need to be told twice. She dressed as quickly as she could and departed. She knew she was a coward for not wanting to attend to Mari, but her friend had been right that Gwen's stomach had been threatening to rebel.

Wrapping her cloak tightly around herself against the chilly morning, Gwen stepped outside, reveling in the crisp air, and set off along the path to the postern gate. It was open, so she didn't have to wait to be let in, and the sentry on duty nodded to her as she entered. She'd temporarily forgotten his name, so she hurried past him with a quick greeting and a wave. Then she stopped and turned back. "Has Sir Gareth passed this way recently?"

"Not recently, madam," the guard said. "He entered before dawn."

"Thank you." It had still been dark when Gareth had left their bed. With the waning of the year, the days were getting shorter, and dawn on the last day of October was hours later than it had been in June.

The first person Gwen saw as she came around the corner of the stables was Godfrid, talking intently to two of his men. He loomed over them, for all that they were big men too, and his face was set like granite. It wasn't a look she had often seen on him outside of those moments when he spoke about Ottar or Ottar's son, Thorfin. Even last night when Godfrid had walked into the hall and seen Cadwaladr sitting at the high table, his expression had been one of cynical amusement.

For Cadwaladr's part, at the sight of the Danes, he had looked like he'd swallowed a whole radish in one go. But other than turning red, he could say nothing once his brother had risen to his feet and flung out his arms in an expansive gesture, welcoming Godfrid and his men into Aber.

When a man had made as many poor choices as Cadwaladr, humiliation could sneak up on him when he least expected it, even if he was a prince.

Gwen halted a few paces away from Godfrid to allow him to finish his conversation with his men, though as he was speaking Danish, she understood none of it. Once he noticed her, his expression softened, and he turned to her.

"Is something wrong?" Gwen said.

"Not at all—" Godfrid broke off from what he'd been about to say. Then he sucked in his cheeks and said, "I forget that I am speaking to Gwen, the wife of Gareth the knight, not a woman of my court. Yes, there is something wrong. One of my men is missing."

"Oh dear." Gwen didn't ask if he was sure. That would be insulting.

Godfrid read her expression, however, and added, "We checked the barracks and the stables. We are two dozen men and have explored the whole castle. It is possible, I suppose, that he found a bed in a room that remains closed to us, but it doesn't feel right that this would be true."

"What's his name?" Gwen said.

"A man named Erik. He's half-Welsh, which is why I brought him, so that he could be another who speaks your language," Godfrid said. "He knows Gwynedd."

"Why would one of your men leave without warning?" Gwen said.

A muscle in Godfrid's cheek twitched. "I fear I have been betrayed. I personally chose each of the men who accompany me and would not have questioned the loyalty of any, Erik among them."

"So he's been with you a long while?" Gwen said.

"Not so much with me as with my father."

"You said he was Welsh. Is Gwynedd his home?"

"He came into my father's service from Rhos, I believe." And then Godfrid froze, realizing, as Gwen did, what he'd just said.

Sweet Mary. "Does Gareth know of this?"

"He has spent the last few hours searching where I could not." Godfrid made a *look there* gesture, and Gwen turned to see Gareth walking towards her from underneath the portcullis. When he came up to her, she put her arms around his waist and pressed her cheek to his chest, while he patted her on the back.

Gwen stepped away, smiling to herself because that was the gesture he used when he wanted her to know that he loved her but was too busy to really show it.

"No luck." Gareth scrubbed at his hair with both hands. "I have one last place to look for Erik."

"Where is that?" Godfrid said.

"Some place I shouldn't show you, but it seems I'm going to anyway, since you're here," Gareth said. "No horse is missing from the stables, which means he can't have gone far or be going far."

"Either that or he had outside help," Gwen said.

Gareth made a disgusted sound at the back of his throat. "That too. Still, he didn't leave by any gate."

"We're going to show Godfrid the tunnel, aren't we?" Gwen clapped her hands together. "I'm coming with you."

"Gwen—"

"It's damp and dark but not dangerous," Gwen said. "And you've never even been down it."

Gareth tsked through his teeth at her. "I keep meaning to, and one thing always overtakes another and drives out the notion."

"What tunnel is this?" Godfrid said, looking from Gareth to Gwen, his eyes alight with interest.

"It's a back door out of Aber in times of need," Gareth said.

"How would Erik have known of it?" Godfrid said.

"He wouldn't have had to know about the tunnels before his arrival," Gareth said. "You know how the men talk, and it's an open secret in Gwynedd anyway."

"A man guards it at all times," Gwen said.

"Guards can be bribed," Gareth said. "Let's see if the one on duty this morning knows anything."

Gwen opened her mouth to suggest that Gareth speak to Hywel about it before they went but then remembered that not only was Hywel not at Aber, but that Gareth's commission had been made clear. King Owain had given them nearly free rein to pursue the investigation as he saw fit. Gareth had come a long way since that bloody road from Dolwyddelan. If Gwen had spied Rhun on the way to the tunnel, she would have roped him in for the fun of it, but she didn't see him. They hadn't done a very good job of freeing him from his stepmother's clutches last night, and she hoped he'd survived the evening still a bachelor.

The guardroom for the tunnel that went north from the castle to the sea was on the ground floor of one of Aber's ancient towers. Extra armor and weapons were stored there, but it had space enough within it for a man to put his feet up on a table in some comfort. Gwen knew for a fact that it was a favorite gathering spot for members of the garrison to entertain each other with dicing or drink.

This tunnel, however, was in the basement of a southern tower, at the bottom of a flight of narrow stone steps. Dank, dark, and chilly, it was the least desirable posting in the castle. King Owain didn't use it as a punishment as he could have. The tunnel's existence made Aber vulnerable, and he needed trusted men to guard it.

A lamp flickered on the table below her. When Gwen, who was in the lead, came around a curve halfway down the stairs, she saw the body of the sentry sprawled on the floor. The soldier was of an age with Gareth, and Gwen knew him only by his nickname, Goch, like Gareth's horse, for his mane of red hair.

Gareth put a hand on her arm to stop her from continuing, passed her on the stairs, and jumped the last three steps to reach Goch first. He put his fingers to the guard's neck and then looked up at Gwen with relief in his face. "He's alive."

At Gareth's touch, Goch moaned and swept a hand across his eyes. He struggled to sit up, and Godfrid and Gareth helped him to sit with his back against the wall. Goch lifted his head, looking blearily at the two men who crouched before him.

"What happened?" Gareth said.

Another groan escaped Goch's lips before he suppressed it. "I hardly know. I was sitting there." He gestured to the overturned chair. "I hadn't considered the possibility that a threat might come from the stairs behind me."

"So you didn't see who hit you?" Gwen said.

Goch shook his head and then winced, putting his hand to the back of his head.

"Where is the man who stood watch with you?" Gareth said.

Goch rubbed his eyes with his thumb and forefinger. "He ... he went to relieve himself." Then his brow furrowed. "No, that was earlier. I don't know what happened to him."

Godfrid had a habit of sucking on his teeth as he thought, and he was at it again. "Who was it?"

"A fellow named Dewi," Goch said.

"Really?" Gwen looked at Gareth, concern in her eyes.

Gareth's brow furrowed. "Dewi was on the beach when we found Tegwen. Maybe he knows something about her death."

"If that's the case, he looked at her and said nothing," Gwen said.

"I realize we don't believe in coincidences, but with the arrival of the Danes, it's possible that what Dewi knows—or fears— has nothing to do with Tegwen's death," Gareth said, "but with the Book of Kells."

Godfrid frowned. "Who is this man?"

"He's been nobody of importance up until now," Gareth said. "I mean that quite literally. And Dewi isn't new to the king's service any more than Erik is to yours or your father's, Godfrid. I joined Hywel's company after he did."

"Gareth, I just had a thought," Gwen said. "Could Dewi know Erik because he came from Rhos too?"

Godfrid clenched a hand and dropped it onto the table in a fist. "What is going on?"

"I can't tell you what may have changed between last night and now, but perhaps we've finally started asking the right questions." Gareth looked towards the tunnel.

Gwen could see him hesitating, torn between chasing after Dewi and his duty, which was to warn the king of what had happened. "I will take Godfrid through the tunnel while you raise the alarm at Aber. You can meet us at the hay barn on the other side with more men and a horse for Godfrid. Perhaps they aren't that far ahead of us. We don't want to risk anyone else obscuring the evidence before we get there."

"As usual, she speaks sense," Godfrid said. "I will keep her safe."

Gareth made a growling sound deep in his chest but nodded. "Hurry." He raced away up the steps.

While Godfrid lit a second lamp, Gwen went to the door to the tunnel and pulled it wide. She glanced back to Goch, who had righted the chair to seat himself at the table, his head resting in the palm of one hand.

"I'll stay here until you return or someone relieves me," Goch said.

"Keep your knife at the ready," Godfrid said.

Goch nodded and pulled out his boot knife, a long blade with a viciously sharp point and a leather handle, worn black with use. He laid it on the table in front of him. Godfrid nodded approvingly, and then he and Gwen entered the tunnel together.

The last time Gwen had come here it was with Hywel, and he'd spent the whole walk reassuring her that everything was going to be fine. Gareth had been waiting for her in the barn at the other end, and it was comforting to know that he would meet them there again. Godfrid hunched his shoulders, since he was tall enough for his hair to brush the ceiling.

"Watch your head when you reach the beams," Gwen said. "I think you're the tallest man who's ever walked here."

That prompted a laugh from Godfrid, and she sensed him relaxing. "You would make a fine leader of men, Gwen."

"You don't like small spaces any more than I do," Gwen said.

"I like the sea."

"I know this is outside your comprehension, but I dislike the sea even more than this tunnel," she said.

Godfrid's white teeth glinted in the lamplight as he grinned at her. "I remember."

The tunnel was less than half a mile long, walkable in ten minutes above ground but an endless journey in the dark. Gwen made herself focus on nothing else but the circle of light thrown out by Godfrid's lantern, which he held out before him. Her heart pounded in her ears, but she kept a hand on the roundness of her belly and told herself that all she had to do was breathe and walk.

Godfrid, however, was focused on their mission and had been keeping his eyes on the ground. They had gone only a hundred feet when he put out a hand to stop Gwen from walking. He crouched low and shone his light on the path. "I've been watching them. We have two sets of footprints."

Gwen bent to look, her hands on her knees. "The guards walk through here every week to make sure it's clear. No breeze stirs the air, so their footprints would remain undisturbed."

"These men were running." Godfrid pointed to the distinct impressions in the soft ground.

Gwen thought she could see what he meant, the way the footprint was deeper at the toes; a man walking had more of a heel-to-toe movement. "We had good reason to think that they came this way. I just don't understand why they thought they had to."

"What do you mean?" Godfrid said.

"I suppose knocking out Goch made sense to them," Gwen said. "But why not leave by the postern gate? With the crowded castle, they could have walked out together plain as day and nobody would have thought anything of it."

"Frightened men don't always think as clearly as those hunting them," Godfrid said.

Gwen grumbled to herself, granting him his point, even if she didn't like it. Cadwaladr had been a fool to have abducted her last year, since she and Gareth hadn't been close to catching him. Arguably, he had been a fool to have murdered Anarawd in the first place. Sometimes guilty men panicked.

"One of the men steps heavily on the outside of his feet as he walks." Godfrid looked up at Gwen. "I wouldn't have said my man had such a gait."

"If we find Dewi, we can check his boots," Gwen said. "It's not something I would know."

They followed the tracks all the way to the ladder that led up to the hay barn. Gwen sighed in relief when they reached it and hoped that no spiders had hitched a ride on her hair when she wasn't looking. Godfrid went up the ladder first. In order to open the trapdoor, he had to push at it with his shoulder. Given the effort involved, Gwen wasn't sure she would have been strong enough to lift it.

"Come on up, Gwen." Godfrid crouched over the hole and reached down a hand for Gwen to grasp. Gwen's belly had grown since the last time she'd climbed a ladder, and she found it awkward to maintain her balance on the narrow rungs. She grasped Godfrid's hand and allowed him to haul her the last few feet until she stood on the floor beside him.

The hay barn was just as neglected as she remembered, though it looked as if King Owain had ordered some work done on one of the walls to shore it up. The intent was to keep it looking dilapidated but not to allow it to actually fall down. Godfrid closed the trap door and scattered hay from a nearby mound across the floor, in order to make it look as if no one had come through the tunnel.

"What do we have here?" Gwen pointed to a corner of fabric that Godfrid had exposed. She pulled at it, and it came loose with a tug.

"That's King Owain's lion crest," Godfrid said. "Now we know Dewi came here."

Gwen held it up and made a noncommittal motion with her head. "We know *someone* was here who didn't want to be seen outside Aber in King Owain's colors."

"I have failed again," Godfrid said.

"What was that?" Gwen said, dropping her arms.

Godfrid laughed. "It is as Gareth has said to me more than once: *never assume.*"

21

Hywel

Hywel was thankful to be riding out of Bryn Euryn, even if the delay meant that he was going to miss Tegwen's funeral. He was already regretting his father's disappointment at his absence. Still, Tegwen was dead, and Hywel's presence at her funeral wasn't going to bring her back. His inquiries at Bryn Euryn, however, might bring her justice.

Instead of taking the high road through Caerhun and the standing stones at Bwlch y Ddeufaen on the return journey, Hywel directed his men to the ferry across the Conwy. They had ten miles to cover, and if they were going to reach Aber with a few hours to spare before sunset, they couldn't dawdle. The weather had remained fine as they left the ferry, but by the time they took the beach road to Aber, it had begun to rain.

The farther they traveled, the more the wind whipped the fine sand into swirls over the road and bent back the bracken and the scrubby trees that managed to survive here despite the poor soil and constant wind. Hywel hunched his shoulders against it, cursing at the raindrops that blew into his face. Before they'd gone half a mile, he was wet, and after five miles, he was soaked from head to foot.

Evan rode to Hywel's right, and the closer to Aber they got, the more alert he'd become. For the last mile, ever since the road had begun moving inland, he'd ridden with his hood pushed back and his head swiveling all around.

"What is it, Evan?" Hywel pushed back his own hood too. Oddly, the rain bothered him less now that he'd given in to it. He wished he'd realized that earlier. He blinked the drops out of his eyes and then shielded them with one hand. Having passed the crossroads where the high road came down from the hills to intersect with the road on which they were traveling, they were hardly more than a mile from Aber. Hywel could practically smell the cooking fires from here.

"Something doesn't feel right, my lord." Evan lifted his spear as a signal to the men. As the company rounded a curve between a field on the right and a series of tree-covered hills to the left, they slowed the horses.

"I can't see or hear anything but the rain." Hywel peered southwest, searching for anything or anyone out of place in the sodden landscape.

Even frowned and put out a hand to Hywel. "Wait—"

But at that instant, the man to the left of Hywel grunted and faltered, an arrow jutting from his shoulder. Hywel had time to rein in sharply before a second arrow flashed between his horse's head and his own and landed in the ditch to the north of the road.

"Get down!" Evan launched himself at Hywel and dived with him for cover.

Hywel's men were well trained and flung themselves off their horses at Evan's shout. Hywel rolled into the tall grasses to the right of the road while others found refuge to the left. Evan threw himself on his stomach beside Hywel, both of them on a downslope, trying to see through the vegetation growing on the rise to the south of the road from where the arrows had come.

"How many arrows has he loosed?" Hywel said.

"At least three," Evan said. "Two horses are down, and Dafydd was hit in the shoulder."

"The archer had to take him down first to get to me," Hywel said.

Evan nodded. "He rushed it."

"You saved my life, Evan," Hywel said.

Evan swept his eyes downward. "I did my duty, my lord."

Hywel grunted under his breath at Evan's modesty, which truth be told was no less than he expected. Evan went back to scanning the hills to the south. Nothing moved on the road but the constant rain, and Hywel's ten men lay still.

"Let me try something, my lord." Evan raised one hand high above his head. No arrow shot through it.

"Get them!"

Hywel didn't immediately recognize the voice of the man who'd spoken, but at the shout, Hywel's men surged from their hiding positions on both sides of the road. Evan pressed a hand onto Hywel's shoulder, keeping him down until he determined the source of the threat. Within a few breaths, three of Hywel's men had a fourth struggling on the ground beneath them. Brushing off Evan's hand with a sour look, Hywel pushed to his feet.

"As I said, no more than my duty, my lord," Evan said.

"You're as bad as Gareth," Hywel said.

Evan bowed his head. "You honor me."

Hywel cracked a smile that he tried not to let Evan see and strode the twenty yards along the road to where the man his company had captured lay. "Get him up."

The man had given up fighting. His hands were tied behind his back, and he'd landed in a puddle, so he was even wetter than Hywel. Hywel's men lifted him from the ground.

"Dewi?" Hywel stared at the man-at-arms, flabbergasted. "Why did you shoot at me?"

"I didn't shoot—I didn't shoot at you. I didn't shoot at anybody!" Dewi eyes went wide in panic at the accusation. "You can see I have no bow!"

"You could have thrown your bow away," one of Hywel's men said.

Evan approached Hywel from behind and spoke low in his ear. "The other man with Dewi got away, my lord. I have sent six of the men to scouring the countryside to the south, but I am not optimistic we'll find the archer. He could have been three hundred yards away when he shot at us. If I were he, I would have loosed my three arrows and run. I don't know why Dewi is here, but I don't think the ambush is his doing."

"Who was the other fellow with you?" Hywel said to Dewi.

Dewi chewed on the inside of his cheek.

"You might as well tell me," Hywel said. "If you're missing from your post, this other fellow is too. Who was it?"

Dewi was used to following orders and, in Hywel's opinion, had never been a great thinker. Hywel waited him out, flicking a hand at several of his men, who shifted with impatience. Hywel didn't like waiting, but he could do it if he had to.

Dewi licked his lips. "It wasn't my idea."

Hywel didn't allow himself to smile at Dewi's capitulation. "Why don't you tell me whose idea it was? We can clear this all up in time for the feast tonight."

"I didn't want to get involved," Dewi said. "Erik said—"

Hywel held up a hand. "Did you say Erik?"

Dewi nodded.

Hywel shook his head at the name. It couldn't be a coincidence. "Go on."

"Erik said—"

Dewi cut himself off for a second time as hoof beats sounded on the road. They all looked west, even Dewi, though his arms were held in a tight grip by one of Hywel's men.

Gareth appeared over the rise with Godfrid (of all people) and another ten men, coming from Aber. Two dogs ran in front of them, making a beeline for Dewi, their tongues lolling out. At a whistle from one of their handlers, the dogs halted. They were within two paces from Dewi by then, and they twitched in anticipation of bringing him down if only they were allowed to.

Moving forward to greet Gareth, Hywel congratulated himself that the two of them had ended up in the same place, though he hoped Gareth knew more about what was going on with Dewi than he did. The company reined in, and the two dog handlers quickly leashed their charges. The animals would be well rewarded tonight.

"My lord." Gareth dismounted, glancing past Hywel to where Dewi stood out of earshot. "Thank you for catching him."

"I'm delighted to have been of service," Hywel said. "What has Dewi done?"

"He and one of Godfrid's men, a man named Erik, fled Aber this morning after subduing one of the sentries," Gareth said.

Godfrid had dismounted too and held out his arms to Hywel, who embraced him gladly. "You should know that someone took a shot at me a moment ago," Hywel said as the two men stepped back from each other.

"What?" Gareth examined the terrain to the south. "Just now?"

"Whether it was Dewi, this Erik both of us are also seeking, or an as-yet-unidentified third man, we haven't yet determined," Hywel said.

"We spotted Dewi and Erik half a mile up the road," Godfrid said. "I don't recall seeing either with a bow or arrows."

"Erik was your man?" Hywel said to Godfrid.

"And a traitor, apparently," Godfrid said. "I wish we were meeting again under better circumstances, but you need to know that Erik served in Rhos before he entered my father's service."

"Your father tells me that Dewi served in Rhos too," Gareth said.

Hywel looked upon Dewi with new eyes, and then said to Gareth, "You'd better tell me what you've discovered in my absence."

Heedless of the rain, which continued to fall, Gareth quickly set forth the events of the past day from his end. Then Hywel gave Godfrid and Gareth a summary of his investigations, including the fact that he'd been contemplating a journey to Dublin in search of Erik.

"How fortunate that I brought him to you." Godfrid coughed. "Sort of."

They walked back to where Dewi stood with his captors.

"We'll see if we can get something out of our prisoner." Hywel stepped in front of Dewi and took a moment to examine him. Dewi kept his eyes downcast, refusing to look up. "A few miles isn't much ground to cover since this morning. What did you hang around for?"

"It was Erik's idea to go to ground until tonight," Dewi said, selling out his companion. "He knew of an empty hut not far from Aber, and we stayed there until we heard the dogs." Dewi cast a resentful look in Gareth's direction. "Better to run than be caught like a rabbit in a trap."

"Why did you run from Aber in the first place?" Hywel said.

Dewi didn't answer immediately, and the way he stared at his feet, digging the toe of his boot into the loose soil of the road, reminded Hywel of when he and Gareth had questioned Ceri and Llelo.

Hywel continued to wait, his eyes on Dewi's downturned head, and Gareth and Godfrid had the sense not to step in. Most men didn't like silence and instinctively would fill it.

Then Dewi's head came up, and he looked at Hywel, his face contorted. For a moment Hywel thought he was going to cry. "I knew I was in trouble the moment I saw her body on the beach."

"You speak of Tegwen's body?" Hywel said.

"Lord Bran swore that nobody would ever find her!" Dewi choked up, his words coming out as a strangled wail.

Hywel rocked back on his heels. "What do you know about my cousin's death?"

"It was an accident! I swear it! Bran backhanded her across the face, and she fell and hit her head on the corner of a table."

The entire company of men, both Hywel's and Gareth's, had been listening with breath held, but at Dewi's outburst, Hywel felt that breath ease out in a quiet sigh as they settled themselves. At long last, they were hearing the truth or something close to it.

"You saw it happen?" Hywel said.

Dewi had gone back to staring at his feet, misery in every line of his body. "I heard it. And then I helped Bran conceal her death."

"You personally were involved in leaving Tegwen's body in Wena's hut?" Gareth said.

Dewi nodded.

"Why not bury her in the garden, or the woods, or drop her in the ocean for that matter?" Gareth said.

"We couldn't risk being seen, and we had no tools!" Dewi said. "The house held only a bed, a table, and a few dishes. The shed was empty. Do you know how hard it is to dig a grave with a spoon?"

Hywel almost laughed. That was something he hadn't ever considered, for all that he'd killed men. He'd never wanted to hide a body, though, and he could imagine the desperate search that must have ensued when Bran found his wife dead at his feet.

"Whose idea was it to put her behind the wall?" Gareth said.

"Bran's," Dewi said. "He made a shroud out of a deerskin he found in a box at the foot of the bed, and we carried her up the ladder to the loft."

"And left her," Hywel said.

"It was all Erik's fault," Dewi said. "He was the one who brought Tegwen to Aber. We didn't even know she was coming until she arrived."

"What were you doing at Aber?" Gareth said.

"I attended to Lord Bran." Dewi lifted his head, a remnant of pride returning.

"Why were you at Wena's hut?" Hywel said. "Bran was supposed to be in Powys with my father."

Dewi's face flushed, and he didn't answer.

Gareth's expression turned menacing, and he stepped closer. "Both Tegwen and Bran are dead, Dewi. But you're not. Telling us everything you know can only help you now."

Dewi licked his lips. They were badly chapped, even with the fall of water on his face. His eyes flicked to the side of the road.

"You have no way out of this, Dewi," Gareth said. "You don't want to hang for a murder you didn't commit."

Even with that empty threat, Hywel was afraid they would have to use harsher methods to compel Dewi to spit out any more information, but then he said, "It was Queen Gwladys who was supposed to come to the hut that night."

A whisper of unease swept among the men, and Hywel held up one hand to stop Dewi from speaking further. Gareth tipped his head to Evan, who began to disperse the men back to their horses. Hywel was still struggling to believe that the truth had been right in front of him all this time, if only Dewi had been willing to tell it.

"Why don't you tell us about that meeting?" Gareth said.

Dewi sneered, realizing he'd struck a nerve. "Gwladys was Bran's lover."

Hywel kept his expression blank.

Dewi waited for a response, but when it wasn't forthcoming, his shoulders sagged. "Oh. You already knew that."

"We did," Gareth said.

"Then why did you ask?" Dewi said.

"To see if you did," Gareth said.

That seemed too complicated for Dewi, who then shrugged. "She'd broken it off with him, but Bran had begged her to talk to him one last time."

It was always the one last time that was the undoing of any secret. Gwladys appeared to have known that, even if Bran hadn't.

"But she didn't come," Hywel said.

Dewi shook his head. "It was Tegwen who came. Lord Bran had sent Erik on an errand to Bryn Euryn, and somehow she convinced him to bring her to Aber."

"That's a fifteen-mile ride if you don't take the ferry," Hywel said. "She must have been very convincing."

Dewi shrugged again. Hywel was growing to despise the gesture. "He would never tell me anything."

Gareth motioned with one hand, silently asking Hywel to step away from Dewi to confer with him and Godfrid. They put their heads together.

"Tegwen would not be the first wife to lie with her husband after-the-fact, thinking to convince him seven months later that the child was born early," Godfrid said.

"When Brychan refused to run away with her, she must have been desperate," Gareth said.

"Nor would Erik be the first Dane to hide a soft heart behind a warrior's countenance," Godfrid said.

Gareth returned to Dewi. "Why did you run?"

"Erik said that it was only a matter of time before someone remembered that we'd both served Bran," Dewi said. "He knew that Prince Hywel had gone to Rhos. He didn't trust me to lie. He said that I either had to come with him, or he'd kill me."

"Did it occur to you that he might kill you once he got you out of Aber?" Hywel said.

At Dewi's wide eyes, Hywel tsked his disbelief.

"Walk me through that night, Dewi," Gareth said. "Erik and Tegwen arrived at the hut. Tegwen went inside, leaving you and Erik to wait outside ... and then what?"

Dewi hunched his shoulders. "I didn't hear all that Tegwen and Bran said. They were quiet at first, and then they started shouting." He looked down at the ground. "Erik and I stayed with the horses until Bran came to get us."

"That's not all you heard, though, is it?" Gareth said.

Hywel had noted that downcast look too, which indicated Dewi was *still* hiding something.

"Nobody can be harmed by Bran now," Gareth said. "It's best if you tell the whole truth."

Dewi's lower lip stuck out as if he were Dai's age instead of Gareth's. "I don't want to hang."

Gareth glanced at Hywel, who answered for him, "My father will be merciful as long as you didn't do anything wrong beyond withholding the true story."

Dewi ducked his head. "Tegwen told Bran that she'd kept his secrets and that he owed her." Now Dewi lifted his eyes to Hywel's face. "She claimed he was responsible for Marchudd's death." Marchudd was Bran's older brother, the eldest son of the three, who'd died in battle in Ceredigion after Bran's marriage to Tegwen.

The three men stood silent absorbing that bit of news, and then Hywel reached around Dewi's back, untied his hands, and began to retie them in front of him. "Is that when he hit her?"

Dewi nodded.

The rope was water-logged and stiff, and Hywel's own hands were cold. By the time they arrived at Aber, the only way to remove the rope might be to cut it. After some frustration with trying to tie the last knot, Gareth stepped in to finish the job while Hywel put his hands to his mouth to warm them.

"Did Tegwen truly know something about Marchudd's death?" Gareth said. "Was Bran really responsible?"

Dewi put his face into his bound hands. "I don't know. It was in Ceredigion." Then he lifted his head to look at Hywel. "You know what that war was like, that last battle in particular."

"Who's to say when a man dies that his death truly came at the hands of his enemy?" Godfrid said.

Hywel nodded. "War is chaos." They'd all lost loved ones that day.

22

Gareth

"Did I miss the funeral?" Hywel said.

"Not yet." Gareth rode beside his lord with Godfrid a half pace behind on the other side. "Tegwen was to be put in the ground as the sun was setting. Your father hoped that the delay would give you enough time to return."

Gareth expected Hywel to express regret or at least grimace that he'd failed to miss the funeral. But instead he opened his mouth and sang:

A bright fort on a shining slope stands;
A girl, shy and beautiful, plays with the gulls.
Though she thinks of me not,
I will go,
on my white horse,
my soul full of longing;
to seek out the girl whose laughter fills my heart,
to speak of love,
since it has come my way.

"Up until this moment, I didn't want to attend, but now I will sing that for her," Hywel said.

Gareth was having a hard time finding his voice. He glanced behind him and saw that several of the men had overheard Hywel's tenor and were clearing their throats and surreptitiously wiping at the corners of their eyes.

"Did you compose that for Tegwen?" Gareth said.

"It has been forming in my mind since I left Aber," Hywel said. "I wish she were still alive to hear it."

"She won't be remembered because she ran away with a Dane anymore but because of your song," Gareth said.

"She was lost," Hywel said simply.

Gareth glanced at his prince. "So you believe Dewi's story?"

"Perhaps not every word, but in the main? Yes."

"Bran must have known that someday the body would come to light. He didn't dispose of her cloak," Godfrid said.

"That close to Aber, everywhere else was equally fraught with peril," Hywel said.

"He should have burned the cloak," Gareth said. "He could have stolen a boat and thrown her body into the sea."

"His wife was dead by his hand," Hywel said. "I submit that he might not have been thinking clearly and would have been concerned primarily for his own skin. He didn't want anyone to see him. He'd come to Aber in secret. He wanted to keep it that way."

"Do you think—" Gareth hesitated, biting his lip.

"Do I think what?" Hywel said.

"He may have known the village children thought the house was haunted," Gareth said. "He probably knew that Cadwaladr met his women there. Perhaps he hoped that if Tegwen was found, suspicion would fall naturally on Prince Cadwaladr. I myself assumed it when we found the body."

"What is the word for such a man?" Godfrid said. "Devious, I think you would say."

"One never knows what a man can do when he's desperate," Gareth said, "as surely as Bran must have been desperate having killed his wife."

"My lord Hywel, your father will be pleased you solved her murder, if not Bran's, in time to lay her to rest," Godfrid said.

"I'll tell you what I'm glad about," Gareth said. "I'm glad that I'm not bringing your lifeless body into Aber, my lord."

Hywel waved off Gareth's concern. "The archer's aim was poor."

Gareth shook his head. "Why now? Why take a shot at you? Bran killed Tegwen. What are we missing that has put you in an archer's sights?"

"You do have a second murder, that of Bran himself," Godfrid said.

Gareth clenched the reins tightly and then forced himself to relax. "I would not have said we were getting close to identifying him."

"And yet, if this ambush is related, our murderer must not agree," Hywel said.

"He has stayed hidden for three years," Gareth said. "What has made him lose his grip?"

Nobody had an answer to that.

"Are you going to tell your father about Tegwen's accusation against Bran?" Gareth said.

"I will have to," Hywel said.

"If I may suggest, my lord," Gareth said, "it would be better if only your father knows what we know. We have inadvertently flushed out another wrongdoer. We want to keep him guessing."

"I agree," Hywel said.

They had finally come off the beach path to the main road that ran past Aber. Torches shone from the gatehouse where a crowd had gathered, forming up on either side of the road to the castle, and Meilyr's drum pounded out a solemn rhythm.

"Tegwen's funeral is about to start." Godfrid bowed. "I am sorry for your loss, my prince."

Hywel nodded absently and dismounted at the crossroads where the track that ran down from the castle met the main road. Gareth waved at the men to dismount and then went to help Dafydd off his horse himself. Dafydd's wound had turned out to be less serious than it could have been because his boiled leather armor had stopped most of the arrow's force. The point had penetrated the muscle of his upper arm, however, and he needed proper treatment before the wound suppurated. Directing another man-at-arms to give him support, Gareth sent Dafydd into the castle by a back pathway that led to the postern gate.

The rest of the men picketed their horses in the grass beside the road. Dewi had been walking with his hands tied in front of him on a lead behind one of the horses, and Evan pulled him off the track behind the other men, keeping one hand on the rope. Dewi hadn't tried to run away, but Tegwen's funeral would present him with the best opportunity, with his guards more focused on the procession than on him.

It wasn't long before Tegwen's coffin passed their position, with Gruffydd, Sioned, and King Owain following immediately behind the pallbearers. Hywel moved towards Rhun, who nodded his head almost imperceptibly in greeting. Mari, who walked next to Rhun, shot her husband a glare and lifted her chin. Gareth couldn't help smiling at his prince's discomfort, confident that he knew what that was about. Gwen walked with Gwalchmai, Llelo, and Dai further back in the procession. At their approach, Evan nudged Gareth's arm. "Go on."

Gareth didn't need a second urging. He took Gwen's hand, and they walked across the bridge that spanned the Aber River to the burial ground of many of Aber's royal family, located to the south of the village. An ancient chapel and hedge surrounded the circular site. By the time the people had filled in every available space to listen to the words of Aber's priest, it was nearly dark. As they lowered Tegwen into the ground and Hywel opened his mouth to sing his paean to her, the rain finally stopped. To the west, the clouds lifted long enough to reveal the sun setting in a fiery ball.

As the last note faded, the congregants murmured their approval. Then, at a nod from his father, Hywel launched into the Latin benediction, one everyone in the audience knew well. It soared above their heads, Gwalchmai's soprano acting as counterpoint to Hywel's tenor.

It was completely dark by the time they made their way back into Aber Castle. With the cessation of the rain, temporary though it might be, candles and more torches had been lit all along the road to light their way—and Tegwen's. Many common folk still believed in their heart of hearts that she needed guidance to her final rest in the next world, despite the exhortations of the Church to the contrary.

Gwen and Gareth held back to allow most of the crowd to leave them behind as he gave her a hurried summary of all that had happened in the last few hours. He'd tried to move out of earshot of Dai and Llelo, but as he finished his tale, Dai appeared at his right elbow. "You should know that Prince Cadwaladr met a man at Wena's hut last night."

Gareth came to a dead halt in the middle of the road. "You boys are going to be the death of me. How do you know that?"

"I saw him." Dai hadn't registered Gareth's glare of disapproval.

Gwen put a hand on Gareth's arm and gave him a quelling look. "What did the man Cadwaladr met look like? Could you see?"

"He was large, with yellow hair." Dai gestured to Godfrid, who was fighting the current of people, coming towards them from wherever he'd been. "Like him."

Once Godfrid reached them, Gareth steered the five of them to the edge of the road, out of the way of any passer-by.

"It's my fault," Llelo said. "I told Dai about going to the hut, and he insisted that *he* wouldn't be scared. Gwalchmai and Iorwerth came too."

Gareth studied Llelo's downturned head. Like at Ceri's hut, Llelo was refusing to look at him.

Gwen stepped in. "Let's start again. The four of you followed Cadwaladr to Wena's hut and saw him meet with a Dane there?"

"No," Dai said, cheerfully oblivious to Gareth's displeasure. "We didn't follow him. He was already there when we arrived. The door was propped open and a lantern lit in the house. We sneaked up to see who had got there first and saw them talking."

"Did they see you?" Gwen said.

Dai shook his head, though for the first time he looked uncertain.

"No, they didn't," Llelo said. "I'm sure of it. They were intent on each other."

"Did you hear what they were talking about?" Gwen said.

"Something about a book," Llelo said.

The three adults exchanged a quick glance. By now, everyone had passed them to return to the castle except for Godfrid's Danes. With a wave of his hand, Godfrid dispersed his men in a defensive perimeter along the road. "What else did they say?" Godfrid said to Llelo.

"Nothing else. Prince Cadwaladr asked if the man had news of 'the book' and reminded him how important it was that he find it."

"Did you recognize the man as one of Godfrid's?" Gwen said. "We have been looking all day for one named Erik, who is half Welsh."

Both boys shook their heads uncertainly.

"Without catching him, we won't know if it was Erik," Godfrid said. "It could have been one of Thorfin's men."

"Why would Cadwaladr want the Book of Kells?" Gwen said.

"For the same reason Thorfin did," Gareth said. "The Earl of Pembroke would make a powerful ally. Thorfin wanted to use it to bring Gilbert de Clare to Ireland. What if Cadwaladr wants Clare's help in gaining power?"

"In Ceredigion?" Gwen said.

"In Gwynedd," Gareth said.

Gareth was really only thinking out loud, but as he spoke the words, a possible plot took shape in his head. There was nothing Cadwaladr wouldn't do to advance his own position and no person he wouldn't betray.

Godfrid put a hand on Llelo's shoulder. The boy had been following the adults' conversation with wary eyes. "What happened next?"

"Cadwaladr rode away, back to Aber, and the big man went off in the opposite direction. We didn't want to get caught, and as it was very late, we returned to Aber too."

Dai was bouncing up and down, as if anxious to speak. Gareth put a hand on top of his head to stop him from moving. "What is it?"

"There was one more thing," he said. "I don't think either of them knew where this book was."

"Why do you say that?" Godfrid said.

"There was a great deal of cursing and kicking furniture," Dai said. "It's how King Owain behaves when he is angry."

Godfrid growled low in his throat. "If you're right, that would be the best news I've heard all day."

23

Gwen

Hallowmas was upon them, and even with the intrigue swirling around Tegwen's death, Gwen was having a difficult time thinking about anything but what the poor girl had looked like when Gwen had first seen her on the beach. Most years, Gwen looked forward to Hallowmas, the dancing and singing in particular, but tonight she felt distant from it.

The feasting was continuing in the great hall, but Gwen, who'd excused herself to use the latrine, didn't return to it, standing instead in the shadow of the stone battlement. The air was damp with the threat of more rain, but she breathed deeply, glad to be away from the hall and the press of people. She was already tired of the smell of sweat and damp wool, and winter hadn't even started.

Dozens, if not hundreds, of candles lit the courtyard of the castle. Some of Aber's villagers had started to trickle away down the hill. Hallowmas was both a serious time and one of joyful celebration. Before midnight, the villagers would light a bonfire from which the hearth fires of every household would be relit.

Sharing food was a way to welcome the souls of family members who'd died, so revelers would leave food on the doorsteps of every house.

She glanced towards the postern gate, which was open, providing easy passage to and from the house in which she and Gareth were staying. Several soldiers stood guarding the door, though they were drinking and eating, so she wasn't sure how much attention they were paying to the people who came and went. With Tegwen laid to rest and her murderer known, King Owain had relaxed the discipline among the men for the evening.

"It makes me uncomfortable too," Gareth whispered in her ear. "Especially since Evan reports that Wena's hut is empty. He saw no sign that either Erik or Cadwaladr were ever there."

Gwen turned to look up at him, her heart lifting as it always did when he was near. "What about the archer who shot at Hywel? A man was wounded and Hywel could have been killed! It's as if the king doesn't care." She gestured to the crowd of people who were surging from the hall, laughing and talking with one another.

"I wouldn't say that," Gareth said, "but he prefers to blame masterless men for that act."

"What masterless men?" Gwen said. "We don't have masterless men this close to Aber."

"Keep your voice down, Gwen."

Gwen turned at Hywel's command. He had Mari on his arm, and in the light of the torches, her face was the least pale

Gwen had seen it in days. It looked as though she had forgiven Hywel for leaving without saying goodbye.

"I'm sorry, my lord," Gwen said. "I'm worried."

Hywel tipped his head to indicate the guards. "Dearest Gwen, this inattention is by design. Those men are drinking well-watered mead."

Gwen's expression cleared. "That's a relief."

"We want to lull our murderer into a false sense of security," Hywel said.

Gareth's brow furrowed. "What are you planning, my lord?"

But Gwen understood. "You're using yourself as bait! How on earth did you convince your father to let you do it?"

Hywel grinned. "He saw the wisdom of catching this murderer sooner rather than later."

"I've already told him I don't like it." Mari squeezed Hywel around the waist with both arms. "I almost lost him already today."

"I'll be fine." Hywel patted her arm, laughing over her head at Gareth and Gwen.

"It would be tempting fate to put yourself in harm's way again," Gwen said.

"I am no more at risk than I would be riding among my guard," Hywel said. "We will have watchers through the night. Most of the villagers won't sleep anyway, so they will think nothing of the activity of our men."

Mari didn't look convinced, but she released Hywel's arm to take Gwen's. "My husband was escorting me to bed, Gwen. Will you retire with me so we don't have to be a party to their stupidity?"

"Of course." If the revelers weren't so loud and raucous, Gwen would have been asleep already.

Mari shot a glare over her shoulder. "He's lucky he almost lost his life today or he'd be sleeping in the stables tonight."

Hywel blew his wife a kiss.

Gwen nudged Mari's shoulder. "He meant well, not waking you."

"He won't make that mistake again," Mari said.

Gwen and Mari passed through the postern gate while Gareth and Hywel stopped to speak to those who guarded the door.

"Gareth will look after him," Gwen said.

"He really is most incorrigible," Mari said.

"That's why you love him."

Mari smiled, unable to stay angry. Gwen was glad to see her friend in a better mood and was about to say so when her attention was caught by a movement at the edge of the trees to the south of the castle. Two figures were standing face-to-face a hundred yards away. Both wore cloaks and were hard to see, since they were well out of the range of the torchlight and only stars shone down tonight.

Gwen watched them for a moment. It looked like they were arguing, but she couldn't hear what they were saying. Then one of the figures went down on one knee before falling to the ground. Gwen let out an involuntary gasp of air, causing Mari to swing around and look where Gwen was looking. Mari squeaked, and although she cut off the sound the moment she released it, the standing figure raised his head and looked towards Mari and Gwen.

Aber's bonfire had just been lit in the courtyard, and its light, combined with the candle-filled turnips that lit the pathway to the house, meant that whoever it was could see the women more easily than they could see him.

The figure hesitated for a moment and then whirled around to disappear into the darkness of the woods beyond.

Gwen finally found her voice. "Gareth!"

Gareth and Hywel reached them in three strides. "What is it?" Gareth took Gwen's arms and turned her so she had to look into his face. She wasn't usually this frozen in the face of danger, but it had taken hardly more three or four breaths for the whole scene to start and finish. The man on the ground wasn't moving, and Gwen feared that she'd just seen him murdered before her eyes.

Gwen didn't have the words to explain; she pulled away from Gareth and lifted the hem of her skirts to run towards the fallen man.

The others ran after her, with Hywel and Gareth passing her once they realized where she was going. The man on the ground still hadn't moved or made a noise, and both men were already crouched over the body by the time Gwen came huffing up, her hand to her belly. Mari had followed too; she leaned her shoulder into a nearby tree before bending over, her hands on her knees, to lose her dinner on the ground.

Gwen wiped Mari's mouth with a cloth that she kept folded at her waist. Gwen felt like puking herself but was managing for the moment to control the instinct. "He's dead?" she said to Gareth.

Hywel held up his palm. It was covered in blood. "He took a knife between his ribs to his heart. Did you see where the killer went?"

Gwen gestured towards the woods. "That way. He could be anywhere."

Hywel peered in the direction she'd pointed. "I can't see a thing. He could be fifty feet away or five hundred." He put his hand to the hilt of his sword and scanned the darkness under the trees.

Gareth flipped back the man's hood, and then Gwen really did fear that she was going to lose her dinner. The dead man was Brychan, Tegwen's lover.

Gareth grunted and then swept a hand across Brychan's eyes to close them. "I feel like this is my fault, at least partly."

"Gareth, no—" Gwen began.

Hywel turned to look down at Gareth. "Why is that?"

Gareth ripped open Brychan's shirt. He hadn't been wearing armor, just a coat and cloak against the night air. "If I hadn't allowed other cares to divert me until this morning, we might have found him sooner, and he might still be alive."

Hywel discarded Gareth's claim with a wave of his hand. "You know as well as I do that Brychan's death cannot be laid at your door."

"The blade was thin." Gareth wiped away the blood, which had stopped pulsing from the wound. "One thrust and he was dead. Gwen could have managed it."

Hywel glanced to where Gwen still stood beside Mari, her arm across her friend's shoulders. "Did you see who did it?"

Gwen shook her head. "Not more than his shape and not much of that."

"Anything you can tell us would be helpful," Hywel said.

"He was of average height, within an inch of Brychan. Slender, or at least not fat. Other than that, it was too dark."

Hywel's lips twisted in dismay. "Brychan must have seen, known, or done something that someone else feared." He went to Mari, who put her face into his chest, not quite sobbing but breathing deeply to control her emotions. Gwen knew how Mari felt, though she was trying to be as calm as the men.

"Yes, but who feared it?" Gareth said.

Hywel looked at Gwen over the top of Mari's head. "I thought at the time that Dewi was telling the truth about Tegwen's death as far as he knew it, and given the corroborating evidence, I still believe it." He indicated Brychan's body with a tip of his head. "This is about something different."

"The Book of Kells, do you think?" Gwen said.

Hywel shrugged. "I couldn't say. We should show Brychan's face to Godfrid. Maybe he knows him. Maybe Brychan spent time in Dublin too."

"Brychan knew his murderer," Gwen said. "I can say that for sure. They were talking before he was stabbed. Their faces were inches apart."

"As I said, one thrust and Brychan was done. He wouldn't have seen it coming," Gareth said. "A weaker man could kill a stronger one that way, simply because of the surprise."

Hywel had released Mari to crouch by the body again, and Gwen wondered if he was thinking of the way he'd murdered King Anarawd. Hywel had been able to approach him because he'd known him, and Anarawd had let his guard down. In that case, Anarawd's armor had slowed but not stopped the blade. Brychan hadn't even had that protection.

Mari was standing a few feet from the body, facing towards the postern gate. "Hywel, regardless of who did this, we can't let everyone know that Brychan was murdered in the woods. The people might panic."

Hywel groaned. "Why does it have to be Hallowmas?"

"We have to do something with the body," Gwen said. "We can't leave him here."

Mari was gathering herself after her shock. "You two put the body in the firewood shed behind the house," she said to Hywel and Gareth. "Gwen and I will act as lookouts."

At Hywel's assent, Mari ran ahead to blow out the candles on the pathway and plunge the manor into greater darkness. A few candles still flickered on the back steps to the house, and she put those out too. Gwen, meanwhile, stood sentry halfway between the woods and the house, and when it seemed all was clear, she waved the men forward. Gareth and Hywel carried the body out of the woods, but when they passed Gwen, she realized they were leaving a trail of blood on the ground behind them.

While Gareth stacked enough wood to last the household inhabitants through the night and divert them from entering the woodshed, and Mari kept watch at the corner of the house, Gwen grabbed a rake from its hook on the wall. Scraping the ground with broad sweeping motions, she worked her way back to the woods with it, churning the soil, grass, and leaves to bury as much blood as she could. Nobody would notice the blood in the dark, but it might be noticeable in the morning and, at the very least, attract wild animals in the night.

When she reached the spot where Brychan had died, she stopped, listening to the distant calls and laughter from the castle. As Gwen's eyes grew used to the darkness under the trees, the world outside the woods grew brighter—or maybe it was the sweep of stars that had appeared from behind a cloud. Gareth and Hywel disappeared inside the woodshed, and Mari now stood on the top steps to the back door, which was open, her silhouette clearly visible against the backdrop of candles she'd relit behind her.

Gwen shivered and looked away. She'd been so focused on her task that she hadn't had time to be afraid of the dark. Now she glanced towards the castle and caught movement out of the corner of her eye. Someone was lurking at the base of the wall, sidling towards the postern gate. Gwen stared at the figure for two heartbeats and then started back towards the manor. She opened her mouth to shout for Gareth, not fool enough to confront a murderer on her own. But before she could catch his attention, a great burst of laughter came from the revelers by the gate. A half-dozen drunken men spilled from it.

Unlike the guards who remained in the courtyard, these men had drunk more than enough mead. They milled around on the pathway leading to the manor house.

"Gareth!" Gwen started to run just as the cloaked figure slipped among them and through them.

Gareth and Hywel didn't appear, but Mari hurried down the steps towards her. "What's happening?"

"I saw him!" Gwen pointed towards the revelers.

"I'll get Hywel," Mari said.

"Gwen!" A drunken man stepped from the pack of men, his arms wide as if he wanted to embrace her. "Where is your husband? He has been far too serious of late, and we mean to make him join us!"

Gwen slowed and then stopped, looking past the man, whose name was Iago. "Did you see who it was who passed by here just now? He wore a cloak and came from over there." Gwen pointed to the wall to the south of the gate.

Iago spun on his heel and waved a hand at his fellows. "It's just us here, right boys? I didn't see anything."

Gareth and Hywel hurried up. "Is everything all right?" Gareth said.

"Gareth!" Iago clapped a hand on Gareth's shoulder. "You're not drinking!"

"And you, Iago, have drunk far too much." Gareth shook him off and guided Gwen through the crowd to the postern gate. "Mari said you saw the killer. Where did he go?"

"Through here, I'm sure of it," Gwen said. "Iago and his friends are too drunk to notice anything but their own amusement."

Two men stood sentry on either side of the doorway. One of them, thankfully, was Rhodri. He'd been on the beach the day before with Gwen. It was his son who'd discovered Cadwaladr's coin pendant.

"A man, hooded and cloaked, came through here just now," Gareth said. "Did you see him?"

"We've seen dozens, my lord, both in and out since you passed this way earlier." Rhodri's brows came together. "I haven't noticed anyone who shouldn't be here, but I don't know the names of everyone at Aber tonight either."

Gareth cursed under his breath. "He belongs here; he must." He gazed around the courtyard, his hands on his hips.

The bonfire had been piled to the height of a man, with the flames shooting higher than that. At least a hundred people were gathered around it, with more on the margins by the craft halls and barracks. Gwen tried to see individual faces instead of the firelight. Then she noticed a cloth bundle by the corner of the stables.

"What's this?" She held up a cloak, thin and brown with blotchy stains in places that someone had wadded up and discarded. Looking at it ruefully, she handed it to Gareth, who cursed again. The cloak was damp, but in the firelight Gwen couldn't tell if the moisture was blood or merely water from the puddle it had been lying in.

"It's rough and cheap," Gwen said.

"It could belong to anyone—from the killer to a villager too drunk to notice how cold he now is." Gareth pounded a fist on one of the posts that held up the stable's roof. "What is going on here?"

"Did Brychan have anything on him that helps us?" Gwen said.

Gareth shrugged. "It's always awkward to go through a dead man's clothes like a petty thief, but Hywel and I did the best we could in the dim light and found nothing of interest. What Brychan knew was in his head."

"And here I thought Hywel was going to be the one in danger tonight," Gwen said.

"I'm concerned now for you and Mari." Gareth tossed the cloak onto a towering stack of wood beside the blacksmith forge. "He knows you saw him, but he got away, and in this crowd, the only way we're going to discover his name is by sheer luck."

"We're getting close," Gwen said, trying to be reassuring. "He's slipped up and killed someone else. He'll know that we've grabbed the end of the thread and only need to tug at it for his world to unravel."

"I won't say you're wrong," Gareth said. "Isn't that always the way of it? As time goes by and more people become involved, the killer's plan gets away from him and spirals out of control."

"There you are!" Godfrid detached himself from some onlookers standing near the gatehouse and strode up to them, grinning. At the sight of their serious faces, however, he faltered.

"What's happened?"

"We have another murder, and we don't know why," Gwen said. "Brychan, Tegwen's lover, is dead."

Godfrid's expression darkened. "My men and I will aid you in any way we can."

"We'll have to ask the same questions we've been asking all over again: if anyone saw anything unusual; if anyone hasn't been where they're supposed to be," Gareth said.

Godfrid snorted. "It's Hallowmas. Nobody is where he's supposed to be."

"We'd better get started, then," Gwen said.

"Not you, though." Gwen found herself being spun around by her husband and directed towards the manor house. "You are for bed."

Gwen didn't dig in her heels, but she didn't come willingly either. It was very unlike Gareth to tell her what to do so determinedly. "You can't think I'm going to sleep? I just saw a man murdered, and you've hidden his body in the woodshed."

"I know, Gwen." Gareth's voice came low in her ear. "But you could try. Mari needs you. And I need you safe. We have a killer running loose inside Aber. I would feel better knowing you were safe outside the walls."

Gwen swallowed down her protest. She liked being involved, and she liked knowing what was happening, but she could just as well skip asking those same questions over again to the drunken inhabitants of Aber Castle. She allowed Gareth to escort her to their room. Hywel met them at the front door, a look of relief crossing his face at the sight of Gwen. He practically pushed her through the doorway to their room. Mari was leaning over the basin in the corner.

"You are a very bad man," Gwen said.

Hywel smirked. "Get her to sleep if you can; try to sleep yourself."

"We won't be long, Gwen," Gareth said. "It is less than two hours to midnight, after which everyone will be even more drunk and incapable of answering our questions."

Hywel scoffed. "In another hour, we're going to be the only ones standing."

24

Hywel

He was a coward. He knew it. And Gwen was a saint. Hywel had no trouble accepting their opposite natures and refused to feel guilty about the look Gwen shot him as he closed the door to the corridor and left the manor house with Gareth. Someone had already relit the candles along the walkway, and the light led them back into Aber.

Godfrid met them inside the gate. "The women are safe?"

That question had Hywel spinning on one heel, grabbing Rhodri's arm, and marching back down the pathway with him. "I need you to stand guard at the manor house."

"My post—" Rhodri didn't exactly stutter, but he was looking at Hywel with a concerned expression.

"Too much has happened during the last two days for me to allow Gwen and Mari to stay in the house without a guard. I need you to stand watch until Gareth and I return."

"Of course," Rhodri said, no longer protesting. "It will be my pleasure."

Hywel returned to where Gareth and Godfrid waited, listening to the tail end of Gareth's description of Brychan's death.

Godfrid was staring at him with bemused horror. "Nothing like this ever happens in Dublin."

Hywel had to laugh. "I very much doubt that."

Gareth then found another sentry to replace Rhodri, one of the few who wasn't completely drunk. Meanwhile, King Owain's man, Adda, appeared, hovering in the entrance to the stables, his eyes searching. When he saw Hywel, he hurried over. "My lord—" He cleared his throat. "We have a problem."

Godfrid's look of continued disbelief was priceless, but Hywel ignored it. "Tell me."

"It's Dewi, the man you captured this afternoon. He won't wake," Adda said.

"No." Two dead men within a single hour was more than Hywel could take.

Gareth stepped in. "Show us."

Adda ushered them towards the back of the stables to a rear room that doubled as Aber's prison when needed. The room hadn't changed since Gareth had spent time in it last year: ten feet on a side with hay scattered across the floor and smelling potently of manure and horse.

Dewi lay facing the wall on a pallet, an improvement from when Gareth had been incarcerated here. With the feeling of having been here before, Hywel put his hand to Dewi's shoulder and rolled him onto his back. His eyes were closed as if in sleep. Gareth put his fingers to Dewi's neck. Hywel expected him to shake his head, but then Gareth grabbed both sides of Dewi's head and rocked him back and forth. "Wake up!"

"He's alive?" Godfrid said from behind them.

"Barely!" Gareth threw a look over his shoulder at Adda. "Get the healer in here."

"I'll get a bucket of water," Godfrid said.

Gareth slapped Dewi's cheeks, and when Dewi moaned, Hywel helped Gareth move him into a sitting position. Godfrid reappeared with a full bucket of water and an empty one as well, and then Adda returned with the healer. Daff wasn't Wena, but Hywel knew him to be capable. Fortunately, Daff also wasn't a man to overdrink.

"What happened to him, my lord?" Daff said.

"I don't know," Hywel said. "He won't wake."

Daff sniffed near Dewi's mouth, as Hywel had done to the guard Madog, mumbled under his breath, and then sprinkled herbs into the cup of water Godfrid handed him. Daff gestured to Dewi's food tray. "Is that what he ate and drank?"

"We think so," Gareth said.

"I'll check it after we get him awake. I'm going to guess that someone tampered with his food, which means we'll need him to puke it up." Daff eyed the prince. "You might want to step back."

Hywel didn't wait to be told twice. He'd been present when a similar treatment had been given to Gareth after Cadwaladr had poisoned him. Daff gestured to Gareth. "Hold his mouth open."

Gareth obeyed, and Daff poured in the liquid, forcing it down Dewi's throat. The guard came awake enough to cough and sputter, and then in a rush he vomited the contents of his stomach into the empty bucket Godfrid shoved in front of him.

Stepping away while Daff administered another dose, Hywel moved to where Adda hovered in the doorway, his hands working nervously in front of him. "Have you been on duty all evening?"

"I came on after Tegwen's funeral, but he was fine then. I'd swear to it!"

"Has he had any visitors?" Hywel said.

Adda nodded his head eagerly. "At least a dozen."

Hywel exchanged a puzzled look with Gareth, who'd overheard. "Why?" Gareth said.

"To mock." Adda raised his shoulders in an exaggerated shrug. "I didn't let any of them but Prince Cadwaladr inside."

Hywel's hands went to the top of his head. "When was this?"

"Right after I first came on duty," Adda said. "Did I do wrong?"

"No, Adda," Gareth said. "You could hardly have gainsaid a prince."

Gareth was right, but that didn't stop Hywel from grinding his teeth.

Godfrid had been following their conversation with a furrowed brow. "Were any of the men mine?"

"Several," Adda said, "though I couldn't tell you their names."

Daff straightened from his crouch beside Dewi's retching form. "When was he brought food?"

"After I came on," Adda said.

"Who brought the tray?" Gareth said.

"One of the serving boys from the kitchen," Adda said.

"His name?" Gareth said.

"I don't know, my lord." Adda shrugged, as Hywel knew he would. Adda was an old soldier who prided himself on his elevated station. He didn't trouble himself with the names of his inferiors if he didn't have to know them.

"What do you think it was, Daff?" Hywel said.

"Not poppy," Daff said, "nor Mandrake, I don't think. Belladonna is my best guess, which is why the emetic should work. He was very fortunate you discovered him when you did, Adda. Who would want him dead?"

"Erik," Godfrid said instantly. "Dewi was the only one who could testify to his wrongdoing."

"Erik would have had a difficult time moving around the castle without being recognized and stopped, even in this crowd," Gareth said.

"Five years have passed since Tegwen's disappearance," Hywel said, "and while Dewi was discreet enough not to allow word of her fate to get out, he could have talked to someone he shouldn't have since the discovery of her body."

"Perhaps he had other secrets," Gareth said. "Perhaps we haven't asked the right questions yet."

"We certainly asked some of them if this is the result." Hywel turned back to Adda. "Did you overhear Dewi's conversation with my uncle?"

"No, my lord," Adda said. "He closed the door behind him, and they spoke softly."

Gareth and Godfrid both growled at the same time. Dewi, meanwhile, moaned and clutched his stomach.

"What do you say?" Gareth said to Daff.

"He'll live, but it may be morning before he's coherent," Daff said.

"We'll leave him until dawn." Hywel looked at Godfrid and then at Gareth, noting the deep circles under his captain's eyes. "Dewi isn't going anywhere."

"I will stay with him in case he has a relapse," Daff said.

"Keep everyone away," Gareth said to Adda. "Nobody is to hear of Dewi's fate until the morning. Is that clear?"

"Yes, my lord," Adda said.

"That includes my uncle," Hywel said.

Adda ducked a nod.

"We'll cover up the window in the cell so nobody can see inside either," Gareth said.

Hywel led the way out of the stables, stopping to observe the dancing around the bonfire with detachment. "Dewi was poisoned, Brychan knifed."

"And you were ambushed," Gareth said. "Our murderer has many talents."

"Or he's panicked and tying up loose ends." Hywel cursed. "If my uncle is involved more than we already know, I am going to kill him."

Neither man blanched at Hywel's invective. Instead, Gareth rested a hand on Hywel's shoulder. "Right now, what I'm most concerned about is all of *us* living through the night."

"Right." Hywel put two fingers to his temple, thinking. "Gareth, speak to the workers in the kitchen and then come find me. My father must know what has transpired."

"Yes, my lord," Gareth said.

"Godfrid, would you mind inquiring of your men if they saw anything unusual tonight?" Hywel said.

"Of course." Godfrid put his heels together. "What are you going to do?"

"I'm going to have a chat with my uncle," Hywel said.

Even at nearly midnight, the hall was full of revelers. The long tables had been pushed to the side, and Meilyr was playing a lively tune while a hundred people danced, both in the hall and outside in the courtyard around the fire. The fire in the hall was out, and as soon as the chapel bell tolled midnight, it would be relit with flames from the bonfire. Hywel's father sat resplendent in the full regalia of his station as King of Gwynedd, Rhun at his side. It looked as if Cristina had retired for the night. Hywel knew from experience that the gathering would descend into debauchery within the hour, and he wasn't surprised that she didn't want to be here to see it.

His uncle sat near the end of the dais and even as Hywel approached, he poured a full cup of mead and drank it down.

Hywel pulled up a spare chair at the end of the table and sat. "Greetings, Uncle."

Cadwaladr shot him a sour look. "What do you want?"

His uncle had never been a happy drunk, so Hywel wasn't surprised to find him morose tonight. Given that, Hywel decided to address him straightforwardly. "Why did you visit Dewi tonight?"

"Who?"

"Dewi. The man who ran from Aber, who is presently residing in the cell at the back of the stables."

"Oh, him," Cadwaladr said.

Hywel waited a beat.

Cadwaladr drank what looked like another half flagon of mead. "I wanted to know where his friend had got to."

"What friend?" Hywel said.

Cadwaladr gazed at Hywel, but his expression didn't hold defiance as much as puzzlement. "You know, the one he ran off with."

"Erik, the half-Dane?" Hywel said.

Cadwaladr snapped his fingers. "That one."

"Why did you want to find Erik?"

"I didn't."

Hywel felt like lowering his head to the table. This was as bad as interviewing old Wynn. His uncle raised his hands above his head, clapping in time to the music and the dancers as the torch that would light the hearth fire wended its way through the crowd. A huge cheer went up as the carefully stacked logs in the fireplace were lit.

"Then why did you go to see Dewi?" Hywel said, waving a hand to gain Cadwaladr's attention.

"You had failed to get Erik's whereabouts out of him," Cadwaladr said. "I thought I'd try."

"Why would you do such a thing?"

Cadwaladr's brow furrowed. "You aren't the only one who can help your father, you know. Since you have been occupied with the Tegwen investigation, I thought I would see what I could discover regarding the Book of Kells."

Hywel stared at his uncle. "My God."

Cadwaladr smirked into his mead.

Hywel rose to his feet, shaking his head. Cadwaladr's story put to rest any accusation of wrongdoing regarding either Dewi, Erik, or whomever Dai and Llelo had seen him meet in Wena's hut last night. He was searching for the Book of Kells. That quest could lay a false front over any number of sins.

"Where are you going?" With his last long gulp, his uncle had gone from self-satisfied to bleary.

Hywel wasn't about to tell his uncle that he was going to speak to the king. "To bed," he said instead.

Cadwaladr raised his cup. "Daw haul ar fryn." *Comes the sun to the hill*, meaning that things would be better in the morning.

Hywel shook his head in disbelief. They could hardly be worse.

25

Gwen

The door to their room burst open, and Dai and Llelo bounded inside. "It's already too big to put out!"

Gwen sat up, staring wildly at the boys, whose shapes were silhouetted in the doorway against the flames behind them. Both Hywel and Gareth were on their feet in an instant, pulling on their breeches and shoving their feet into boots. Gwen helped Mari out of bed, while Hywel slammed the door shut behind the boys, though not before a billow of smoke had followed them into the room.

"I managed one good look. The flames are already scaling the back wall." Hywel crossed the floor to the window.

Gareth swung the shutter wide. "I'll go out first and catch the girls. It's hardly a drop at all."

Gwen thanked whatever foresight had prompted Taran to give them one of the rooms on the first floor. But the manor housed other guests, who may well have gone to bed late, drunk, and would be hard to wake. Gwen didn't hear footsteps on the floor above her. She prayed that some of them hadn't found their bed at all tonight and were sleeping safe at a table in the hall, their heads on their arms.

In the few moments it took for Gareth to hop over the windowsill and drop to the ground, Gwen grabbed the dress she'd worn yesterday, her cloak, and her boots, and threw them out the window, followed by Gareth's sword. Gareth was tall enough to still be able to see inside, and he held out his hands to Gwen, who scrambled over the sill and into his arms. Gareth set her down and immediately caught Mari, who followed close behind.

Gwen didn't know that her heart had ever pounded so hard. She ran to the postern gate, screaming to the soldiers who guarded it, finding it incomprehensible that they could not have noticed the danger only a few dozen yards away. Finally, a man poked his head through the doorway. Gwen was relieved to see it was Rhodri, still awake even at this late hour.

"Raise the alarm! Fire! Fire!" Encompassing the danger in a single glance, Rhodri ran across the courtyard towards the gatehouse and barracks.

Fire was the danger of any dwelling, which was why the kitchen was often kept separate from the main buildings in a castle or in the lower level of a keep where the walls could be made of stone or dirt. Gwen tried to calm her breathing, resting in the doorway of the postern gate. She understood, now, why nobody in the courtyard had noticed the smoke: the bonfire was still blazing, although few people remained around it.

At Rhodri's call, every man who could still stand poured out of the great hall and the barracks, passing Gwen at the gate.

Rhodri returned too and put a hand on her shoulder. "Are you all right?"

Gwen nodded, still breathing hard but less panicked than before.

It was a matter of a few moments to collect the necessary buckets; Hywel organized the beginnings of a human chain from the creek that flowed to the east of the manor house. With each new arrival, the line grew longer and the buckets of water flowed from hand to hand with greater speed. The hope now, given how quickly the fire had spread, was to prevent the fire from spreading to the surrounding trees or the castle. The manor house itself had been a lost cause before Gareth had set Gwen on the ground.

Gareth came out of the front door with a woman hung over his shoulder. He'd thrown a soaking wet blanket over them both, and Gwen tried not to cry after the fact at the danger he'd been in. Gareth laid the woman on the ground, and Gwen ran to her. She started coughing and trying to sit up.

"That's the last," Gareth said.

"How many—?" Gwen choked back the question, gazing up into Gareth's face.

"We got everyone out," Gareth said. "Several of the rooms were empty."

Gwen bent her head, hugely relieved, and then Gareth put a hand on her shoulder. "I need to see to the security of Aber."

"Could the fire be merely a diversion?" Gwen said.

"That's what I intend to find out if I can. Stay here." He was off at a run to the postern gate.

Llelo and Dai were standing in the creek, at the start of one of the lines of people passing buckets to put out the fire. Gwen was about to join their group when her father puffed over to her and threw a blanket around her shoulders. "Are you all right?"

"I'm fine. Really, I'm fine," Gwen said. "We should help with the fire."

"You'll catch your death of cold out here," Meilyr said.

"I have clothes somewhere." Gwen spied her small pile of belongings by a tree thirty feet from the manor house. Mari sat next to them, pulling on one boot. "Where's Gwalchmai?"

Meilyr pointed with his chin to the line of water carriers. Gwalchmai had joined Llelo and Dai.

"If you see to them, I'll join you in a moment," Gwen said.

Meilyr grunted his assent and moved off. Gwen knew that he loved her, but she also knew that Gwalchmai's welfare was paramount in her father's eyes. She no longer begrudged him that fact, and since she was well, she didn't waste any time feeling disgruntled at coming in second yet again. And to be fair, he had brought her a blanket first.

"Take the blanket, Mari," Gwen said when she reached her friend, who still sat under the tree. Mari held Hywel's sword in her lap, while Gareth's leaned against the tree behind her.

"What are you going to do?" Mari handed Gwen her dress.

"Help."

Mari put the sword aside to assist Gwen with her clothes, but after she dressed, Gwen stopped her from following her to the creek. "You stay here and rest. Let me do this for both of us."

Mari subsided without further protest, indicating how unwell she really felt. With one last glance back at her friend, Gwen headed off to join the lines of water carriers, only to find that that King Owain himself had taken a spot two people ahead of her. At the sight of Gwen, he motioned for the men between them to change places with him, which they did without question.

"A bad business, Gwen," he said.

"Llelo and Dai woke us," Gwen said. "If not for them, we might not have escaped."

"Are you sure you should be here?" he said.

"I'll stop if I feel unwell, but every hand helps," Gwen said.

King Owain nodded, still looking grim. "The people are worried. Some are saying that Tegwen lies restlessly." He leaned closer to Gwen. "I spoke at length with Hywel and Gareth before they retired last night."

Gwen was glad she didn't have to be the one to update the king on the latest events. "Ghosts don't start fires, any more than a ghost murdered Brychan or poisoned Dewi. Next they'll be saying that Bran has risen from the dead to walk with her."

"I feel responsible," King Owain said. "It was I who directed you to speak to Brychan but then didn't order a watch set on him so we would know where he was at all times."

Gwen grabbed another bucket from her neighbor on the other side and handed it to the king. Her arm was growing tired, and the muscles in her belly were aching, but she wasn't going to stop now, especially if King Owain was willing to confide in her. "You were distracted—"

"I've been distracted for months," King Owain said. "I feel at times as if my kingdom is slipping through my fingers."

That was far too frank a statement for her to reply to, and she wondered if King Owain was still a little drunk from the evening's festivities.

"You don't say his name but I know what you're thinking," King Owain said.

Gwen swallowed. "Sire?"

"You wonder if my brother has had more of a hand in these events than he's said or we've discovered. Tomorrow, with the holy day over, he will return to Merionydd for a long winter of idleness."

"Perhaps you could find something to occupy him?" Gwen said. "Stephen and Maud are still at each other's throats."

King Owain guffawed under his breath. "A little war is in order, do you think? One that my brother can sink his teeth into?"

"I don't like war," Gwen said. "I fear for my husband and our friends, but if Cadwaladr is searching for the Book of Kells to use as leverage for his own meeting with Gilbert de Clare, it is a short hop from there to speculating that he wants more than Ceredigion."

"Bran was plotting against my life and sleeping with my wife," King Owain said.

Gwen looked away.

King Owain noticed. "Hywel told me. I find a deep well of anger in my belly at all that has happened in my kingdom that I knew nothing about, and it makes me concerned about what else I don't know."

Gwen was grateful that she had been living in the south when Tegwen disappeared and that Gareth hadn't yet joined Hywel's company. Those events had completely passed her by. She handed another bucket to the king.

"Rhun and Hywel—"

"They are fine sons," King Owain said, "but though Rhun will be king after me, he lacks the suspicious mind that a king needs. I am counting on Hywel to protect him when my time comes."

"You know he will," Gwen said. "But you don't have to worry about that for a long time to come."

"One never knows," the king said. "When Gareth and Hywel return to Ceredigion after the Christmas feast, I expect you to remain at Aber. I cannot have all three of you departing at the same time. Hywel will arrange for his informants to report to you in his absence."

Gwen's surprise was such that she stopped moving, and the man beside her prodded her into action with the edge of a bucket. "But Gareth—"

"Gareth will not object when I tell him that this duty will keep you out of greater trouble," the king said.

Gwen swallowed hard. She didn't know how it had happened, but it seemed that she'd been promoted.

The conversation had her worried, however. The king seemed particularly maudlin tonight, perhaps not surprising given the death around them, but an uncomfortable sensation started in her belly that he'd had a premonition of his own death. She would mention it to Hywel at the first opportunity.

"When you speak to my son, tell him that it would be better for him to swallow his pride and admit what he doesn't know than to lose everything we've gained in Ceredigion."

Gwen gaped at the king. He couldn't have read her mind, could he? Before she could ask what he was talking about, Gwen felt a drop of water plop onto the top of her head. At first she thought it was spray from a swung bucket, but then another drop came. And then another. She held out a hand. Rain splattered into it. King Owain tipped back his head, relieved laughter escaping his lips.

"Pardon the ramblings of an old man, Gwen. We will not falter now. God is on our side."

26

Gareth

The hall was crowded for the last celebratory meal at Aber Castle, with the bonus of yet another strange event to gossip over. The villagers from the surrounding area, even if they had slept at home the night before, had come to help with the cleanup of the fire and stayed to celebrate Calan Gaeaf. King Owain had insisted that the festival be celebrated properly. Gareth was in wholehearted agreement, even if it felt like they were spitting into the wind.

The guards had left the front door open, since people went in and out of it in a constant stream anyway, and the press and stench of people inside was already a little too much. They had spent all morning in prayer in the chapel, thankful to have survived Hallowmas with no more deaths. The manor house lay in ruins and the body had been burned beyond recognition. With the crowds dispersing by the end of the day, or at the latest by tomorrow, Gareth felt his opportunity for finding the answers to the rest of his questions slipping away. He glanced up to the high table where Hywel and Godfrid sat beside each other. As an honored guest, Godfrid could remain as long as he liked, but he would be leaving soon too, on his quest to find Ottar's son, Thorfin, and the Book of Kells.

Gareth's eyes narrowed as he registered Cadwaladr's absence from the high table. The man always wanted to be at the center of attention, but he liked to mingle with the common folk at times because it made him look magnanimous. Gareth—and many others—knew that to be a pretense, but Cadwaladr was the brother of the king and because King Owain tolerated him, everyone else had to too. Gareth cast his eyes around the hall, looking for the wayward prince; he was about to rise to his feet to better see over the top of others' heads when Gwen put a hand on his arm. "Are you all right?"

"Of course. Why?" he said.

"You've been ripping at that meat with your teeth as if it's someone's throat, and now you've forgotten about your meal altogether."

"I was looking for Prince Cadwaladr." Gareth gave a slight laugh. "I'm sorry. I realize I'm not good company right now."

"How about we take a walk?" she said. "I need some air too, and it will give you a chance to look for him outside. Perhaps Dewi is now capable of speech."

"You know me so well." Gareth got to his feet and helped Gwen to hers. Cristina had kindly loaned Gwen one of her gowns, a deep burgundy which set off her dark hair and eyes. "I wish one of the kitchen workers had noticed someone who didn't belong there last night."

"But they didn't," Gwen said. "They're run off their feet and have been for days. Besides, it seems more and more likely that the murderer is someone we know—someone who belongs at Aber and wouldn't be noticed."

"The murderer did return to the castle," Gareth agreed.

Gwen tipped her head so she could look into his face. "Is that why you're searching for Cadwaladr?"

"Cadwaladr is a slippery bastard," Gareth said. "Besides, I need something else to think about besides Bran and Tegwen and everything we still don't know about their deaths."

"This isn't a failure, Gareth," Gwen said. "Bran killed Tegwen. We do know that."

"I am trying to believe it was an accident," Gareth said.

"It doesn't matter now," Gwen said. "They're both dead."

Gareth scowled. "He could have done a hundred things with her body instead of hiding it in Wena's hut and putting out that she'd run off with a Dane. That is not the act of an innocent man."

"You need to let Tegwen go," Gwen said. "That's what last night was for."

"If only the murderer had known we were hours from closing the investigation," Gareth said. "Instead, Dewi and Erik flee Aber, someone shoots at Hywel, Brychan is murdered, Dewi is poisoned, and the manor house set afire, all within the space of a single day. Now we have more questions than when I awoke yesterday morning. If we already know Bran killed Tegwen, who is behind these other incidents?"

"We'll solve this case like we solve every other. By asking questions, like you and Hywel have been doing." Gwen canted her head. "And hopefully, with a bit more luck than we've had so far."

"Brychan didn't have any luck," Gareth said.

"You are sour this morning," Gwen said.

Gareth grumbled under his breath. "A killer is walking free. I can't breathe easy."

They stood on the top step to the keep, and Gareth felt Gwen take a deep breath beside him. The air was moist and warm. More rain would come soon, but thankfully, it had held off during the worship service for All Saints' Day, since the chapel hadn't been large enough to hold everyone, and the residents of Aber had overflowed into the courtyard. Gareth and Gwen had found places inside, but looking at Gwen's pale face, Gareth wished he'd paid more attention to her and had found a better place to pray, or perhaps skipped the service entirely.

He took her arm, and they headed away from the hall, looking for a quiet place to be together.

"I keep seeing that man with Brychan, watching him fall," Gwen said. "People are saying that Aber is haunted by all the deaths, but someone real started that fire and someone real poisoned Dewi." She sighed.

Gareth had already talked to Hywel about taking Gwen home to Anglesey tomorrow. Hywel had said that he would bring Mari and leave her there with Gwen, before the two men set out to help Godfrid with his quest. Hywel, it seemed, intended to come along on that adventure too.

Evan appeared in the doorway to the stables. "Dewi's awake, my lord."

"Sir Gareth!"

Gareth turned at the shout. The drunken soldier from the previous night, Iago, stood underneath the gatehouse, waving his arm above his head urgently. Torn between two duties, Gareth gave Gwen a quizzical look.

She released his arm. "Go. I'll talk to Dewi with Evan."

"I'll find you after I see what Iago wants," Gareth said.

Gwen and Evan disappeared into the darkness of the stables, and Gareth loped towards the gatehouse, anxious to clear up whatever this was so he could get back to Gwen. Then Gareth saw who was beside Iago and pulled up ten yards from the gatehouse, his mouth dropping open in surprise.

"Hello, Sir Gareth." The woman before him smiled. "I see you have been keeping well."

"Prioress Nest!" Gareth caught the arms of his old mentor, who was standing with a young companion, also a nun. Both wore the heavy undyed robes and head coverings of their vocation. "What are you doing here?"

"I fear the community you so lovingly protected is no longer, my friend," she said. "We came to grief, finally, last year. Those of us who survived found refuge with a community of women at Conwy."

Gareth's stomach clenched with a momentary guilt that he hadn't been there to protect them. Nest gave him a compassionate look. "Gareth."

He shook himself. "You've been so close all this time? Why haven't you contacted me before?"

Nest narrowed her eyes at him. "We are pledged to a life of quiet contemplation. I would never have come to Aber at all if it wasn't so urgent." Then she frowned. "Where are your manners, sir?"

"Of course, of course!" Gareth accepted his chastisement with bowed head, pleased that she was here at all. He gestured towards the great hall. "Come inside. There is plenty of food for everyone. King Owain has not scrimped on the feast, despite the difficulties of the last few days."

Nest indicated the girl next to her. "This is Bronwen, a novice."

Bronwen was carrying a large, heavy package in her arms. Gareth looked at it curiously but didn't ask its purpose, just held out his arms to take it from her. Nest shook her head and grasped it instead. "Patience."

She seemed intent on having her own way and strode up the steps to the keep in front of Gareth. Once inside, she went directly to the end of a nearby table where there was enough space for them to sit. Iago had come with them, and Gareth held up a hand to indicate that he should wait by the door in case he was needed.

Nest didn't take a trencher for herself or for Bronwen but swept the remains of the previous diners' meals aside with one arm. Then she set the package on the table between them. "I heard you were looking for this."

Gareth stared at the wrapped package and then up at Nest.

"We learned of the arrival of three Danish ships at Aber almost before they landed on your shore," Nest said. "My contacts assured me the Danes had been welcomed into Aber Castle, so I knew it was time to find you."

"I don't understand." Gareth's head felt thick and slow, like it was stuffed with day-old porridge.

"A man brought it to us." Nest pinched her lips together as if fighting back amusement. "Not that bringing it to us or leaving it with us came about of his own volition. A fisherman found him at the bottom of his longboat, the only survivor of a storm."

"When was this?" Gareth said.

"The end of September," Nest said. "The storm was a bad one."

"I wouldn't know," Gareth said. "I was in Ceredigion with Prince Hywel."

"I don't know what happened to the rest of the men who sailed with him, but the man was alone with few possessions." Nest put her hand gently on the package. "This was clutched to his chest, wrapped in many layers of oilskin and sealed tight. The fisherman brought it and him to us. Unfortunately, the man himself never woke."

"You're telling me that this is the Book of Kells?" Gareth said, still disbelieving. "Why didn't you come to me sooner?"

"That's the second time you've asked me that," Nest said reprovingly. "I was waiting for a sign that would direct me towards the proper course of action."

Gareth rubbed at his chin. "And you found that sign now?"

"The man who stole it was a Dane, and Danes have come to Aber looking for it. It is not mine to keep, and I cannot return it to Kells. But you can."

"The Dane who came to Aber wants to return it too," Gareth said. "He is a good man."

"He is a Dane." Nest's voice hardened. "Too many houses such as mine have been sacked by Danes for me to ever rejoice when I see their sails on the water. We learned to run and hide a long time ago." Then she shot Gareth a thoughtful look. "Though there have been times when fighting seems to have been the proper course of action."

"I will introduce you to Godfrid, and perhaps you will feel differently." Gareth smiled at Nest's icy and skeptical expression. "Allow me at the very least to introduce you to King Owain. This is news we can all celebrate." He rose to his feet, his heart lighter than it had been in days. It was one mystery solved, and he hadn't even had to leave Aber to do it.

"Wait." Nest caught Gareth's wrist. "There's one more thing I must speak to you about. I understand that you buried Tegwen ferch Cadwallon yesterday."

Gareth sank slowly back down to his bench. "Yes, we did. Did you know her?"

"Not I," Nest said, "but our order had dealings with her."

Gareth's mind had been full of his good news and its consequences. The finding of the Book of Kells coupled with

Thorfin's death was going to rock Dublin to its very foundation. But now he focused again on Nest. "How so?"

"A few days before she disappeared, she came to us. Our convent lies near Bryn Euryn. She asked about joining our community."

"Tegwen wanted to become a nun?" Gareth said. That seemed the least likely thing he'd heard about her.

Nest gave him a sad smile. "She said she did. I thought you ought to know."

"Thank you for telling us," Gareth said. "Though I suppose the investigation is over now. We have a witness who attests that her husband killed her."

"She loved her husband." Bronwen spoke for the first time, and from her wide-eyed look, seemed shocked to have spoken at all. "But she was afraid of him too."

"Do you know that for certain?" Gareth said.

Bronwen nodded. "She told me so when she visited. We were of an age, so I was allowed to show her around the convent. She claimed to know a great secret about him but wouldn't speak of it to me—" Bronwen glanced at Nest, who nodded reassuringly for her to continue. "The leader of our order would have taken her in right then and there, but she insisted she had to go back. We never saw her again ..."

"I'm sure she was grateful to have had someone to talk to," Nest said soothingly.

Bronwen nodded. "That's what I said to the other man who came around asking about her."

Gareth took in an audible breath of surprise. "What other man?"

"It was after she disappeared," Bronwen said, clearly surprised at his surprise. "Long after."

"Who was this?" Gareth said. "Was it her husband, Bran?"

"No, no. Not her husband, someone else," the girl said. "Older."

"You didn't tell me about this." Nest fixed her eyes on Bronwen.

"I just remembered," Bronwen said, showing a glimmer of spine by not wilting under her superior's glare.

"When was this?" Gareth said.

Bronwen's chin wrinkled up as she thought. "Maybe ... three years ago?"

"Did the man give you his name?" Gareth said.

Bronwen shook her head, her expression uncertain. "I'm sure he did, but I don't remember it." Then her face brightened. "But you can ask him yourself. He's right there." She pointed towards the high table. "It's man on the end."

Bronwen was pointing to Gruffydd, Tegwen's grandfather. Gruffydd had been talking with Taran. Bronwen's gesture must have caught his eye because he looked in their direction and saw Gareth staring back. Gruffydd put a hand on Taran's shoulder, mouthing apologies, rose to his feet, and almost before Gareth could blink, had disappeared through the doorway to the kitchens at the back of the hall.

"What's wrong, Gareth?" Nest said.

Luck had reared its reluctant head at last. "We need to raise the alarm," Gareth said, though Nest would have no idea what he was talking about. "It was Gruffydd all along!"

27

Gwen

Dewi's chin stuck out, his expression mutinous and defiant. "I don't know what you're talking about."

"I need to know who else you told about Tegwen's disappearance and death," Gwen said, "or anything about what you witnessed the night she died. Someone poisoned you last night, and I can't believe it was for no reason."

Evan and Goch, who had recovered from the blow to the head Dewi had given him, had dragged him out of the stables into the daylight. They set him on the same stump by the kitchen door that Gwen had sat on two days ago to talk to Gareth and Hywel. Dewi's hands weren't tied, but he had no weapons, and his face was drawn and white from his ordeal. According to the healer, he'd been sick until he had nothing left inside him and had lain shivering and feverish until dawn.

This time, Gwen had banished the kitchen boy to chop his wood elsewhere. The only reason they were out here at all rather than in the cell at the back of the stables was because it reeked of sickness—among other things—and Gwen's stomach couldn't take it.

"I didn't tell anyone!" Dewi brushed his lank black hair out of his face. It had come undone from the tie at the base of his neck. "Do you think I'm a fool?"

Gwen did, but she tried not to let her skepticism show on her face. He'd obviously kept Bran's secret well enough to have survived this long. "What about Erik? Could he have talked? We're trying to figure out why someone tried to kill you."

"Erik wouldn't have talked," Dewi said, "and he wouldn't poison me either."

"He's long gone anyway," Goch said.

Fugitives had been known to double back, but Erik would know that they were searching for him. He couldn't show his face in Aber; thus, Gwen had to agree with Goch. At the very least, Erik didn't murder Brychan and then retreat *into* Aber.

"Particularly in the last few days, did you mention to anyone anything about the events of that night?" Evan said. "You knew Tegwen. You could have let slip that you'd been near Aber with Bran around the time she disappeared."

Dewi screwed up his face in a parody of thought. "No, I didn't."

"You could have mentioned it accidently, perhaps to impress a girl you were wooing?" Goch said.

Dewi made as if to dismiss the question, and then his brow furrowed. "Well, I talked to my half-brother, of course."

Evan leaned in. "When was this?"

"Moreover, who is your half-brother?" Gwen said.

"The first time was years after Tegwen died," Dewi said, answering Evan's question first. "It can't be important now."

"What did you tell him?" Evan said.

"He said that he knew Tegwen before her marriage to Bran and wondered what had happened to her. I didn't tell him that she'd died," Dewi added hurriedly, "only that I thought there was more to the story. I might have mentioned that I saw her not long before she disappeared, but he knew I worked for Bran, so why wouldn't I have seen her? How could this be important now?"

Gwen put her face into Dewi's. "Who. Is. Your. Brother?"

Dewi looked around as if expecting to see him in the courtyard. "His name is Brychan. We didn't see each other for years while I was in Rhos and he was in Dolwyddelan and Bala, but then we reconnected by chance in Ceredigion during the wars there and then again a few years ago after he returned to Gwynedd."

Gwen knew her mouth had fallen open. She didn't know what to say.

"Dewi doesn't know, Gwen," Evan said.

Dewi glanced at Evan. "Know what?"

Gwen put her hand on Dewi's shoulder and tried to speak as gently as she could. "Brychan was murdered last night."

Dewi goggled at Gwen. "What? He can't have been! Why would anyone do that?"

"Did you confess your knowledge of Tegwen's death to Brychan after we found her body?" Gwen said.

Dewi's face went blank.

At that moment, there was a commotion in the kitchen and Gruffydd, Dolwyddelan's castellan, burst through the doorway. He skidded to a halt in front of Dewi, his eyes widening. "I thought you were dead!" And then he seemed to come to himself, gaping at Gwen, Evan, and Goch, who were watching him in various stages of surprise and consternation.

He stared at them for two heartbeats, and then as Gareth flung himself through the open doorway from the kitchen, Gruffydd fled, running flat out for the postern gate.

Gareth put up a hand. "Stop him!"

The guards at the gate looked at Gareth, confused expressions on their faces, and then at Gruffydd as if to say, "Stop *him*?"

"Out of my way!" Gruffydd made a sweeping motion with his arm.

"Yes!" Gareth was younger and a little more fit than Gruffydd, but if the sentry hadn't pulled the postern gate closed at the last moment, Gruffydd might have escaped. Fortunately, the sentry knew an order when he heard one, and he was more comfortable taking orders from Gareth than from Gruffydd.

Goch and Evan had run after Gareth. Gwen followed at her usual slower pace. By the time she reached the postern gate, Gareth had Gruffydd pressed to the closed door and was tying his hands behind his back. With a word from Gareth, Evan removed Gruffydd's sword from his belt and a knife from his boot.

"This is ridiculous. I have done nothing wrong," Gruffydd said.

"Then why did you run?" Gareth said.

"You have misunderstood," Gruffydd said. "I ate something that disagreed with me and was hastening outside of Aber before I humiliated myself in front of everyone."

"You seem healthy enough to me," Gareth said.

Gruffydd hacked and coughed, which seemed real enough to Gwen. She almost believed his story. She might still have believed it if Evan hadn't at that moment turned Gruffydd's knife over in his hands and, with a curious expression on his face, shown it to Gareth.

"That's blood." Evan traced a thin line near the hilt with his finger. Narrow with a fine point, the knife looked like it would match the wound too, if they had a wound to match.

"Don't be absurd," Gruffydd said.

Gareth leaned closer, keeping a hand pressed between Gruffydd's shoulder blades and prodding his feet apart. "You've had a momentous few days."

"I don't know what you're talking about," Gruffydd said.

Gareth tsked through his teeth. "The irony is that until you murdered Brychan, poisoned Dewi, and set fire to the manor house yesterday, you'd kept your hands clean. What made you fall apart so suddenly?"

"He murdered Brychan?" Dewi had come to a halt beside Gwen, who'd completely forgotten about him in the capture of Gruffydd.

Gareth glanced behind him. "Stay back, Dewi."

Dewi didn't hear him—or couldn't hear him. "Why?" The word came out a wail.

Gwen didn't answer Dewi because she didn't know, and she was hoping someone was going to tell her soon.

"Murder, poisoning, and arson. Am I missing something?" Gareth said.

"And then there's the matter of your attempted murder of me." Hywel had come up behind Gwen and stopped at her left shoulder, between her and Dewi. Dewi had gone up on the balls of his feet and came down again only when Hywel put a heavy hand on his shoulder to keep him still.

"I didn't shoot at the prince," Gruffydd said. "That was Brychan."

"Who happens to be conveniently dead and unable to gainsay you," Gareth said.

"Brychan is the archer," Gruffydd said.

"I don't believe you." Hywel released Dewi and closed in on Gruffydd. "I think you murdered Bran too."

Gruffydd didn't answer, a sneer contorting his features. "I admit to nothing."

"It is as I suspected," Hywel said. "Brychan was the one with the courage, not you."

Gruffydd spat on the ground. "Brychan went only where I pointed."

There was a silence as Gruffydd seemed to realize what he'd said. He clenched his jaw. Gwen stood stunned. She'd spoken with Brychan at length and believed what he'd told her. If he'd murdered Bran, then he'd lied to her face. She felt like a fool to have been so trusting.

"What's the penalty for conspiracy to murder the Lord of Rhos?" Gareth said as if asking Hywel about the weather on Anglesey.

"You can't pin Bran's death on me." Gruffydd's features were twisted with hate.

"But you did murder Brychan," Gareth said.

Gareth had Gruffydd's cheek pressed to the wall. Gruffydd's mouth worked, and Gareth spoke in his ear. "We have the loose thread now. All we have to do is pull at it and your entire world will unravel. Better to confess to what you did do and only owe *galanas* to Brychan's family, than refuse to talk and be accused of Lord Bran's murder as well as Brychan's. Think of Sioned."

"I am thinking of Sioned. I didn't murder Bran." Gruffydd seemed to think that if he repeated the phrase often enough, someone would believe him.

Gareth flipped Gruffydd around to face his audience and gazed at him, unbending. Gruffydd's eyes flicked to Hywel. And it was only then that at last he nodded. "Brychan demanded that I give him money so he could leave Gwynedd forever. He told me that he feared you were getting too close. We fought. That he's dead was an accident."

"What—you accidently stabbed him through the heart with your boot knife?" Hywel said.

"It was an accident," Gruffydd said again.

Gwen felt even sicker inside.

"What about Dewi, here?" Evan said.

"The penalty for murder by poison is a hanging," Gareth said. "You're lucky he's alive. You'd better hope he stays that way."

"Dewi was at the hut the night Tegwen died," Gruffydd said. "Brychan told me Dewi was there when Bran killed my granddaughter." And like Brychan before him, it was as if Gruffydd broke in half. He bent forward, choking on grief as fresh today as it had been five years ago when Tegwen disappeared. "Bran didn't deserve the title of lord."

Gruffydd lifted his chin, tears streaming down his cheeks, and raised his voice. Gwen turned, confused as to whom he was speaking, and saw that the courtyard behind her had filled with onlookers. "Brychan came to me a few years after Tegwen's disappearance with what little proof he had that Bran might be responsible. That he might have killed her. I found more."

"You questioned the nuns at the convent near Bryn Euryn," Gareth said.

"Them among others. The moment I saw you speaking with the nuns, I knew it was over." Gruffydd's next words tumbled out of his mouth in a rush now that his long held secrets had become known. "Bran received no punishment for his crime, while Sioned and I suffered, never to know where she'd come to rest, never able to visit her grave. In order even to see Tegwen's children, we had to pretend to Bran that we suspected nothing." He paused, and the hatred that rose in Gruffydd's eyes had Gwen retreating a pace. "It was intolerable."

"You murderous bastard!"

While Gwen had stepped back at Gruffydd's confession, Dewi had moved closer. With a cry of pain and anguish, he plucked the knife that Evan had been twirling between his fingers and launched himself at Gruffydd.

Gareth saw him coming and pulled Gruffydd sideways, falling with him to the ground as Dewi's knife descended. The blade missed Gruffydd's heart, instead sliding along his right ribcage. Dewi ended up straddling Gruffydd with Gareth sprawled underneath them both. It all happened so fast that nobody else was able to intervene until Dewi's arm came up for another thrust, at which point Hywel caught him with both arms around his torso and, with Evan's belated help, hauled him away.

Gareth managed to scoot out from under Gruffydd, who lay in a helpless ball in the dirt, his knees pulled up to his chest and his hands still tied behind his back. Blood soaked his left side, but he was alive. Hywel kicked away the knife that Evan had knocked from Dewi's hand and stood above both men, his hands on his hips, glaring down at them.

Then a women's voice came from behind Gwen. "Don't hurt him, please." Sioned rushed past Gwen to throw herself over Gruffydd's prone form. "He never killed anyone. He's only telling you that he did to protect me."

28

Hywel

"**C**ome here, Godfrid. We have a present for you." Gwen was practically hopping up and down in her glee as the big Dane made his way towards where she, Hywel, and Gareth had gathered at the far end of one of the long tables near the dais.

Godfrid halted two paces away, his gaze taking in each of them and then the wrapped package on the table. Disbelief and hope warred together in his expression. "That's not—"

Gwen clasped her hands together and went up on her toes. "It is!"

Hywel reached out and carefully unfolded the wrappings that had kept the Book of Kells safe on its long journey.

Godfrid moved forward, dropping a hand onto Gareth's shoulder as he stopped beside him. "You are a miracle worker."

"It wasn't my doing," Gareth said.

"That's not true, Gareth," Gwen said. "Prioress Nest sought you out because she trusts you."

Godfrid growled. "You're starting the story at the ending again."

Gareth grinned.

In addition to not witnessing Gareth's encounter with Prioress Nest, Godfrid had also missed all but the very end of the drama with Gruffydd and Sioned. Once the Book of Kells was stowed safely in Aber's treasury until such a time as the winds turned favorable and Godfrid had concocted a strategy for its return, he demanded they tell him that story from the beginning too. Many of the guests had already departed for their homes, the story of Tegwen's death and its resolution on their lips, and everyone left in the great hall was well into a mellow mood. Feeling charitable towards all, Hywel sprawled in his seat, his ankles crossed in front of him and his arm across the rail of Mari's chair.

"Let me see if I understand this correctly," Godfrid said. "According to Dewi, Tegwen died after Bran struck her and she fell against the corner of a table. Bran, Dewi, and Erik left her in Wena's hut—I must see this place before I leave, Gareth—and put out that she ran off with a Dane."

"Yes," Gwen said.

"I am offended that Bran blamed one of my own for the loss of his wife," Godfrid said. "But then, we Danes are the stuff of legends."

Gwen smacked Godfrid's shoulder, but his look of self-satisfaction didn't leave his face. Gareth couldn't blame the big Dane for his contentment. His quest had ended in success, barring the loss of Erik, who had yet to be caught.

"Three years later," Gareth said, "Dewi tells Brychan a tiny piece of the story. Brychan turns to Gruffydd, who begins asking questions he hadn't known to ask before and learns more about her disappearance. Both Brychan and Gruffydd believe absolutely that Bran killed Tegwen and concoct the plan to murder him."

"By ambush." Godfrid nodded. "Brychan, who loosed the arrow, gets away clean."

"Moving to the present day, once Tegwen's body is found and our investigation moves into full swing, Sioned, who knows the full story even if she wasn't a participant in the ambush of Bran, panics. She's afraid that we are close to uncovering the truth about her husband's role in Bran's death and convinces Brychan to take a shot at me." Hywel straightened in his seat at the memory. "Having failed, Brychan returns to Sioned and demands payment to keep quiet. She slips a knife between his ribs instead."

"Why would Brychan be so foolish as to listen to her in the first place?" Godfrid said.

"She threatened to expose him as Bran's killer if he didn't help deflect the investigation," Gareth said.

"What about Dewi?" Gwen said.

"Dewi told Brychan of his involvement in Tegwen's death, and Brychan told Sioned. So Sioned poisoned Dewi," Gareth said. "If Erik wasn't still at large, he would have been in danger too."

"And the fire?" Godfrid said.

"Sioned saw Gareth and me move Brychan's body," Hywel said, "but she didn't know that we'd recognized it in the darkness nor that Brychan had talked to Gwen at length about his relationship with Tegwen. That conversation, if not the one with Dewi, Brychan had kept to himself."

"Plus, a fire is always a good distraction," Gareth said, "with the added benefit of murdering us if she got lucky."

"If not for Dai and Llelo, she might have succeeded," Gwen said.

Gareth shot Gwen a questioning look. "Did we ever find out where those scalawags had been and why they were still awake?"

Gwen laughed. "Dearest husband, I think we don't want to know the answer to that question."

"Sioned then confessed all to Gruffydd," Hywel said, continuing the story, "and when Gruffydd saw Prioress Nest in the hall with Gareth, he panicked. Once caught, he chose to take all of the blame."

"The fact that Sioned had killed Brychan with Gruffydd's knife made his confession much more credible," Gareth said, "not that I would have ever suspected her of any of this."

"Sioned did what she did because she wanted to protect her husband," Gwen said. "She loves him."

"And Gruffydd loves her," Hywel said, "which is why he did what he did."

"It is astonishing that she attempted so much in so short a time," Godfrid said, "but I can see how as a woman and the grieving grandmother, she was above suspicion. Who would question her movements or her absence from the hall in her time of grief?"

"Last night, Sioned asked her husband and maid to leave her alone in the chapel, when what she was really doing was meeting Brychan in the woods and murdering him," Gwen said. "Who would gainsay her request to be left alone during the revelry? No one."

"What is to become of Sioned and Gruffydd?" Godfrid said.

"Payment for their crimes will pauper them. They will lose everything," Gareth said. "But for the fate of Tegwen's daughters, I suspect neither would care."

Hywel tapped a finger to his lips. "I will speak to Ifon. He will take the girls in."

"I think your father, my lord, would have preferred not to have learned any of this," Gwen said. "But I'm sure he's happy to know that Cadwaladr was not at the heart of it."

"This time," Hywel said darkly. He still couldn't decide if that fact was a relief or a disappointment.

"That's the problem with secrets," Godfrid said. "Given time, they fester."

Gwen nodded. "The core of their lives was rotten, and it proved their undoing."

"There's a lesson there for us all," Godfrid said.

At Godfrid's last words, Hywel straightened in his seat. *A lesson. A lesson for us all.* He stood abruptly. "I have to see my father."

Hywel felt Mari's curious look, but he simply kissed the top of her head and left the room. Certainty had taken hold of him. He'd been struggling for weeks with his burdens, worrying continually about the two lords he'd left in charge of Ceredigion. They had been deposed from their lands by Normans and regained them only at Hywel's hand, so their commitment to Hywel was absolute. Or so he hoped.

But a kingdom wasn't won or maintained on hope.

He found his father going over the kingdom's finances with Taran, discussing the cost of rebuilding the manor house and what tithes might come in from the upcoming slaughter of sheep and cattle in each cantref. Hywel stood in the doorway for a moment without them seeing him.

He knew he was hesitating and cleared his throat to get their attention. "Father."

King Owain had been bending over the table, reading the papers in front of Taran, who was seated. The king straightened to his full height and looked at Hywel. "Son."

Hywel took a step into the room. "I have been a coward and a fool, Father."

Owain jerked his head at Taran. The steward rose hastily to his feet and departed, though not before resting his hand on Hywel's shoulder as he passed by him on his way into the corridor.

Hywel's father remained standing where he was, waiting.

Hywel spoke again. "I have told you of our gains in Ceredigion, and of the sacking of Cardigan, but what I haven't told you is what I have failed to do. What I am failing to do." And then like when Gruffydd had confessed his crimes, Hywel found his next words tumbling out of his mouth: his decisions, many of them wrong; the forces arrayed against him, which the attack on

Cardigan Castle was unlikely to stem; the losses of men and horses that he had avoided elucidating clearly to his father for months; and his stark awareness of his own inexperience.

"If you remove me from my position because of my failures, it would be far better than for me to lose Ceredigion for you entirely," Hywel concluded. "My hope is that it hasn't quite come to that and that you can forgive me for coming to you for help. Or rather, not coming to you for help sooner."

Hywel's father rubbed at his chin as he thought about his answer. Hywel shifted from one foot to another. His stomach had fallen into his boots when he'd entered his father's office initially, but Hywel had meant what he'd said. Finally admitting that he didn't know what to do or how to do it had lifted a huge weight from his shoulders.

Then his father came around the desk, and to Hywel's astonishment, he came right up to Hywel and embraced him. Then, taking a step back, he said, "It takes a brave man to admit to his own ignorance. You are neither a coward nor a fool, son. To say that I am proud of you would be to understate the case."

Hywel gaped at his father for a heartbeat, and then cold relief flooded through him. Suddenly, he could breathe again.

"Now, why don't you get Taran back in here, and between the three of us, we can solve our little problem of Ceredigion."

Hywel had hoped that a return to Aber would provide him with a respite from his troubles. As he pulled up a chair opposite his father and Taran, he decided that he'd been looking at this journey the wrong way round. Trouble wasn't something he could run from or to. It followed him everywhere he went. It hadn't been a respite from trouble that he'd needed, or that he'd come to Aber to find.

It was clarity.

And it was a rare man who could find that all by himself.

29

Gareth

Gareth paced back and forth at the end of the corridor. Queen Cristina, herself delivered of a healthy son named Dafydd shortly after Calan Gaeaf, had given up her room for Gwen's lying in. Gwen had woken at dawn with pains, endured a full day of laboring, and now it was past midnight and still their child hadn't been delivered.

Sometime around sunset the pains had closed in around Gwen, and the midwives had whisked her away to Cristina's room. Gareth had started drinking then, stopped a few hours later, and had been pacing back and forth in front of the fire in the great hall ever since. Other residents of Aber waited with him, occasionally shooting glances in his direction, but otherwise had the sense to leave him alone.

"She is well, Gareth." Seeing the way things were going, Hywel had brought a chair to the end of the closest table and reclined in it, his ankles crossed and his boots on the table top. He sipped at his cup of mead. "They would have told you if she wasn't."

"It's gone on so long!" Gareth stopped his pacing and gazed at the empty doorway. He couldn't hear anything that was happening upstairs from here.

"God isn't going to take her from you now, not when He and Gwen have conspired so perfectly to keep you here for the birth," Hywel said.

Gareth glanced at his lord, worried that this comment had been accompanied by discontent, but Hywel was smiling.

Hywel and his men, Gareth among them, had intended to begin the journey to Ceredigion after Epiphany. That was nine days ago. Although the weather had stayed mild through December, it had turned to winter in January and here it was, the middle of the month, and the snow fell as heavily today as it had fallen a week ago, making the roads impassable and ensuring Gareth's presence for the birth of his child.

"Laboring this long is normal." Hywel dropped his feet to the floor and joined Gareth for a circuit around the hall. "When Eira died, they told me hours earlier that it wasn't going well. Gwen's mother too."

"If she's going to die, I can't be out here and her in there."

"She's not going to die."

"You don't know that!" Gareth shook Hywel off. He'd reached the breaking point and was going to start throwing chairs like King Owain. Before he had to choose a chair to throw, however, one of the midwives appeared in the doorway and canted her head. Gareth bounded towards her.

"If you would come with me, my lord, your wife would see you now."

Gareth's breath caught in his throat. In later years, he would say that he had no memory of the journey from the great hall to Cristina's door, which the midwife opened for him. A second midwife, a woman twice Gareth's age, turned as he entered. Gareth drank in the sight of the child in her arms and then looked past her to Gwen, who rested in the bed. She lifted her head to smile at him, tears fresh on her cheeks.

"It's a girl, Gareth," she said.

The midwife adjusted the baby's blanket and placed her in Gareth's arms. Wiping away sudden tears of his own, he sat beside Gwen on the bed and put his forehead to hers, finding himself unable to speak.

"Your lady wife did very well," the midwife said. "Both she and the child are strong and healthy."

"Thank you," Gareth said. "Thank you for everything."

With a knowing smile at Gareth's near incoherence, Gwen reached for the baby, who'd begun to root around. "Let me feed her before she cries."

Gareth settled beside Gwen with his back against the headboard. A servant finished bundling together the used linens and departed, leaving the door half-open.

"Is it safe to see her?" Hywel's voice came from the corridor.

"Yes, my lord," the servant answered.

Hywel appeared in the doorway, bracing his shoulder against the frame and smiling. "Have you chosen a name? My father waits in the hall."

Gareth gently stroked the back of his daughter's head. "Tangwen."

"The king won't mind that we want to honor Tegwen with a piece of her name?" Gwen said, looking quickly up at Hywel. "Given all that happened, we didn't feel right about taking it entirely." Both names—as well as Gwen's own—had the same root, which meant 'pure' or 'white', but while Teg meant beautiful, Tang was the word for peace.

Hywel blinked, and then he bowed. When he looked up again, Gareth thought he saw tears on his cheeks too. "Tegwen *was* beautiful, and so is your daughter. But I would choose peace too."

As Hywel departed, Gwen leaned against Gareth. "I'm so glad you're here."

Gareth kissed his daughter and then his wife. "I swear to you now that I always will be."

The End

Historical Note

I am often asked what parts of my books are 'true' and what are not. I jokingly say that my stories are as historically accurate as I can make them except when they aren't, but the research that goes into them is extensive in order for them to represent medieval Wales as accurately as possible. While Gareth and Gwen themselves are fictional characters, the court of Owain Gwynedd, his sons, wives, and their circumstances, really existed.

The problem with researching this era is that so few contemporary documents remain.

We do know, for example, that Kells was sacked by the Dublin Danes in the summer of 1144. We know that Hywel burned Cardigan that same summer. We also know that Cristina gave birth to a son, Dafydd, very shortly after her marriage to King Owain. What we don't have access to is the rest of the story. Imagining what might have been is why I write these books.

Gilbert de Clare, the Earl of Pembroke, had to wait a little longer for the chance to invade Ireland, and in the end, it was his son, Richard, who accomplished it. The deposed King of Leinster sought help regaining his kingdom and invited the Normans in. As Gwen pointed out in *The Fallen Princess*, however, once the Normans laid eyes on the prize, it was all but impossible to get them to leave.

As a side note, *Calan Gaeaf* (or All Saints' Day) and *Nos Galan Gaeaf* (or Hallowmas), which take center stage in *The*

Fallen Princess, are just two of many traditions that were incorporated into the Church as Christianity made inroads into Wales. *Nos Galan Gaeaf* is the Welsh equivalent of Samhain, which has become our Halloween, a traditional day within Celtic societies when the veil between the human world and the Otherworld thins. The Church in the medieval era was ever-present and laid its own traditions over the top of older traditions that it inherited.

Calan Gaeaf is one of those traditions. See my post here for more information: http://www.sarahwoodbury.com/calan-gaeaf/

About the Author

With two historian parents, Sarah couldn't help but develop an interest in the past. She went on to get more than enough education herself (in anthropology) and began writing fiction when the stories in her head overflowed and demanded she let them out. While her ancestry is Welsh, she only visited Wales for the first time while in college. She has been in love with the country, language, and people ever since. She even convinced her husband to give all four of their children Welsh names.

She makes her home in Oregon.

www.sarahwoodbury.com

CPSIA information can be obtained
at www.ICGtesting.com
Printed in the USA
FSOW04n1053291215
15088FS